"Morning, Red."

The man's voice was so deep, his overused, outdated greeting so easy and familiar that, for the first time in her life, Caitlin felt her face flush with embarrassment. "Where am I?"

"According to your directions, you're home. If not, then we've invaded someone else's privacy for the last three days."

"Three days? What have I been doing?"

"If you don't know, then I haven't given it my all." He sighed, then chuckled softly and drew a fingertip down her spine. "Feeding."

For three days? She was in bed with a man who possessed the chiseled body and face of a Greek god and she couldn't remember the feel of his body on, or in, hers?

"Who are you?"

"Ladies first."

"Caitlin St. George."

The man froze, his eyes widening for a split second before he moved away from her and shifted into the form of a smoky dragon before disappearing.

DRAGON PROMISE

DENISE LYNN

Published in Great Britain 2015
by Mills & Boon, an imprint of Harlequin (UK) Limited,
Eton House, 18-24 Paradise Road, Richmond, Surrey, TW9 1SR

© 2015 Denise L. Koch

ISBN: 978-0-263-91750-5

89-0915

Harlequin (UK) Limited's policy is to use papers that are natural, renewable and recyclable products and made from wood grown in sustainable forests. The logging and manufacturing processes conform to the legal environmental regulations of the country of origin.

Printed and bound in Spain
by CPI, Barcelona

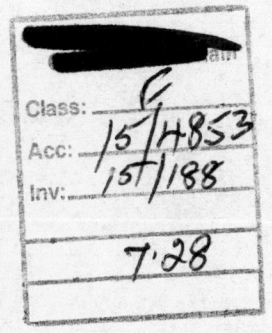

Denise Lynn, an award-winning author, lives in the USA with her husband, son and numerous four-legged "kids." Between the pages of romance novels she has traveled to lands and times filled with brave knights, courageous ladies and never-ending love. Now she can share with others her dream of telling tales of adventure and romance. You can write to her at PO Box 17, Monclova, OH 43542, USA, or visit her website, www.denise-lynn. com.

Braeden was for Brenda, Cameron for Cheryl...

And for my sister Sandy, I grant you Sean,
along with all of his passion and his magick.
With much love, always.

Prologue

Ancient castle ruins on the east coast of Ireland—
October 3. Two years ago

Candlelight flickered in the drafty cell, casting eerily dancing shadows on the wall behind the altar. Pacing before the altar, Nathan the Learned paused to stare into the undulating flames, before gazing down into a crystal bowl. The water filling the bowl had been blessed by the light of a full moon to lend more power to his scrying.

He scried not for hints of what the future held, because he knew that once his deeds this night were completed, his future would be secure. Instead, he wanted to see the past. Not just a hazy memory of days gone by, but a clear reckoning of what had brought him to this long-sought-after moment of greatness.

With one hand on the head of the naked, bound

woman kneeling at his feet, he waved the other over the bowl. The water rippled outward from the center, as if disturbed by a falling pebble.

A wavering image of a medieval castle appeared. *Mirabilus.* The medieval stronghold where it all began so very long ago. The water stilled, permitting the reflection to become clearer. A cold breeze, not unlike the one he'd felt that fateful night, brushed across his cheek. The shape of an amethyst dragon formed over the image of the castle. It wavered as if trying to take flight and then it cracked, splintering into a million pieces, just as it had that fateful night. He then saw himself as a child hiding within the darkness of a curtained alcove as the High Druid, his uncle Aelthed, killed his own brother—Nathan's father. The terror of the child flowed into the man he'd become, settling cold in his belly. He had vowed revenge that night and would soon taste the victory he'd craved for so long.

The image of childhood faded, permitting a new one to appear. Again Nathan saw himself, this time a man full grown, leaning over the High Druid Aelthed as he lay gasping his last breaths upon his bed. He cared not that the wizard suffered in his final moments. The man deserved whatever pain and agony plagued him—not just for killing Nathan's father, but for also seeing to it that he had been laid to rest in an unhallowed grave, unable to ever attain life after death. Worse, when the time had come for Nathan to be named Dragon Lord of Mirabilus, the honor had gone to another, along with the ancient family grimoire and the two remaining dragon pendants.

Nathan shook with unforgotten rage. Oh, yes, the wizard had paid dearly for those mistakes. As Aelthed's soul had sought escape from his withered body, Nathan had trapped it in a wooden puzzle box that locked with such an intricate, complicated set of moves no one would ever be able to free his soul. For nearly nine centuries, Aelthed's soul had remained imprisoned. And for most of those years, Nathan had kept the puzzle box close at hand, guarding it like a prized possession.

Until he'd dropped it while trying to escape death at the talons of a Drake's magical dragon when he'd tried to destroy the eldest Drake and his wife.

Now all the items he needed—the puzzle box, the pendants and the grimoire—were together under the protection of the current Dragon Lord. From what he could discern, the Drakes had been unable to break the spell holding the wizard's soul captive. So, just as he'd planned, Aelthed's spirit was still confined, waiting for Nathan to set him free.

Once again the image faded. This time it was replaced by the reflection of his son, pale and cold in death. Nathan screamed in agony and waved the recent, too painful image away.

Tapping the handle of the braided leather whip he held against his thigh, he seethed. A few years ago he'd nearly lost his own life to the current Dragon Lord. Sorely wounded, he'd nurtured his hatred and desire for power, using that dark energy to survive. Which was more than what could be said for his son. The Dragon Lord's twin had taken his sole remaining son—once again preventing him from reaching his goal.

He cursed the Dragon Lord and his family. They were the only obstacle in his way—the only thing that kept him from attaining supreme power.

For all these centuries, the Drakes had stood between him and his place as Hierophant, supreme ruler over all.

But no more.

This time he would gain possession of the Drake family grimoire, those accursed pendants and the ancient puzzle box—along with its spellbound occupant. Once all of the items were in his hands, he could finish the spell he'd worked on for centuries, and then the position of Hierophant would be his. And when he alone held supreme power, nothing and no one would ever again be able to repudiate his will.

Nathan laughed. And this time he wouldn't have to lift a finger to defeat the Drakes.

They thought themselves unreachable, hiding behind a specialized security system that made breaking in to Dragon's Lair undetected, impossible for anyone possessing more than human capabilities. And they were far too cautious, their sixth sense too well developed for him to be able to attack them away from their stronghold.

But he had another option at hand. He glanced at the woman kneeling on the stone floor before his altar. A necessary link. With her help, this time he would use a Drake to beat them.

Now that the full moon had finally risen, he was anxious to set his perfect plan into motion. He screamed at her, "Say the words!"

When she refused, he snarled and then raised his arm asking, "Do you enjoy the bite of pain?"

At her silence he flicked the whip in his hand, making it hiss and whistle as it snaked toward its victim. The crack echoed in the nearly empty chamber. The tips of the braided leather scored her naked back, adding yet another row of bloody lines to the pale flesh.

Her shoulders flinched, but she gave no other sign of giving in to the agony—yet.

Nathan narrowed his eyes and trembled with a surge

of unbridled lust. This gypsy mage could give him many weeks of untold pleasure. Even after his rather ardent lovemaking last night, she was still lovely. The lingering traces of his touch on her luscious breasts and full hips only made her more desirable. He saw the bruises as his marks of ownership, and he ached to once again possess her.

Not just yet. Soon. His mind whispered for him to be patient, and Nathan drew in a long, shuddering breath.

First he needed the ancient curse against his enemies to be spoken. He had repeatedly tried activating the simple yet powerful curse himself and found only failure. He'd studied the curse's history over and over until discovering that it was not Druid. It was of Romani origin, and he was certain this beautiful gypsy mage possessed the magic to give the curse life. He'd cloaked himself in the allure of youth then seduced her with the promise of riches and whispered of nights filled with tender, fulfilling lovemaking.

But when she'd seen his true self, discovered his lies and the reason for the curse, she'd sworn to never say the words. Her reaction made him more certain she could bring the curse alive and one way or another, he would force her to do so.

Nathan dropped the whip at his feet and grabbed a handful of her thick, raven-hued hair. Tugging on it until the hairpins he'd used to secure the luxurious tresses atop her head and away from her back slipped free.

He slid his other hand along her neck, closing his fingers one by one tightly over her windpipe. "Do you seek death out of some misguided notion that it will save those I wish to harm?" He leaned down and whispered against her ear. "It will not work. If you refuse me again, I know another mage...another *gypsy* mage...one much younger than you who will be more than grateful to escape your fate."

The woman tensed beneath his touch, obviously realizing that he spoke of her younger sister.

"Perhaps we will try one more time." He relaxed his hold around her neck slightly.

She swallowed hard and then nodded.

He released her and stepped back to retrieve the whip and send it sailing to snap loud on the floor beside her. "Say the words."

When she bowed her head and began to whisper, Nathan lashed his weapon once again across her back, shouting, "Louder, so I can hear you!"

"Not a dragon born—" she paused, gasping as if the words burned her throat more than the lashes across her flesh "—yet a dragon you shall be."

Nathan tossed a pinch of dark reddish powder into the flickering candle atop the altar. When the flames danced around the dragon blood, he nudged the woman, ordering, "Finish it."

"Once this beast has taken form, it will answer only to thee."

Nathan dropped clippings of his own hair into the candle. As the stench of burning hair filled the air, and the flames of the candle sparked, he proclaimed, "I am thee."

He stared down at the woman. Now that the curse had been given voice, his lust vanished. While there was no way to know how long it would take for the curse to work, her task had been completed. The time had come to end their partnership. "I fear I have no further use for you, my dear."

He let the whip fly again and again, chuckling as it cracked loudly across her shoulder. Disappointed that she didn't beg for mercy, or so much as raise a hand in her own defense, he worked the deadly weapon until her ragged breaths were nothing more than a few mewling gasps.

Drenched in sweat and gasping for breath himself, Nathan let the whip fall from his hand and leaned over the dying woman now curled in a ball on the floor. She opened one swollen eye and whispered, "St. George will set you free."

He growled at her and then shrieked, "You bitch!" before drawing what little life force she had left from her body.

With her last choked breath, she once again whispered, "St. George will set you free."

Chapter 1

Outskirts of Detroit—One year ago

"Man, now that is one fine-looking piece."

"Yeah, how'd you like to have a taste of that?"

Inwardly seething, Sean Drake's only physical display of disgust was a slight tightening of his grip around the beer bottle in his hand at the juvenile comments the thugs in the booth behind him were making about the woman who'd just taken a seat at the bar. Their antics and crude behavior were starting to chafe at his last nerve.

These men were petty thieves and thugs. One was a large, hard-drinking bully, and the other his smaller, junkie buddy. Both low-life slugs.

He'd run into them a few weeks ago when they were casing the neighborhood around his current apartment. They'd been looking for their next target, and he'd made certain to accidentally bump into them that night to thwart their plans.

He should have killed them instead.

Had he followed his gut instinct, they wouldn't be here tonight, intent on harassing someone weaker and smaller than themselves. He wasn't about to let that happen. He didn't care what trouble they brought on themselves, but they wouldn't be permitted to hurt anyone else.

Sean tossed back the bottle of beer he'd been nursing and realized with a start that it was time to go home. Not to his sparsely furnished, one-bedroom apartment at the edge of the city, but home to the forested mountains and Dragon's Lair. He choked back a laugh at that thought. Barely eight months had passed since he'd left the Lair, but it felt like years. Actually, he hadn't simply left. Confused, half-dead and afraid for his life, he'd run away in the middle of the night.

It had taken him most of this time alone to come to the conclusion that he'd deserved the beating the Dragon Lord had given him. After all, his unwillingness to control his new, and unwanted, powers had put not just himself at risk, but he'd also become a danger to his brothers and their families. As the Dragon Lord, Braeden had been forced to choose between knocking some sense into the new changeling, or killing him.

Thankfully, even though it would have been within his rights as the lord, his brother hadn't chosen to take his life. Sean knew he should have been grateful, but at the time, the boulder-sized chip on his shoulder hadn't allowed him to see reason. Instead, he'd convinced his sorry self that everyone hated him, that nobody understood him—basically, he'd reacted like a spoiled, self-centered child.

But he hadn't been a child. He'd been a relatively normal twenty-six-year-old adult with a college degree, and more wealth and opportunities than most people would see in a lifetime. He had a good position in the family business and a family who'd cared about him.

Until just over a year ago, when he had been torn from a dark dream by the sounds of a striking whip and an evil cackle, followed by what sounded like a raggedly chanted curse. He hadn't been able to make sense of the breathless words, just snippets of a woman's pain-filled voice. A demonic urge to change into a dragon had filled him. With it came an unrelenting need to seek Drake blood. Since he wasn't a changeling, he had chalked it up to being nothing more than remnants of a nightmare.

His shape-shifting into a dragon would have been fine as far as Braeden or Cameron were concerned. Since both of his older brothers were changeling wizards and possessed dragon blood from birth, they would have welcomed his newfound ability. But it wasn't fine with him. He had always been the normal one, the human brother without any power to read minds, transfer thoughts, slide into dreams, shift into a dragon or materialize someplace on a whim.

For many long weeks after the nightmare, he'd been edgy, moody, confused and unreasonable. As the next month passed, instead of fading away, the troubling urges from that dark dream grew. At the time, he'd thought he was losing his mind. But then, when the dream turned real and he had shifted to dragon form, he'd felt invincible and driven with only one purpose in mind—to kill his brothers. Aunt Danielle had been convinced that he'd been cursed—and since he had heard bits of a chanted curse in his nightmare, he agreed with her assessment, but could do nothing to break whatever spell had been cast over him, except wonder who had cast the spell and why.

Cameron had spent the next two months trying to teach him how to use this new unearthly power and how to control his urges, but Sean had been reluctant to accept his brother's training. One night, in a moment of what he could now only consider pure insanity, he'd shifted into dragon form and attacked Braeden.

While he'd known that as the Dragon Lord his brother was a powerful wizard, he hadn't truly known just how powerful until Braeden's beast gave him a beat down he'd survived only by some miracle.

Sean rubbed the side of his neck. Just remembering that night made his scars burn like fire. How would his brothers—and their beasts—react when he showed up at Dragon's Lair? Would they let him come home? If so, what would it cost him to gain entry back into the family fold?

A sudden flash of sensual heat flowed through him, interrupting his musings and drawing his attention to his surroundings. The brilliant green eyes of his slumbering dragon flickered open. The black, elongated pupils narrowed and widened, dilating with curiosity and interest.

Sean tensed, focusing on the unexpected awakening of his inner beast. He controlled the urge to shift and then studied the other occupants of the bar. Who—or what—had roused the dragon from its slumber?

His gaze settled on the exceptionally attractive woman at the bar—the one the thugs were still drooling over as they kept up their running commentary of what they'd like to do to her.

Their shallow imaginations leaned more toward control and force than pleasure. The urge to show them exactly how control and force felt grew stronger by the minute.

Yeah, it was definitely time to go home before he did something that would terrify the humans of this world.

Curious about the woman, and his dragon's rapt fascination with her, he rose from his seat at the booth and grabbed his empty beer bottle from the table. Seemed the perfect time to get another one.

Crossing the uneven floor of the seedy neighborhood bar, Sean knew he was ready to pay whatever price his brother demanded. In an effort not to draw unwanted attention from his family, he'd avoided touching his bank account. Now, he was tired of drifting, tired of picking up one meaningless job after another just to eat and beyond tired of trying to act normal among humans who would never understand or accept what he'd become.

Sean leaned over the empty stool next to the woman, put the bottle on the worn bar top and nodded when the bartender reached to pull a fresh longneck from the cooler.

Intentionally turning to face the woman, Sean breathed in deeply. He couldn't quite put his finger on it, but instead of some floral or botanical perfume, her scent was enticing—like exotic spices and promises. Lusty promises that curled around him, twisting, swirling, drawing him ever closer.

He leaned in until his lips were mere inches from her cheek. When she turned her head to look at him, her scent grew stronger, filling his mind and his blood with the need to possess her. He wanted to taste her deep red, full lips, run his fingers through those auburn- and coppery-colored waves curling halfway down her back and get lost in the warmth of her brandy-hued eyes.

When she didn't lean away from him, he motioned for the bartender to refill her drink then tossed the money for the beer and her drink on the bar.

"Thank you."

Her low, throaty whisper raced warm and enticing across his face, leaving him almost trembling with lust. The dragon's rumble of desire deepened to a guttural roar, demanding he claim this woman as his own.

Surprised by both his and the beast's intense responses, he was certain this was no mortal woman. He freed his senses and brushed his mind briefly across hers.

Instead of discovering nothing of interest, a rush of familiarity, of like meeting like, confirmed his assumption—she was another preternatural. His knowledge about others of his kind was limited, gained from the few details his family had provided and from stories told by a vampire he'd run across a couple of months ago. It didn't require an abundance of knowledge to know from the instant, sensual heat of her returned touch and the seductive half smile playing across her mouth, that she was a succubus looking for much more than just another drink.

Her sense of desperation swept over him. She wasn't seeking just a quick night of pleasure. Sharp, painful pangs of hunger gnawed at his gut—she needed to feed from someone strong enough to withstand the draining she would unleash on them.

More than able to satisfy her craving, Sean smiled back at her. She could feed on his life force for days without draining him.

Before he could understand exactly what was happening, or offer protest, Sean's beast gently blew an in-

visible puff of fire and smoke in her direction, marking
the woman as his.

Didn't the dragon understand that the two of them
were one being? The beast couldn't claim a mate without committing Sean to the same person. He resisted
the urge to gasp at the implication. Of course the beast
knew exactly what it had done.

Sometimes Sean wished he'd have paid more attention to what his brother had tried to teach him. Even
though he didn't possess the ability to materialize elsewhere or slide into another person's dreams like his
brothers did, he was able to shift and to communicate
telepathically. While it made him more like them, more
of a Drake perhaps, he still didn't understand his beast
the way his brothers did theirs.

Why had his beast chosen this moment to mark a
woman when it had never considered doing so before?
Was it because he'd recently been thinking about returning to Dragon's Lair and his family?

And why this woman? Sean held back a chuckle.
The answer to this question was obvious. He wanted
this beguiling temptress with every fiber of his being.

She said nothing, but the slightest widening of her
eyes let him know she'd felt the mental brand.

He pushed the drink he'd bought closer to her then
grabbed the beer, deepened his smile and nodded before
returning to the booth without saying a word.

Caitlin watched him leave. A less-perceptive woman
might have been deflated by his nonverbal response,
interpreting it as a dismissal. However, she knew better. He may not have spoken words, but his brief touch
across her thoughts had felt like a warm, possessive
caress against her cheek. His inner beast had marked
her, meaning this was no mere mortal man. Whatever

nonhuman traits he possessed were apparently from the animal kingdom. But his mental touch hadn't permitted her entry into his mind to tell her which one.

However it didn't require any degree of perception to notice that he hadn't simply *walked* away—he'd sauntered, swaggered—as if confident of her interest and daring her to follow him.

Caitlin curled her fingers around the glass he'd pushed toward her. The imprint left by his touch was still warm under hers. Beneath the warmth churned a hunger as deep as her own. She shivered with anticipation, knowing her bed wouldn't be cold or lonely tonight.

Of more importance had been the feeling that his interest in her was purely physical—an interest that she welcomed with relief. Because of a vow to her mother, she hadn't fed in over a month, and now blood flowed through her veins like a thick, slow-moving sludge. The lethargy weighing her down was nearly unbearable; she needed something—someone—to refill her life force.

The fastest, easiest way to gain the life-giving power she needed to survive was to simply suck the force from another being. However, that required her to know when to stop before completely draining the *donor*, and right now her hunger would make that nearly impossible.

But the most pleasurable way to obtain what she needed, the fairest way for the other participant and the longest-lasting method was through hot, intense sex. Finding a willing partner wasn't a problem, since as a succubus, men and women were always drawn to her whether she summoned the attraction or not. Unfortunately, most humans didn't possess enough life force, or the driving need—a near-insatiable hunger—to survive mating with her.

Hence the reason for promising her mother that she'd refrain from feeding on them—again. Since this man wasn't human, he stood a better chance of living through the event.

The old cliché "killing two birds with one stone" came to mind. She would still be honoring her parents' request by not seeking out a human, and by morning she might gain enough life force to last weeks.

She raised the glass to her lips and then paused before putting the drink back on the bar without taking a sip. Already weak and slow, Caitlin knew the booze would only make her feel worse. She'd come in here as a last resort, looking for a *donor*, not to get drunk.

Now that she'd found what she wanted—what she so desperately needed—it was time to go. Not for one second did she worry about him finding her. She'd strategically leave enough of her scent lingering in the air that he'd find the way to her home with ease.

"Aren't you a hot little thing?"

Hot? Always. *Little?* Caitlin resisted rolling her eyes at that description. She hadn't been a *little thing* since she'd hit just under six foot tall at age twelve.

A yellowish glare from the streetlight at the end of the alley danced in the droplets of sleet rolling down the thug's drawn blade. She forgot about his comment and took another step back from the two men stalking her, luring them farther into the dark alley.

They'd been in the booth behind the changeling at the bar. She'd heard their crude comments when she'd entered, felt them watching her when she'd left the bar, and she'd seen their reflections in the smoked-glass window as they followed her out. She'd expected *him* to follow her, but these two were another story.

With a quick touch of her mind to the humans, she discovered that while their goal also included sex, it wasn't the passionate kind they wanted. She quirked an eyebrow at their stupidity and kept walking backward.

They had corralled her into the alley a block away from the bar where no one would see them—mistakenly thinking she was an easy target. She might be drained, but her tired muscles and slow reactions would still be more than enough to handle these two.

One man swung a knife at her, laughing as she jumped back from what he thought was a lethal blade.

"Yeah. Come on, cut her, cut her." The smaller of the two men squealed like a child. From the glassiness of his eyes, the lack of meat on his bones and the jerkiness of his movements, he was obviously juiced on something more than beer.

The changeling with a body even she would die for approached frowning, but said nothing to stop the other two men. He hung back. A quizzical expression drew his brows together as if he was waiting for something.

"Do you want my help?" She jerked slightly at the intrusion of his silent query.

"No." Caitlin scoffed at his offer, adding, *"You know damn well that help with these two isn't what I want from you."*

Once again he gave her a smile full of promises and passion.

She drew her full attention to the thug with the blade, and because the question was usually expected in these situations, she asked, "What do you want?"

Knife man smiled. "Why, darlin', we want you."

Of course he did. Everyone wanted her whether the desire was mutual or not. Caitlin shrugged out of her unzipped jacket, letting the buttery-soft black leather hit the wet pavement. "Oh, big boy, all you had to do was ask."

Her unexpected, brazen comment stopped them in their tracks. Only the twitching drughead seemed upset by the sudden turn of events. But his most dangerous response was to twitch faster.

Needing just a drop of energy before taking on these two humans, she reached out with her mind and touched the junkie, recoiling instantly from the contamination and disease he carried deep in his soul. No way in hell would she place a finger on him and risk poisoning herself needlessly.

She focused on the knife wielder. He possessed a vile darkness that wouldn't kill her, but it would eventually make her physically ill. From their encounter in the bar, she knew the changeling would give her the opportunity to heal herself long before she became sick.

The blade sliced through her silky tank top and across her rib cage as the thug closed his hand boldly around her left breast. "Teasing will get you killed."

Caitlin didn't flinch at the knife tip's burn. The lost blood would soon be replenished, and the cut would heal momentarily. And while his hold on her body irritated her, it didn't hurt.

But he'd ruined her favorite top. That was completely unacceptable.

She tilted her head and smiled before placing the palm of her hand against his cheek. "Teasing?"

The knife fell from his hand, his pupils dilated and he moaned raggedly with a sudden, unexpected flare of lust. Humans were just so damn easy. She threaded her fingers through his dark, greasy hair. Resisting the urge to shiver with disgust, she cupped the back of his head and drew him closer, whispering, "I would never tease about anything as important as a new top."

When their lips nearly met, she exhaled softly, filling him with mindless desire and near-excruciating need.

His eyelids fluttered closed—he was hers to do with as she willed. Caitlin tightened her hold and inhaled almost every last ounce of his life-giving force until he whimpered like a little girl.

"Enough."

The preternatural's one-word command shocked her into releasing her grip on the human. She let him drop to the pavement like a rock. Nobody outside her parents, or the royal circle of elders, gave her orders. Who did he think he was?

The junkie stared down at his buddy in open-mouthed shock. Jerking his head and shoulders, he screamed, "What? What the hell did you do?"

Mr. To Die For popped the little guy on the jaw and dropped him with one hit.

Caitlin staggered, gasping in confusion and worry at her sudden inability to function, or focus. She'd known she would be ill from sucking the life out of the thug. But not this quickly, never this fast. This wasn't normal. Something was wrong. Her heart thudded fast and hard inside her chest. What was happening to her? What was so different this time around?

She stumbled and then bounced off the garbage Dumpster. Just great. Her parents would be so pissed off if she went and got herself killed now.

"Come here." The male she'd wanted pulled her against him right before she collapsed into a puddle. Cupping her chin, he tipped her head up and brought his lips close to hers. "Eat. Drink. Whatever it is you do."

She weakly slung an arm around his neck. "How romantic."

"Yeah, that's me, Mr. Romance at your service. Shut up and feed."

"Not a vampire." Her words sounded disjointed to her ears.

"No shit."

Caitlin's stomach cramped; her legs shook. Had he not been holding her so securely, she wouldn't have remained on her feet for much longer.

When her arm slipped from around his neck to dangle uselessly, she knew there'd be no way she'd be able to exhale anything from him. Hoping his intent was truly to help her, she whispered, "Kiss me."

The first touch of his lips against hers sent a lightning-charged zing of energy clear to her toes. She sighed with the most exquisite longing, forgetting even to draw in his energy as she reveled in the utter completeness of the moment for a split second before darkness overtook her.

Caitlin's first awareness was the feel of cool, satiny-smooth sheets against her flesh. Her second was that she felt more alive than she had in months. She opened her eyes and gazed into the grassy-green depths of the eyes staring back at her.

"Morning, Red."

Normally, that clichéd endearment would send her ire skyrocketing, but his voice was so deep, his overused, outdated greeting so easy and familiar that for the first time in her life, she felt her face flush with embarrassment. His one-sided smile—a seductive, knowing smirk—only lent more heat to her cheeks.

Confused by her odd reaction, she asked, "Where am I?"

"According to your directions, you're home. If not, then we've invaded someone else's privacy for the past three days."

Three days!

She sat up quickly, glancing around to make certain she truly was home. The deep forest green of the walls were adorned not with any feminine ornamentation, but with only the tools of her trade—a centuries-old broad sword and a pair of even more ancient crossed daggers—mounted near the door let her know they were indeed in her bedroom. No other woman would have decorated their bedroom in such a manner. Satisfied with her location, she held the sheet tightly to her neck. "Three days? What have I been doing?"

"If you don't know, then I haven't given it my all." He sighed then chuckled softly and drew a fingertip down her spine. "Feeding."

For three days? And she couldn't remember any of it? She was in bed with a man who possessed the chiseled body and face of a Greek god and she couldn't remember the feel of his body on, or in, hers? Either she'd lost her mind, or he was some type of preternatural she'd never met before.

She closed her eyes tightly, trying desperately to remember. Then slowly, bit by bit, the fog started to clear, permitting snippets of their time together to trickle into her mind.

They'd met in a bar and had been attracted to each other from the beginning.

His inner animal—the part that made him preternatural—had marked her. She wasn't certain why it had done so, only that for some reason it had chosen her. More importantly, she hadn't turned him away.

Images of the thugs in the alley floated through her mind. When she'd become sick immediately after draining the one attacker, this man, the one now in her bed, had been there to catch her before she fell to the wet pavement. He'd given her energy—his own life force, without question.

A shiver of lust raced down her spine as more, broken bits of memories poured forth. Not quite visual memories, but more like remembered feelings. The warmth of his mind-robbing kiss as his tongue had swept across hers. And the certainty of his touch when he'd stroked and caressed her to a fevered pitch that left her gasping for air and wanting so much more.

All of this was so foreign to her, so strange. She'd never let a man into her bedroom. She'd never been so swept away by a kiss that she'd lost the ability to think. She'd never met a man who could willingly fill her life force and live.

Never before had she desired, longed for, lusted after a man who possessed an inner strength that was on a level she couldn't quite understand, and while it excited her, it also frightened her.

Though she could remember the feel of his touch, the taste of his kiss, she couldn't pull his name from her memories. It was an odd time to ask, but she wanted to know.

Caitlin took a breath, looked at him and asked, "Who are you?"

He tugged on the sheet, dragging it down to her waist, and sat up far enough to slide his tongue along the curve of her breast. "Ladies first."

She shivered. How many times had he done that the

last few days? Caitlin swallowed her moan. Had she enjoyed it as much as she did now? "Caitlin St. George."

The man froze, his eyes widening for a split second before he moved away from her. His smile faded into a deep, menacing laugh, wiping away her desire to lean in to his caress.

Fear slid in behind her lingering passion, pushing it away, flowing over the warmth to bury it with a cold, foreboding chill. Maybe she should have asked *what* he was, instead of *who*.

Before she could part her lips to voice her question, he shifted into the form of a smoky dragon and was gone.

Chapter 2

*Dragon's Lair, Drakes' Resort
in East Tennessee—today*

"Sean, we have a problem."

Without taking his attention away from the lines of coding on his monitor, Sean reached out to absently hit the button on the intercom. "What now?"

"The security alerts are going insane. Again."

"Be right there." He saved the program he'd been debugging, shrugged into his suit jacket and headed out of the private office in his suite.

Sean reminded himself to be patient. Harold was doing the best he could. The security tech had called in sick this morning, and he didn't have time to sit and watch the monitors himself.

The rest of the family had left for the family's medieval stronghold on Mirabilus Isle a few days ago, and he wasn't about to call either of his brothers, or his aunt, home for something this minor. Not when this was the first time since his return they'd left him in complete charge of the Lair.

So when Harold, the family's right-hand man, sometimes chauffeur, mechanic and occasional handyman, had volunteered to watch the cameras, Sean had accepted his help.

Of course, today was the day when everything that could go wrong, did. Now, for the third time this morning, Sean's new tweaks to the system were having fits.

Walking into the basement security room, Sean glanced at the half-round bank of monitors. "Which one now?"

"The lobby." Harold rose and moved out of the inner circle.

Well, at least it wasn't in the kitchen again. Sean sat down and swiveled the task chair back around to glance at the screen to the lobby.

The temperature bar at the bottom of the monitor was blinking red—something very hot, or on fire, was in the lobby. He knew if he turned the sound on, that the alarm would be barking in time with the blinks.

"I didn't see anything out of the ordinary." Harold leaned over his shoulder, pointing at the check-in counter. "But it went off when she entered."

A woman stood at the counter. Either the modified alarm system was a total bust, or it was finally doing its job correctly.

Sean tapped in another view of the counter and cursed softly.

The system was working just as it should—monitoring the temperature of the guests' bodies and alerting the security staff to the presence of a nonhuman.

She hadn't changed much since he'd last seen her. A little paler, with lines of distress marring her forehead, making her appear drained and weak. Shadows of worry framed her amber eyes. If anything, her apparent vulnerability made her more enticing now than before. Caitlin St. George—the magic dragon slayer—was checking in to Dragon's Lair.

When she'd first told him her name, he had gotten the impression that she didn't realize what her name even meant. But then, since he'd refused her entry into his thoughts, she hadn't known who, or what, he was, so there'd been no reason for her to put two and two together.

Actually, other than her name—which could be nothing more than a strange coincidence—he'd had no reason to vanish the way he had. Granted, she was a St. George and he a Drake—the dragon slayer and the dragon—but as far as he knew, the days of killing dragons had ended centuries ago.

Yet at hearing her name, something sharp and menacing had poked at his dragon, enraging it beyond reason. So he'd done the only thing he could upon discovering he'd been sleeping with what his beast seemed to distrust—laughed at the complete irony of the situation and then vanished from her life.

What was she doing here at the Lair? Something was obviously wrong. But why would she come to him? After the way he'd deserted her so abruptly, it made no sense for her to be here.

Sean cleared the event from the system and reset the lobby's alarm. "There you go, Harold. It's all reset now."

The man frowned at him and asked, "Who is she?"

He brushed by Harold, answering on his way to the elevator, "An old friend."

"How old?"

Sean knew what Harold was asking in his round-about way. He wanted to know if this was someone he'd met during those long, endless months his family all referred to as "Sean's dark time."

Knowing Harold wouldn't like the answer and that the man wouldn't be able to keep the information to himself, Sean hit the close button on the elevator's panel and said, "I met her at a bar in town." It wasn't exactly a lie—he *had* met her at a bar, in a town, just not a bar in this town.

Checking his reflection in the smoke-tinted mirrored wall, he straightened his tie and raked his fingers through his hair. Why his appearance mattered was beyond him. It wasn't as if his beast was going to let either of them remain dressed for long.

Stepping out of the elevator when it stopped a floor above, he crossed the resort's lobby, almost missing a step as a nearly forgotten bolt of raw lust surged through him, awakening the slumbering dragon within.

He could feel the beast turn its head to stare intently at the woman. He heard the ragged chuff as it picked up her scent and recognized the mate it had hungered for, yet oddly wanted to avoid.

He rolled his neck, fighting the urge to give in to the heated desires washing through him and leaned over the counter next to Caitlin to tell the clerk, "I've got this one, Brandy. Give me a suite key on thirteen." He glanced at the floor, then asked, "Do you have any bags?"

St. George was cool, collected—unlike her response at their last encounter. She didn't flinch, didn't even bat an eyelash. However, she stared at him, her eyes shimmering, and swallowed hard, apparently as affected by his presence as he was by hers. "My luggage is in the car. I don't need a room, but we do need to talk."

Sean placed the keycard back on the counter and nodded toward the row of elevator doors. "If you'll follow me?"

She seemed hesitant, not moving until he placed a hand on her shoulder. "Come on, Red, I'd really hate to embarrass both of us right here in the lobby."

That, too, was a lie. At this minute he didn't care where they were, or who was around. He wanted nothing more than to shred the clothes from her body with his talons and taste every delectable inch of her naked flesh.

Beneath his touch he felt her flare of lust roar to life, only to cool just as quickly. Sean wasn't fooled by her controlled disinterest—it was a method of self-preservation that she'd obviously learned, and perfected, during this last year.

Damn shame, actually.

She let him guide her to the elevator. Once the door slid closed behind them, he moved in, stalking her, backing her into a corner. "Welcome to Dragon's Lair."

She pushed against his chest. "I said we need to talk."

Talking was the furthest thing from his mind. Sean leaned against her, his chest pressing into the softness of her breasts. He narrowed his eyes as the heat of her body drifted into his. "Talk about what?"

"You do remember what I am, don't you?"

With a soft throaty growl, Sean nodded. "Yeah, mine."

"Really? Your abrupt departure said the exact opposite. Trust me, I am *not* yours."

Sean settled his thighs more firmly against hers and

feathered his lips against her neck. "You'll soon forget that I ever left so hastily."

Caitlin closed her eyes at the reminder of their last encounter. It had taken days, but eventually all of her memories had flooded back and she'd remembered every second of the time they'd spent in her bed.

She hadn't been as uninvolved as she'd first hoped. In fact, if her memories were accurate, she'd urged him on a time or three and had begged—*begged*!—him to stop teasing her, to end his achingly hot torment of her body more than once.

Never before had any man satisfied her so completely—and lived.

Her body seemed to hum as it, too, remembered and hungered for a command performance. She placed her hands flat on his chest, biting back a sigh at the feel of his muscles beneath her palms. "Please."

He clasped both of her hands with one of his own and dragged them down the length of his chest and past his waist. "You don't need to beg—at least not right now. We can save that for later."

When he bent his head to once again feed her shivers with his lips, she turned slightly and sank her fangs into his neck.

He pulled free from her bite, still smiling. "New trick?"

"A gift from my father. You should be grateful that unlike him, I don't suck blood."

"Oh, sweetheart, there isn't anything you could do to me that I wouldn't like."

"Sean, please." She shoved him farther away and paced along the back of the elevator. "I'm not here on a pleasure run. I need your help."

Her worry settled cold in his blood, effectively cool-

ing the wayward desire. He watched her carefully. Her
stride as she paced was brisk and determined. Yet she
repeatedly curled and uncurled her fingers while shooting him brief darting glances. Nervousness was mixed
in with her worry.

Sean silently swore. How did he so instinctively
know that without delving into her mind? What was
this *thing* between them? Why the instant attraction
before and again now, and why did he so easily pick
up on her moods? And why was his beast so conflicted
between desiring her and wanting to tear her to shreds?

The only thing he understood about any of it was that
he didn't like it—at all. It was an interruption in his life
that he didn't need right now. This was something he
couldn't control. And the safety of his family and his
own life depended on his ability to control the vile urges
demanding their deaths that still haunted him at times.

Without looking, he reached over and hit the stop
button. When the elevator bounced gently to a halt, he
asked, "I haven't heard from you in nearly a year, what
sort of help do you think I'd be willing to offer?"

She paused to look at him with narrowed eyes. "I
gave up trying to contact you after about four months."

"I never received a call or any other contact from
you."

"If by *other contact* you mean telepathy, I can't do
that unless I can see you. So summoning you with my
mind was out of the question. Since you'd shifted into a
dragon, it wasn't that hard to guess your identity. There
aren't that many dragon clans left, and the way you reacted to hearing my name made it fairly obvious you
were a Drake. After that, finding the phone number to
Dragon's Lair was easy." She resumed pacing, her arms
crossed against her body. "Unfortunately, I kept getting

the wrong Drake. I spoke to your aunt. The last time I called she told me that you were recently engaged and to leave you alone." The look she turned on him was frigid. "So I did."

He felt her rising anger. However, it was nothing compared to his own. *Engaged?* That was the best Aunt Dani could devise? "When was this?"

Caitlin shook her head and sighed as if bored with this conversation. "The first time was about a month after you disappeared from my bedroom."

She'd called while he was still debating whether to come home or not. Which explains why he had never received word that she'd called. However, he'd returned to the Lair shortly after that, so why hadn't his aunt mentioned the calls?

That was something he'd take up with Danielle later.

"I'm sorry. I wasn't living here then."

"Ah."

He was taken aback by the shortness of her answer. "I am not engaged."

She rolled her eyes and shrugged. "That doesn't matter."

"What did you—"

She turned to face him, throwing up her hands to stop him from talking. She screamed in frustration and then nearly shouted, "Our son has been kidnapped!"

The beast reared back and growled with enough force to send him stumbling backward. The growl turned menacing as it vibrated inside his chest. Between that unexplained bout of temper and the sudden roaring in his ears, he wasn't certain he'd heard her correctly. After taking a deep breath and shaking his head, he asked, "Our what?"

"Son. Our son."

"That isn't possible."

"Yes," she shot back. "It is possible." She covered her face with a shaking hand for a second before adding, "I don't have the time, nor the inclination, for this."

He repeated, "It's not possible." He would have known. The beast should have known. This woman had been marked as its mate, why hadn't the beast known, or at least sensed this had happened?

"Damn it!" she yelled. "Do you think I sleep with so many men that I don't know who the father of my child is?"

"No." His mind swirled with an effort to make sense of this. First, however, he needed to defuse her anger before she managed to give the beast a reason to be uncontrollably enraged. "That isn't what I meant. Calm down. Give me a minute to—"

"Would you like a calculator?" She jerked her purse from her shoulder, rummaged inside and slapped her smartphone against his chest. "Here. We were together a little over a year ago. He's three months old. You do the math."

Sean cursed and pushed the phone aside. "I assumed you were on the pill."

Not only was it lame, it was the flimsiest excuse he'd ever used. Especially since he knew what her response would be.

"Oh, of course you did. And I suppose you also assumed that human birth control pills would somehow be effective?"

He closed his eyes at the expected reply. He'd never had to worry about any type of danger inherent with spur-of-the-moment sex, since his beast had the uncanny ability to sense when something wasn't quite right and would steer him away from the encounter. As for birth control—his brothers had assured him that it was a nonissue since he could only impregnate his... *mate.*

Sean wanted to kick himself. Once they'd walked into her bedroom he'd been so wrapped up in lust, need, desire and her that he'd never given a second thought to the fact his dragon had marked this female at the bar. How had he let himself get so out of touch with reality? It wasn't as if he could blame the alcohol—he'd only had two beers. Regardless, intoxication wasn't an acceptable excuse for anything. Especially not for this.

Caitlin dropped the phone back inside her purse, and then she grasped the lapels of his suit jacket. "I don't care if you believe me or not. I know he's your son, and he's in danger."

Sean looked down at her as he willed the snarling dragon to calm down enough for him to think. "I never said I didn't believe you."

"He's just a baby." Tears welled in her eyes. Her chin quivered. "Please, help me."

He could hear the beast's roar in his ears, saw it thrash back and forth in his mind. The dragon was feeling trapped and angry, but the woman in front of him was afraid and worried. His beast would soon get over its hissy fit. However, Caitlin couldn't be expected to do the same. He stroked her cheek and brushed away a falling tear. "Yes. Of course I will."

She fell against his chest with a cry. "Thank you."

Ignoring a sudden bout of heartburn caused by the dragon's displeasure with this entire situation, Sean restarted the elevator and then, against his better judgment, he wrapped his arms around her. "It'll be fine. We'll get him back safely. Have the kidnappers asked for a ransom?"

She nodded against his chest.

"That's good. Money isn't an obstacle."

"The ransom isn't money."

The kidnapper didn't want money? Then what was the demand? "So you've talked to the kidnapper?"

The elevator doors whooshed open, and Caitlin stepped out of his embrace. She shrugged one shoulder and then said, "In a manner of speaking, yes."

Sean frowned at her elusive answer. "My suite is right around the corner. We can talk there."

He escorted her down the hallway in silence. Once inside his apartment suite, Sean crossed the living room to open the sliding door to the balcony. A blast of cool, late-autumn air flowed into the suite. He breathed in deeply, hoping the crispness of the air would help to quell the uneasiness in his chest.

Stepping away from the door, he motioned Caitlin toward the sofa. "Would you like something to drink?"

She shook her head as she settled into a corner of the couch.

Instead of taking a seat himself, he perched on the arm of the chair across the room from her. "Why don't you start at the beginning."

"The day before yesterday, something broke into my room while I was napping."

"Something?"

"Yeah—*something*." She shrugged. "At first I thought it might be you, until the icy evilness of it washed over me, taking away my breath."

As far as he knew, that type of evilness could belong to only one being. A sickening feeling in the pit of Sean's stomach formed, growing with each passing word of her explanation.

"It was as if it knew I'd realized the thing's vile intent, because it conjured a spell that threw me against a wall and pinned me there until it exited with our son in tow."

"Can you describe it?"

"At first it was wispy with no real identifiable form."

That explained why she'd thought it might be him. His dragon form was little more than smoke unless he—or the Dragon Lord—willed it into something more solid.

"And when it started to take shape, it was like a beast from a nightmare." Her lip quivered, but she quickly turned her head away as she continued, "A monster has our son."

Sean's beast growled with rage. Not with a vague undirected anger like it had upon first seeing Caitlin, but with murderous intent toward the wizard who had taken its offspring.

"You'd said it spoke to you and demanded ransom?"

She nodded, but didn't answer.

Sean rose and crossed the room to kneel before her. He stroked her cheek, coaxing her to look at him. "What, Caitlin? Tell me, what does it want?"

"The book, the box, the emerald and sapphire pendants." She stared at him. "And for you to complete your task."

Sean jerked back as if he'd been burned. While the items demanded as ransom told him that his suspicion had been correct—Nathan the Learned had his son—it gave him no clue as to what task he was supposed to complete.

Caitlin edged around him and stood up. With her hands pressing into her stomach, she moved across the room—away from him. Staring out the open balcony doors, she asked, "How are you involved with this... this thing?"

"I'm not." Even though as far as he knew he wasn't working with any malevolent being—at least not of his own free will—his answer felt...off...not quite right somehow. It felt as if his subconscious was vaguely aware of something that hadn't yet fully registered in his brain yet.

"Then why did it place so much importance on this task of yours?" She leaned against the doorjamb. "It laughed when it repeated itself more than once."

"*It* has a name—Nathan—"

"No!" She spun around with a cry before he could complete his sentence. "Not Nathan the Learned?"

Tightening his grasp on the arm of the sofa, he frowned. What did a succubus know about a Druid wizard? He straightened and turned to face her. "How do you know about Nathan?"

"My father is a vampire."

He rubbed his neck. "I already gathered that much."

"He's been around long enough to have run into the Learned a time or two. Besides, my father has a seat on the High Council of our kind, so there isn't much he doesn't know, or hasn't heard." She shrugged again. "And what he doesn't know, my mother can usually find out."

He almost didn't want to ask. "And your mother is a...what?"

"Dead."

Sean resisted the urge to vanish. A few years ago he would have walked out of the apartment at such a senseless answer. But he'd seen and learned so many things the last two years that he was fairly certain this wouldn't be anything new. "Dead as in a zombie?"

Her eyes widened. "Gross. No. Dead as in physically deceased."

"Ah." Feeling foolish, he offered condolences. "I am sorry for your loss."

"No need. She's still here."

Maybe he hadn't learned everything just yet. "What?"

Caitlin rolled her eyes. "She refuses to move on without my father, so her spirit is still here."

"That raises more questions than I want to get into right now. But I don't suppose your mother can find out where…" He paused, realizing that he didn't know the child's name.

"Sean."

"What?"

"Sean. His given name is Sean Alexander Drake II."

Just. Simply. Wonderful. Since there was no way for her to know that what she'd done in naming the boy went against centuries of Drake tradition.

"Is there a reason you made it so easy for him to be found by any dragon slayer out there?"

She shrugged. "Since I'm the slayer, it actually didn't cross my mind. Besides, his name had nothing to do with you or what you are."

"Right." He didn't buy that for a minute. "Then why make it so obvious he's my son?"

"Because it was the easiest way to piss off my parents."

"And I'm sure you succeeded."

"Completely."

Why she'd want to enrage her family in such a manner was a question left for another time. "I don't suppose your mother can find out where Junior is being held?"

She cringed visibly at his use of *Junior.* "Sean—his name is Sean."

"Can she find out where Sean is being held?"

"She already has. He's in a castle ruins on the east coast of Ireland."

Sean found it interesting that the wizard had holed up about as close to Mirabilus Isle as he could without being easily detected. His family had taken the larger jet, but Braeden's personal one was still in the hangar at the airport. He pulled out his cell phone and directed Harold to have the jet fueled and ready to go as quickly as possible then tapped it off without explaining why. He and Caitlin needed to get to Mirabilus, and she had no means of otherworldly transportation.

Turning his attention back to Caitlin, he asked, "Does your mother know if he's harmed the baby?"

"Our son is fine—for now."

That was a relief. Although there was no telling how long that might last. A flash of heat coursing down the back of his head, then down his spine, distracted him.

"He'll be safe for a week."

Sean frowned at the way she'd answered his question before he'd asked, and then he realized her intrusion had caused the flash of heat. "Stay out of my head, Caitlin."

"I'm sorry. Since we're physically so close, it's just easier."

"Easier isn't always right." Before, at the bar, she hadn't complained about him delving into her mind, but he wondered how she would react to the same type of trespass now and reached out to brush her thoughts.

His touch seemed to crack the mental dam she'd been using to rein in her needs. At first a trickle of weak, nervous energy flowed free. Then, as if the dam burst, the hunger she'd been holding back rushed out, nearly overwhelming him. Her raw, aching need was stronger now than it had been the night they'd first met. She was literally starving to death.

He studied her closely. While her copper-streaked auburn hair still fell in waves down her back, the shimmering luster had dulled, as had that twinkling spark in her amber gaze. Her attempt to hide the circles beneath her eyes might have worked from a distance, but now, standing before her, he could see the darker areas where the makeup had worn away. Her face seemed thinner, and her cheeks gaunt.

He lowered his focus, briefly noticing the line of padding in the shoulders of her jacket, before seeing the stark definition of her collarbone.

Sean cursed silently. This hadn't happened in the hours since their child had been taken. Without thinking, he backed her against a wall, pinning her forcibly with his body. "What have you done, Caitlin?"

"What are you talking about?" She pushed at his shoulders. "Nothing. I've done nothing. Let me go."

He ignored her feeble attempt to free herself. Instead, he opened himself to the emotions battling for escape—an avalanche of need, hunger, anger and fear cascaded against him—a tide of emotions he could easily calm, if she'd let him.

Her hunger and craving tore at him, creating a sudden urge to care for her. He didn't question the urge; she was the mother of his child and his dragon's mate. She was his responsibility, and he would do whatever he must to ensure her well-being.

Seemingly over his early bout of anger, his beast chuffed in agreement and then sniffed the air around her. Sean wanted to groan at the lack of life force surrounding her. How many weeks, or months, had she gone without feeding? How many more would pass before she perished?

"You've done nothing?" He slipped a hand beneath her jacket and felt her ribs. "Nothing?" The dragon raged with an unfamiliar worry. Fighting to control his own concern at what she'd done to herself and the beast's anxiety, Sean said, "You will be of no use if you are dead. You need to feed."

She sighed raggedly and leaned against him. With her lips against the hollow of his neck, Caitlin agreed. "I know."

Letting one claw form, Sean hooked the dragon talon into the neck of her silky blouse, warning, "If this is a favorite top, consider it gone."

"Don't," she whispered, but offered no resistance.

"You are spent." He trailed a line of kisses along her cheek. "Let me help."

At her soft sigh, he shredded the fabric and then slowly traced the smooth curve of his talon across her stomach, drawing a moan from her lips.

She shrugged out of her jacket and torn blouse, letting the clothing fall to the floor, and placed her hands against his chest. "What are you going to do to help?"

Her touch was like ice, cold and lifeless against his skin. He again sensed her fear and hunger. He knew the fear would only be calmed once her child was back safely in her arms. But her hunger twisted in his gut with an unspoken desperation that only increased his desire to feed her.

"First you are going to gain some strength." He retracted the claw and covered her hands with one of his own. "Then we're going to Mirabilus to get our son back and kill that bastard wizard once and for all."

When she only nodded, he dipped his head to ask in

a whisper, "What use will you be to the child if you've starved yourself?"

She tried to free her hands, but he held them securely against his chest. "I'm fine."

Sean laughed softly at her lie. "You are far from fine." He pulled her into his embrace asking, "When did you last feed?"

"I don't remember."

He cursed at the shakiness of her answer, released her from the circle of his embrace, swung her up into his arms and headed down the hall toward his bedroom.

She stared at him in shock. "What are you doing?"

"I would think that was obvious." He kicked open the door, crossed the room and dropped her onto the bed.

When she scrambled, almost backstroking toward the far edge of the bed, he easily grasped her legs and pulled her back to him. Kneeling on the bed, he leaned over her and held her head between his cupped hands. "Why didn't you come to me?"

Caitlin swallowed a cry of frustration at the concern she heard in his voice. She could claim that she had tried everything to contact him, but they'd both know that was a lie. Even though she'd been unable to reach him via the phone, she could have searched for him, driven here to Dragon's Lair. While tracking him down might have angered him, he would have come to understand the need.

Or she could say she hadn't wanted to tell him about the baby, but she would know the strength of that lie. She had wanted to tell him, wanted him by her side during the pregnancy and delivery, but her parents and the High Council had insisted vehemently that she hold on to that secret, going so far as to imprison her—a near death sentence for her—when they discovered that she had reached out to him by calling Dragon's Lair.

Still, at this moment, she'd be safer back in her cell. This was the last place she wanted to be—and the only place she longed to be. Beneath his unwavering stare, she finally answered, "Because I don't want to need you."

His easy smile was her undoing. That smug, knowing, self-satisfied, all-male half smile was enough to make the walls she'd painstakingly erected around her emotions crash to her feet as nothing more than tiny shards of broken glass.

His gentle touch stroking her cheek, brushing the hair from her face, tracing her lips, coaxed a strangled cry from her.

Blinking back unwanted tears of shame and disgust at the ease of her surrender, she slipped her arms around him and whispered, "Damn you to hell, Drake."

"At least I won't be lonely with you by my side."

Between his feathery kisses, she exclaimed, "I hate you."

Again with that smile, he answered, "I know."

"I'd rather we didn't—"

He covered her mouth with his, effectively cutting off her words.

When his tongue swept across hers and he exhaled, his breath filled her. It warmed her and fed life into her starving soul. He had every reason to be angry with her, but still he freely shared his life force. How could she not set aside her misgivings?

It didn't matter that she was a St. George, a slayer of dragons, or that he was a Drake and supposedly her mortal enemy. Nor did it matter what her family or the High Council thought best. She needed this—she needed *him*.

She had craved his touch for so many months now that she no longer cared what her parents or the council had said. They were wrong—all of them were wrong. They'd insisted that her obvious path was to kill the dragon and had expressed disappointment that she hadn't done so when she'd had the chance. But she knew with a certainty she couldn't explain, that her only path in life was to not *kill* the dragon. Without the beast, and the man, she feared she might be the one who died.

Without releasing her, his cell phone hit the nightstand right before she heard their clothes rustle to the floor and felt the cool breeze rush across her flesh. She greatly appreciated some of his more than handy skills.

He rolled onto his back, pulling her atop him, and broke their kiss. "Now, if you're done complaining and protesting, let me help you. Take what you need, Caitlin."

She sat up to straddle him, her hands flat on his chest. His expression was serious, no hint of teasing quirked his lips. His heart beat strong and steady beneath her palms, no uneven thumps to give evidence of a lie.

She wanted to accept his offer, but knew full well that she was so starved for his touch that things might get out of control this time. If she drained him, killed him, she'd never see her son again, and she'd spend the rest of her life running from his family. Worry for his well-being prompted her to admit, "I don't know if I can stop myself."

"Darlin'," he drawled in his best tough-man voice, "I think we both know full well that you can't hurt me."

When she still hesitated, Sean reached up to thread

his fingers through her hair. He cupped the back of her head, and she shivered at the tingles running across her scalp.

His bright green gaze held hers, and she swore she could see the dragon within coaxing her closer as the man pulled her down. Memories of their last time together filled her mind, heated her blood and gave her the oddest sense of belonging. Coming here had been the right thing to do.

When their lips barely touched, he challenged, "I dare you to try draining me."

How could she possibly resist such an offer?

Chapter 3

Sean knew Caitlin would be unable to resist his challenge. He relaxed beneath her as she hungrily kissed him, inhaling as much of his energy as she could.

Knowing that a kiss, a drawing in of his breath, would never be enough for her to gain full strength, he slid his hands down the smoothness of her back, chasing the rising goose bumps with his fingertips, and grasped her hips to lift her.

He wanted her healthy and whole—needed her to be at her very best for what was to come. It would take both of them to defeat Nathan and rescue the child. And she would need all the strength she could summon for what would come afterward.

He shifted beneath her and eased her slowly down the length of his erection. Her moan echoed his as she curled her fingers into his shoulders, her nails pressing hard into his flesh.

Sean closed his eyes, savoring what was more than just a physical union of their bodies. This intimate act was more than just a way to replenish Caitlin's energy, or to satisfy the hunger between them.

It was a way to feed their beasts—to soothe the anger emanating from their souls. The growing heat of their bodies, the touch of their lips, transformed the hurt into a power that could very possibly keep them both alive.

Through a thick fog of desire he heard the security alarm scream from his office down the hall. His cell phone vibrated off the nightstand.

Before he could respond to either, Caitlin rolled off him with a harshly gasped curse. Her wide-eyed gaze flew to the bedroom doorway. "Mother! What are you doing here?"

Sean quickly spelled their clothing back on, swallowed hard and then rose from the bed. He stared at the uninvited, semisolid, still-forming woman walking into his bedroom. "Mrs. St. George?"

His beast twitched, backing away in the same manner it did when confronted by an angry Aunt Danielle. Sean rolled his eyes at the adolescent behavior of his dragon.

Mrs. St. George ignored him. Instead, once fully visible, she pinned Caitlin with a hard glare. "I thought we discussed you having anything to do with this… this vile animal."

Animal? The dead wife of a vampire thought *him* an animal? Sean was amazed at the woman's audacity.

"Like it or not, Mother, he is my son's sire."

Narrowing his eyes, Sean frowned at the term *sire*. He was the child's *father*, not his overlord. But that was a detail he'd take up with Caitlin later. For now he chose to silently watch the byplay between the two women.

He hoped it would give him a chance to catch his breath and regain some composure.

"This is how you defy the council? They gave you orders to keep your mouth shut and to stay away from this beast. Instead, you lied to us about where you were going and like some cheap whore, come running to the enemy's bed?"

"He is not *my* enemy."

Mrs. St. George flung her arm out and pointed a shaking finger at Sean. "That is a filthy beast. Your father would run him through with a sword and roast him on a spit like the pig he is, if he knew what you were doing."

The dragon within shook off its initial apprehension at Mrs. St. George's appearance. He focused his growing rage, intent on self-preservation, on the older woman. Never before had the desire to kill been so strong and overpowering—not even when he'd felt driven to murder his brothers. Who did this…ghost… think she was to threaten him in such a manner? *Roast him on a spit?* Sean clenched his fists tighter at his sides as he fought the unrelenting urge to shift into dragon form, rear up and do a little roasting of his own.

"What the hell is going on here?" Braeden materialized in the doorway, breaking the beast's murderous focus by his unexpected appearance. Had Sean been thinking, he would have realized that Harold would eventually contact Braeden, who would then spell himself directly into the middle of the action.

While he was grateful for his brother's timely interruption, Sean groaned at the speed Harold had obviously used in contacting his brother, instead of ordering the jet. "I've got this. Go back to your wife."

His brother cocked an eyebrow at him before studying Caitlin, who was still on the bed, flushed and look-ing as rumpled as the sheets beneath her, and then at her mother, who had turned to face him. A smirk lifted the corner of his mouth. "Why, Mrs. St. George, how's the hubby doing these days? Does his leg still bother him?"

Sean frowned in confusion. His brother drifted into his mind to fill in the missing piece. *At the last meeting of the heads of the preternatural families, St. George and I had a minor...tiff. He lost.*

Caitlin's mother stiffened at Braeden's question and raised her chin a notch. "That's Baron St. George to you, Drake."

Braeden leaned casually against the doorway and inspected his fingernails as if bored. "*Lord* Drake."

Sean knew his brother's nonchalant stance was noth-ing but an act. The deep steadiness of his voice had been a dead giveaway. He waited to see how Mrs. St. George would react to the Dragon Lord's reminder of who held the higher rank. Regardless of the families involved, St. George was just a baron in his circle, and while titled, he still answered to others. Braeden was the High Lord in his, answering to no one.

Finally, with a look that could kill a mortal, Mrs. St. George dipped her head slightly in deference. "The baron is well, my lord."

Braeden straightened and walked into the bedroom. "So, anyone care to explain what's going on here? Why has Lady St. George come to the Lair?" He paused by the bed to stare down at Caitlin. "And why is the dragon slayer's child in a dragon's bed?"

Caitlin corrected him. "My father's daughter is no longer a child, nor is he the dragon slayer. I am."

Braeden arched his eyebrows at her statement. Before the situation could get completely out of control, Sean insisted once again, "I can handle this."

Caitlin's mother visibly shook before exclaiming, "My daughter bore that vile beast's spawn!"

Sean cringed when he saw Braeden stiffen. This wasn't how he had wanted his family to find out.

Without asking permission, Braeden stroked Caitlin's cheek. His touch lingered far too long for Sean's comfort. He might not have been born a preternatural, but he knew enough about his brother to realize Braeden was mining information whether Caitlin wanted him to or not.

Finally, after what felt like hours, but was in fact mere seconds, Braeden lowered his arm and turned to glare at Sean. It was obvious from the darkness of his eyes and the tick in his cheek that he knew everything. "Could you have been any more foolish?"

"I…" Sean trailed off at the elongating of Braeden's pupils. Now was not the time to poke a stick at the one being that could kill him and his child's mother in the blink of an eye.

"You do understand what this means?"

"Yes." Of course he did.

Now.

He was mated…

For life.

Not only was the child his responsibility, so was the mother. Getting Caitlin to understand that would be the questionable part.

"Good. Have you thought about getting into Nathan's stronghold?"

"Haven't had time yet. I was seeing to another… problem first."

Braeden shot a hard gaze from him to Caitlin and

back. "And you thought relinquishing a portion of your own strength would help the situation?"

His dragon bristled at the insinuation of weakness, but Sean wasn't going to argue this with his brother at this very tense moment. So he simply nodded.

Thankfully, Braeden didn't press the issue. Instead, he said, "This explains your need for a jet. Mine will be ready within the hour. In the meantime, figure this—" he paused to wave a hand between the two of them then continued "—*problem* out. I'll head back to Mirabilus and nose around Nathan's stronghold. Either I, or Cam, will be in touch." Braeden nodded toward the older woman. "For future reference, whatever you do, don't let her, or her husband, get anywhere near my nephew."

Sean opened his mouth to ask why, but before he could utter a single syllable, Braeden was gone.

Still refusing to meet his gaze, Caitlin's mother stepped closer to the bed. Addressing her daughter, she said, "I will not have some beast telling me what I can or cannot do."

Beast? She called the Dragon Lord a beast in his own home? Sean had reached the limit of his patience. "Get out." When she didn't move, he let his dragon give the order. "Get. Out."

The raspy, deep command got her attention, although not in the manner he'd intended. She turned to look at him with all the concern of someone being pestered by a gnat. "I beg your pardon?"

Her shoulders sagging, Caitlin implored the older woman, "Mother, please, just go."

"Not without you, I won't. Your father has secured Baron Derek's signature on the prenuptial agreement. It seems that after careful consideration, and a substantial increase in the dowry, the baron is willing to ignore your childish escapades this last year. Besides, the elders have located a suitable family for the bastard you bore, and they'll be at the manor the day after tomorrow to collect him."

She turned to address Sean directly. "Now, if you'll just hand over the items we need for the ransom, we'll be on our way."

The woman couldn't be serious. He glanced at Caitlin, but she kept her head lowered, refusing to meet his gaze. They were going to give the baby to strangers? Just like that? Without even consulting him first?

It wasn't as if the two of them were too young or immature to care for a child. And it most certainly wasn't as if either one of them couldn't afford to care for the baby. There was no logical reason to give the child away to strangers. And to talk about it so callously, as if they were doing nothing more than giving away a lamp, was more than he could tolerate.

Rage burned in his chest. But he didn't know who he was angrier with—Lady St. George for her unforgiveable rudeness, or Caitlin for acting as if this was all fine with her. He could deal with Caitlin later. Right now, however, he wanted her mother gone.

Sean didn't bother trying to hold his temper. The woman didn't deserve any type of restrained behavior from him. She could count herself lucky that he didn't unleash the dragon spitting and snarling inside him.

He strode across the room until he stood between Caitlin and her mother. Staring down at her, he once again ordered, "Get out of my apartment. Get out of the Lair. Now!"

She sighed and then motioned Caitlin to join her. "Come, it is time to leave."

"No!" Sean yelled at her while reaching back to hold

on to Caitlin's shoulder, keeping her pinned in place on the bed. "*You*, get out of here. She stays."

Lady St. George's eyes widened, and she grew more opaque with each passing second. Right before she completely disappeared, Sean said, "And don't come back."

"That wasn't necessary."

Sean spun around to look down at Caitlin. "I didn't ask for your opinion, did I?"

When she rose from the bed, he asked, "Where do you think you're going?"

"They aren't going to let me stay. I need to go home."

"*Let* you stay?" He didn't even try to hide the sarcasm in his voice. "What are you, ten years old?" Sean pointed at the bed. "Sit down. You aren't going anywhere."

"But—"

"But nothing." He interrupted her. "Oh, that's right, *Baron Derek* is waiting for you." The physical act of simply saying those words aloud sent the beast into a raging fit.

She shrugged her shoulders and said nothing.

"What makes you think I'm going to let the mother of my child marry another man?"

"What do you care? It's not as if I was ever going to marry you."

Sean laughed at her. "Oh, darlin', I don't remember asking you to marry me."

"Then what the hell are you talking about?"

He hadn't planned on giving her the news in this manner, but now was as good a time as any. "Didn't your daddy tell you? Must have been an oversight on his part. Why do you think he's so anxious to get you wed to someone else?"

She sighed and looked away. "Because he's tired

of hearing others talk about his daughter in such a degrading manner."

"Yeah, right, Caitlin. You know better than that. Do you really think St. George cares what anyone else says or thinks?"

"When it comes to me, yes, he does. He hates the dishonor I've brought to his door."

"You brought a baby to his door—my baby. Since when is there dishonor in creating life?"

"When that life is conceived out of wedlock and isn't of royal blood, there is plenty of dishonor."

And here he'd always thought Braeden had cornered the market on acting like a medieval lord. Apparently, he'd been wrong. Sean made a show of looking around the room. "In what century do you people live?"

She raised her hands, only to lower them back onto her lap. "You don't understand."

"Oh, hey, I get it. Wealth and power don't replace titled nobility in your little world." He moved closer to her. "Actually, it's you who doesn't understand. The reason your father is marrying you off as quickly as he can is because he knows that dragons mate for life."

"Mate?" She jumped up from the bed and glanced toward the door. "You talk like an animal."

"Of course I do." If she thought she was going to make a break for it and get out of this room, she was sadly mistaken. He stepped close enough that he could feel her confusion. "Do you forget *what* I am?"

Before she could answer, the wispy form of his dragon rose up from him, surrounding him. He stood in the center of the smoky creature and stared at her as his beast leaned forward to capture her gaze.

Spellbound by the glittering stare holding her captive, Caitlin shivered at the display of control and power before her.

Sean crossed his arms against his chest and asked, "Are you afraid, Caitlin?"

The beast lowered its head, sniffing her, chuffing her scent, and then rose up, its mouth open, fangs bared, growling in obvious displeasure.

"You should be afraid. Far more afraid of me than you are of your parents."

Caitlin respected her parents, didn't want to disappoint them any more than she already had and yes, to a certain extent, she did fear their wrath. However, her fear of him had the added element of possible death— hers. Summoning as much bravado as she could, Caitlin stared at him, asking, "You plan on terrifying me to prove that point?"

"No. But you need to understand there are no options for you."

"There are always options." There had to be.

"No." He circled her slowly, his beast moving with him. "Any option was lost when you carried the child to term. Had we not been mated, it's doubtful you would have been pregnant in the first place and even if by some chance you had, you would have lost the baby long before it was born. It's the nature of the beast—a way to prevent unwanted changelings."

A tiny part of her mind wondered if that was the reason her parents had essentially locked her away during her pregnancy. Since she had been ravenous the entire time, they'd said it was to protect the human population. Had they lied? Had it been done in hope that the baby would perish? *No.* She swatted down the thought. Even though they had withheld this mating information, she was certain they would never stoop so low. "Even if that's true, and we are…mated…it doesn't mean we have to have anything to do with each other once Sean is rescued."

"True. You're right." He agreed with her but then added, "However, there are two problems with having no contact. No matter what happens, you will never marry another man. Ever." The smooth curve of a talon traced her spine, making her shiver with fear and unexpected longing. "Do you understand me?"

"No. I don't. That doesn't make any sense. We aren't in love. We have no intentions of marrying each other."

"Perhaps not. But dragons mate for life."

He'd already said that. "And?"

"I can never take another mate while you live."

She closed her eyes. This was too much. She heard his words, but they made little sense. Pinning her gaze back on his, she asked, "So, if I don't stay with you, you'll spend the rest of your life alone?"

"Since I have no intention of raising a son without a mother, no, I would not live alone."

That meant— Her mind screamed. *Wait a minute!* No. He couldn't be serious. Could he? She felt as if she were choking on her own breath. "You would kill me?"

He lifted one eyebrow. "How dark is that cave where your mind goes?" He shook his head. "No, I have no intention of killing you. But you are my mate. You are *my* child's mother. And that's where the second problem comes into play. If you want to see the child grow up, you'll need to live here and trust me, you aren't doing so with a husband in tow."

Her stomach knotted at the implication. "Are you planning to take him away from me?"

"Absolutely. He is mine." A low, menacing growl

raced hot against her ear. "What do you care? You were going to give him to strangers."

She trembled with dread. Her heart ached at the idea of losing her son forever. "That wasn't my idea."

"I didn't hear you argue with your mother about it."

Argue with her mother? That would have been a fine waste of time, since the woman would have simply ignored her. Never, for one second, had she worried about giving her son away—she'd had every intention of escaping with him and disappearing for good. "You don't understand."

"What don't I understand? That you were going to give my child to another family in the St. George clan?" His voice was tight with what she recognized as anger. "What were they going to do with him?" He grasped her arms and threw her mother's words in her face. "Run a sword through him and roast him on a spit like a pig?"

"No!" She tried to jerk free. "It's not like that."

"Then tell me what it is like." His hold on her arms tightened. "Tell me how much love and affection the child would have received from a clan who so obviously despises what he might become."

"Stop it. You don't know what you're talking about."

"It does make me wonder, though. Would you have attended the child's funeral wearing black? Would you have mourned his death? Or would you have avoided the event altogether?"

Her heart beat hard and fast, making breathing difficult. The smooth huskiness of his voice, more beast now than man, frightened her more than she ever thought possible. She kicked at him, twisted her arms to claw at him.

He threw her onto the bed, landing on top of her. She

swung her fists. When he did nothing more than laugh, she bared her fangs and hissed.

Sean nearly laughed in her face. "You want fangs?" He turned her head with the palm of his hand, shoving her cheek into the pillow, holding her still, and sank the tip of his fangs into the tender curve where her neck met her shoulder.

His bite laced anger through Caitlin's growing horror. She struggled to shove him away, but he tightened his hold, sending a wave of pain shooting across her shoulder.

"Let me go."

His beast only growled, making her wonder who was in control—the man or the dragon.

Immortality had been her birthright from her father. She'd always taken comfort knowing that outside of having her heart, or head, ripped from her body, or starving to death, nothing would end her life.

However, with Sean's deadly fangs lodged so close to her neck, her immortality was in grave danger. The sticky warmth of her own blood soaking into her clothes only served to confirm the danger.

Submit.

The deep raspy voice of the beast flowed into her mind. But submitting to him wasn't an option. While the Drakes and St. Georges may have become slightly more civilized these last few centuries, after today that would change.

Her resistance gained her another deeper level of pain as his jaw tightened and he shook her.

Submit.

How? Caitlin sobbed at the futility of trying to fight this beast.

Caitlin, for the sake of our child, submit.

This deep voice, while still raspy and hoarse, did not contain the undertone of a beast. It was human, and its plea touched not just her mind, but something deeper, too.

With a sob, she fell lax beneath him.

After one final halfhearted shake, he gentled, releasing her, then soothing her injured flesh with his tongue, wiping away the blood and the pain as he tended the wound. His touch knitted muscle and flesh until it was once again whole.

Satisfied the injury had been healed, Sean lifted his head to look down at her and warn, "Don't ever fight me again."

"You have to be kidding. I'm supposed to bow to your every whim out of fear for my life?"

He heard the angry bravado in her trembling voice. Relieved that her terror had begun to subside, he lightened his tone. "See how easily you understand?"

"You are not some commanding deity that I need to mindlessly obey."

"Damn pity. However, it doesn't change the fact that I am responsible for your well-being and safety. It's instinctual. Things will go easier for you if you just do as you're told."

When she didn't respond to his flippancy, or statement of fact, he rose from the bed. "I need a minute alone, and I'm sure you could use some time to yourself, too. But we obviously have a plane to catch, so be quick." He glanced around the bedroom. "You said your luggage was in your car?"

She nodded and Sean headed toward the door. "I'll have it sent to the plane and your car parked in the garage. Join me out front when you're ready."

Caitlin waited a few minutes after he'd left the room

before she rolled over and buried her face in the comforter on the bed. Why had she come here? What made her think that Sean would help her get their son back without any conditions of his own? She'd known he was a dragon changeling. She also knew what that meant—demanding, possessive and oh, so arrogant in his assumption that he alone was right. Yet she'd never had so much as a second thought about coming to him.

Her breath hitched, and she swallowed the urge to cry. Was her son warm? Was he dry? Had he been fed? Did they hold him when he cried?

They wouldn't know that he didn't like to be rocked; he'd rather be bounced. So if they rocked him, it would only make him more upset, more agitated. What if his anxiety was more than they could handle and prompted them to do something horribly reckless?

Dozing in the corner of the ancient puzzle box, Aelthed opened his eyes and tilted his head to one side with a frown. Something was…different. There was a certain *something* in the air swirling about his eternal jail.

It felt like… He leaned forward, his arms wrapped around his bent legs, studying the chemistry in the air. It felt like animal lust.

Need.

Desire.

He shook his head. From where had this emotion come? Who was the object of such primordial passion?

Even after more than eight long centuries of captivity, he understood and recognized the intense longing that charged the air swirling about him like lightning in a thunderstorm.

The dragon twins were already mated, so neither of them were the target. And he knew that it was not

Danielle Drake. Her passion was for him, and it felt warm, comforting, enticing and nothing at all like this brewing storm.

"No." Aelthed rose and paced, hoping the movement would clear his mind of what was impossible. "It can't be."

The newest changeling wasn't a dragon born. It couldn't be him. His beast and power came from a curse alone, not from family blood. So why would that dragon's emotions flow all the way from Dragon's Lair to Mirabilus, into his cell and mind? Unless... Aelthed frowned. Was there more to this curse than he'd first feared?

Sending his thoughts out into the air, he whispered, "Danielle, come, talk to me."

Just saying her name eased the tension from his body and the frown from his face. Danielle Drake possessed far more than just guardianship of his prison— she possessed his heart. Since he'd forced himself into her hands a couple years ago, he'd come to care for her deeply and he was well aware she shared the same feelings for him.

After Nathan the Learned had dropped the box that kept Aelthed imprisoned at the feet of the Dragon Lord's wife, Alexia, they had put him in the basement with their weapons and forgotten about him. Which suited him fine, because it gave him the chance to listen and learn.

When it became necessary to gain assistance, he'd sought out Danielle Drake. Aelthed laughed softly remembering the first time he'd spoken to her. At that moment he'd been grateful for two things—that Danielle was telepathic and that his nephew Nathan had kept him updated on the current languages through the decades.

Otherwise he never would have been able to converse with the woman.

He might have only been a spirit imprisoned in a puzzle box, but that didn't stop him from noticing how beautiful she was with her womanly curves and long raven tresses. He'd been drawn to her from the first moment she'd touched his box and made him gasp at the warmth that had flooded through him.

She was so easy to talk to, quick of wit and old enough to know her own mind. Which she had to be, considering she'd raised her three nephews alone after their parents had been killed at Nathan's hand. It was a shame she'd never married, never had the opportunity to share a life and experiences with someone her own age. But she'd insisted more than once that her life had been full and she was content with her lot—especially now that she had Aelthed to share her joys and troubles with.

He'd once lamented the huge difference in their ages and she'd laughed at him. While it was true that he was over nine hundred years of age and she only sixty-two, he'd only lived as a man for eighty of those years. As far as she was concerned, he wasn't all that much older.

He didn't argue with her logic, because it made no difference while he was locked in a wooden cube.

Within moments, he felt her warm touch on the box as she lifted it from her nightstand. "What is it, Aelthed? What do you need?"

He shivered at the low, seductive timbre of her voice. Oh, to be alive again, to be a man capable of gathering her into his arms for an embrace, a kiss, a prelude to making love. A wry smile briefly crossed his lips. Dreams and wishes were all he had and of late, they weren't nearly enough.

Opening his mind to his surroundings, he brought her into view. He nodded with approval at the way she'd been wearing her hair down lately, instead of twisted up into a tight bun. She looked younger, more alive with the raven tresses streaming along her back. Forcing his attention back to the subject at hand, he asked, "Your nephew, the youngest one, is he still back at Dragon's Lair?"

He felt the woman's hesitation before she answered, "Yes, he is."

"And tell me, Danielle, what troubles him?"

She sat on the edge of her bed and sighed. "I'm not sure of all the facts since Braeden just returned from the Lair. But it seems Sean got a vampire's daughter pregnant. She had a son, and he's been kidnapped."

A vampire? The changeling lusted after a vampire? "Good heavens, not St. George?"

"Of course. Would one of the Drake boys choose anyone…normal?"

Aelthed chuckled at her long-suffering tone. Even though she'd done a fine job, she never should have had to raise three Drake males on her own. "No. It would make your life all too boring if they did."

Danielle nodded in agreement. "I suppose so." She placed the puzzle cube on a pillow and stretched out on the bed. "So, what can you tell me about St. George?"

"Well, it's your great-great-great-grandsire's fault that he's a vampire. If I recall the rumors correctly, the two of them got into a fight—the dragon and the dragon slayer—and when the dragon managed to knock the slayer out, he left the man tied to a tree in the forest assuming someone would come along and free him."

"I can guess the rest." Danielle snorted. "He was found by a vampire, not another human."

"Yes. Which explains the deep-seated hatred between the two families."

"Not that they ever would have been the best of friends in the first place."

"Perhaps not, but we can do nothing about the past. Only the future. How did the cursed changeling get a vampire pregnant?"

"She's not exactly a vampire. Braeden says she's a succubus."

Aelthed considered that possibility then shook his head. "Doubtful. I think the Dragon Lord may be mistaken on this one. Although I am willing to guess that if she's not a full blood-sucking vampire, that she may be a psychic soul-sucking one. Does she have fangs?"

"I don't know. I haven't met her."

"This babe she bore, is it human—or otherworldly?"

"I'm not sure." Danielle shook her head and sighed. "But since its mother isn't human, doesn't it stand to reason that the babe might not be, either?"

More to himself than anyone else, Aelthed mused, "I wasn't thinking of the mother."

Danielle's frown deepened. "Surely you don't think this curse on my nephew carried over to his child?"

"Considering the oddities of late, it's something we need to consider." Even though Aelthed could already guess her answer, he had to ask, "I don't suppose you know if the babe has shown any habits that might be considered…purely Drake?"

"I can't answer that, either. I know nothing more than you." Danielle picked up the cube and held it out before her. "Right now all I know for certain—" she drew the cube closer and then dropped her voice to little more than a whisper "—is that your nephew, Nathan the Learned, has the child and is using him as leverage to get his hands on the grimoire...and you."

Chapter 4

Caitlin awoke with a start, uncertain where she was at first until a warm hand brushed down her arm. Then it all came rushing back—her arrival at Dragon's Lair, her mother's intrusion and boarding the plane.

When they'd boarded, she hadn't paid much attention. It'd been easy enough to fall asleep when they'd left Tennessee, but not so much now. Even though she was still exhausted, she looked around the dimly lit cabin. The only description she could think of off the top of her head was air yacht. The Drakes' private jet wasn't a short-hop plane. From the size of it, the baby could easily do transcontinental flights with ease.

The interior looked nothing like any plane she'd ever flown on before. She stretched her legs out before her, pressing her back into the baby-soft leather of the seat. No wonder she'd fallen asleep so quickly; this was easily the most comfortable recliner she'd ever sat in before.

From behind black-padded doors toward the rear of the plane, Sean's voice drifted across her ears. Apparently, he was on the phone again, meaning she was free to go snooping.

Caitlin felt the side of the chair for a button to lower the leg rest. Instead, the one she pressed extended the chair out into a bed. Comfortable? Yes, but not what she wanted. She pressed another button and this time righted the piece of furniture to a chair and then swiveled away from the window. She rose and stepped around the chair next to hers—there were four of them, one on each side of the aisle and the chairs could swivel to face each other if the people seated wanted to hold a conversation.

Behind this setup was another, but while still recliners, the chairs were more like airplane seats in that they didn't swivel around. Between the two sets of chairs was a table that folded down against the wall.

She turned around and walked past the swivel recliners into a small kitchen—or galley, she supposed—and pulled open the fridge to take a bottle of water. The closed doors beyond the galley probably led into the cockpit. She had no desire to see what was there, so turned around and walked into Sean's chest.

"Looking for something?"

"No. Just being nosy."

He laughed. "It's a winged travel home. Braeden does nothing in half measures." Pointing down the aisle, he added, "On the other side of the first set of doors is the head…bathroom. Double sink, shower, toilet. Beyond that is another set of doors that leads to another cabin with more private seating for four. Beyond that a soundproof door concealing the bedroom, where there's two sofas that fold out to beds."

Then he slid open a small panel on the wall next to the galley door and pressed a button. A huge screen slid down in the center of the cabin. "And if you want to watch a movie, you can do that in any of the cabins. Including the head, except that screen's a little smaller."

Caitlin widened her eyes. "Impressive."

"No half measures whatsoever."

"I can't imagine his travel trailer."

Sean laughed. "Where did you get the idea that Braeden goes camping?"

"No?"

He escorted her to the double chairs. "Hardly."

They no sooner sat down than his phone rang again. "Excuse me." He rose and walked down the aisle.

She turned her attention out the window to see only the blackness of the night. They were headed to the Drake family's medieval stronghold on Mirabilus—an island somewhere in the Irish Sea.

It was said that the glamour spell cast over the isle, more than a thousand years ago, still held, and that any mortal who looked upon it saw nothing but mist and fog obscuring their vision.

She couldn't begin to imagine a magic that strong. What sort of power did it take to cast such a permanent spell? This island had been in his family's possession since the beginning of time. What sort of powers did he and his brothers hold?

Caitlin glanced toward Sean before looking back out at the expanse of darkness. He was still on the phone. Had one of his brothers discovered something about her son? She folded and unfolded her hands, fighting the impatience gnawing at her. It had only been a few hours, but her worry for her son made her anxious and left her wondering why this seemingly top-of-the-line plane was taking so long to get to Mirabilus.

"Soon." Sean sat back down and covered her fidgeting hands with one of his own. Obviously, his call had ended. "We'll be there soon."

When she only yawned then nodded in response, he slipped his arm across her shoulders and pulled her against him, asking, "Tired?"

"Very." But the knowledge that they were getting closer to her son now had her nerves on edge. Besides, his fingers circling her shoulder, and the warmth of his side against hers, had her wishing for something more than sleep.

Even though she didn't feel his presence in her mind, his deep chuckle let her know that he was tuned in to her thoughts and she tried to pull away, but he simply swept her into his arms and across his lap as if she were nothing more than a rag doll.

"Where were we before your mother appeared?"

The warmth of his breath whispering against her ear sent shivers down her spine. Caitlin sighed and pushed against his shoulder. "Not in public." She had no intention of joining any mile-high club.

"There's no one here." He made a show of looking around the empty cabin. "It's not as if we're aboard a commercial airliner."

"Was that your brother on the phone?" She tried to change the direction of their conversation before it got out of control.

"Of course." While he followed her lead with the conversation, he didn't stop caressing her shoulder. In fact, the free hand he'd placed on her stomach was now inching higher.

"Anything I should know? Did he discover something about little Sean?"

"No. We were discussing our living arrangements at Mirabilus."

"What do you mean by *our* living arrangements?" She sucked back a soft gasp as he brushed his hand along the underside of her breast.

"As in where we'll be sleeping."

He'd easily, and all too conveniently, ignored the intended emphasis she'd placed on the word *our*. Caitlin wished she could just as easily ignore the warmth of his hand that had trailed away from her shoulder to steadily stroke the sensitive spot beneath her ear. With all of the calmness she could muster, she asked, "Any reason we can't have separate rooms?"

"A few." He leaned his head down to rest his lips behind her ear. "For one thing, while it may be a castle, it doesn't have near unlimited supply of empty rooms."

"Uh-huh." She closed her eyes, savoring the rush of sexually charged pleasure rippling to life. She really should stop him.

And she would…soon.

"For another thing—" he paused to graze her earlobe with his teeth then continued "—why wouldn't we share a room?"

His lips joined in the play along with his teeth. She wasn't certain which would make her lose focus first— the light nips from his teeth or the gentle suckling of his lips. She'd had no idea earlobes could be that sensitive. Caitlin leaned away, but he just followed along.

"We aren't a couple." For some reason her tone didn't sound too sure of that fact even to her own ears.

"No?"

He brushed his thumb across her breast. Her nipples

strained through the layers of clothing to get closer to his touch. She gritted her teeth to keep from crying out with longing, swallowed hard and finally said, "No. We aren't."

He caressed her thigh, making her jump in surprise. When had he moved his hand from her breast? While she was still sorting through that quandary, he asked, "So, we don't have a child together?"

"Yes, we do." She grabbed his hand, stopping him from sliding it between her thighs.

"So at some point in time we were most definitely a couple."

She couldn't argue that point. However, she responded, "We were only together a few nights."

"And days."

He relaxed the hand on her leg. Caitlin followed suit, easing up on the confining grip she had on his hand. Sean entwined his fingers through hers and lifted their joined hands to his lips.

Wondering what he was up to now, she looked at him. The shimmer of his eyes warned her that she wasn't going to agree with whatever plot he was devising.

He kissed the back of her hand before moving his lips to hers.

She closed her eyes, not fighting the kiss or the empowering breath flowing into her, feeding her sorely depleted stores. Her mind seemed to spin in a whirlwind of colors that beckoned her to lose herself in the brilliant maelstrom.

Then a touch, the stroke of palm against flesh, unfettered by clothing, brushed slowly down the length of her body.

Caitlin froze. He'd slipped into her mind with his kiss

and she'd been too weak, too tired to sense his presence until he was inside. But that didn't mean she had to quietly accept his intrusion.

She pulled away from his kiss, but he held her close and whispered, "Accept my offer, Caitlin. I have enough energy for both of us, and I freely give you whatever you need."

When she hesitated, he rested his forehead against hers and said, "I swear to you, we can argue and fight about it later. There'll be plenty of time. For now, if you won't feed for yourself, do it for our son. He needs you."

Unable to withstand the lull of his voice and the heat of his mental touch, she relaxed in his embrace, accepting the return of his kiss and the strength he offered.

Sean knew this wouldn't last for long. The Caitlin he remembered from their brief tryst would never have rested so pliantly in his arms, permitting him to have his way. Nor would she have surrendered so easily to his physical, or mental, touch. Doing so attested to her near starvation.

She wouldn't have done this to herself. The thought that anyone would have starved her in this manner sent his blood boiling. And the thought that they'd probably done so because of the child added his beast's rage to his own. They would pay—with their lives if the dragon had any say in the matter.

Her throaty moan tore him from the darkness of his thoughts. He frowned, realizing that this mental play, this stroking and touching, no matter how focused, wasn't going to be enough to satisfy the hunger tearing at her.

Sean knew he couldn't do this without his beast's help. After all, that had to be where the magic originated, so he hoped the brute would behave himself. He gave control of this mind play to the dragon, trusting the beast wouldn't harm his own mate.

While they physically stayed in the seat they shared, in his mind the dragon came to life. A mass of foggy mist swirled into the form of the beast before dissipating, only to return in the shape of a man. He glanced over his shoulder and for a split second, Sean saw the elongated emerald gaze of his dragon.

The power and lust in that brief glimpse sent a shiver down his spine. But the tremor evaporated, replaced with a heat so intense Sean wondered if they'd burn alive.

A woman appeared out of the lingering mist. Not any woman, but Caitlin. A timid smile crossed her lips, but her amber-hued eyes held a wariness that couldn't be denied. She didn't trust the beast—didn't trust him to hold control.

He'd have to prove her fears baseless.

He reached for her and the plane lost altitude as if it would fall from the sky. It took a moment for Sean to realize the motion of the jet was real—it wasn't some imagined feeling of bottomlessness.

The Fasten Seat Belt light blinked on. At the same time, the pilot's voice filled the cabin. "Sorry about that. We've hit a pocket of turbulence. Should be out of it soon."

It was all Sean could do not to growl in frustration. This was one of the many reasons he didn't like flying in planes—the utter lack of control.

Caitlin scrambled back into her seat and fastened her seat belt. She was flush, shaking, and it didn't take a genius to know it wasn't from the plane's sudden movement.

He leaned over and captured her lips beneath his.

Their kiss was brief since that wasn't his intent. When she parted her lips, he exhaled as much of his energy and power as he could, willing her to absorb what little he could offer in this manner.

She stroked the side of his face, rested her hand against his cheek and slowly inhaled. Her fingers against his skin trembled. When she started to pull away, he cupped the back of her head and held her steady. Regardless of what she thought, or feared, she couldn't drain him. His beast would never permit such a thing to happen.

Once her heartbeat slowed, and her fingers stilled, he released her. "Will that hold for now?"

"Yes. Thank you." She turned away to stare out the window.

The plane hit another patch of turbulence and she grasped his forearm. "Sean!"

He patted her hand. "It'll be fine."

"No. Look!"

He followed the line of her finger to the outside of the plane. The turbulence hadn't been caused by any weather formation. The dark shape of a demon beast near the tip of the wing was the reason the plane's flight pattern had been so erratic.

"What is that?"

Sean had the distinct impression that he somehow knew this demon, but how? "I think the question is *who* is that, not what."

"Fine, then, who is it?"

"I would guess our son's kidnapper."

Caitlin gasped. "Do something."

While reaching for his cell phone, Sean looked at her to ask, "What exactly do you want me to do?" He wasn't about to slip into the demon's mind to try forcing him away, and he wasn't able to materialize on the outside of the plane. If that thing was Nathan the Learned, as he feared, he would be literally risking not just his own life, but those of Caitlin and their child, as well.

He hit speed dial on his phone. "Cam, we have a problem here."

Not bothering to wait for an explanation, his brother rushed into his mind and pulled out just as quickly, leaving Sean reeling from the rush.

Within seconds, two dragons appeared behind the demon.

"Your brothers?" Caitlin asked.

He studied them briefly then shook his head. "No. Cam and his wife, Ariel."

Surprised, she asked, "She's a dragon changeling, too?"

"Only when she's pregnant." At her questioning look, he explained, "She takes on the abilities of the baby she carries." Which obviously meant another Drake was on the way soon.

"How did they get here so quickly?"

Sean explained, "Just like Braeden, Cam is also able to materialize where he's needed in an instant. Since he was most likely with Ariel, it's a fair bet she demanded to come along."

"But how did he know what was happening? Are they watching us?"

"In a manner of speaking, yes. This jet is Braeden's pride and joy. He was probably keeping his awareness on it and knew when trouble threatened."

The dragons double-teamed the demon with a diving-bombing aerial assault. They worked in perfect unison, and Sean could only imagine the exhilaration they felt at their spiraling maneuvers. The demon beast was no match for the two larger and faster dragons, and it quickly disappeared into the night sky.

Cam hung back long enough to peer in the window at Caitlin. She leaned away. "What does he want?"

"Thank you. Now go home." Sean tapped a finger on the glass. "He's just being nosy. He'd never admit it, but it's a common ailment for him. Especially in beast form."

"Sort of like a dog?"

The dragon reared back as if it had heard her comment, which he probably had, and spun away.

Sean snorted in amusement, but said in a more serious tone, "I'm not too sure that's the way to talk to something who just rescued you."

"I wasn't thinking." Caitlin sighed. "I'll apologize later."

The seat belt light blinked off.

His phone rang. Sean absently looked at the caller ID before responding to Caitlin. "You do that, but right now get some sleep. We'll be at Mirabilus soon."

She shook her head. "I can't sleep."

There were things he couldn't do like his brothers could, but this wasn't one of them. He placed his palm over her eyes and whispered, "Sleep, Caitlin, just go to sleep."

Once certain she was resting comfortably, he rose and disappeared into the rear cabin to return Braeden's call.

Someone touched her arm, startling her from her odd dreams of demons, dragons and wizards.

"Caitlin. We're here."

She blinked the sleep from her eyes and frowned before turning an accusing glare toward Sean. She'd been unable to fall asleep until he'd placed his hand over her eyes and ordered her to go to sleep. How many other powers did he have that would also prove unwelcome? "You knocked me out."

He ignored her and moved away to the already open exit door. "Coming?"

She followed him down the steps onto the runway and into a waiting limo. "You have everything at your fingertips, don't you?" She winced at the snippiness of her tone.

"And you don't?" Sean shook his head at her comment. "If it all disappeared tomorrow, I'd still know how to survive. Would you?"

Caitlin looked down at her lap. He'd basically been decent to her during the entire trip. He could have grilled her about what had happened in his bedroom with her mother, but instead he'd seemed to have declared an unspoken truce—at least for now. What was wrong with her? Why on earth was she picking the stupidest fight possible? "No, probably not."

He reached over to cover her folded hands. "Is this really an argument you want to pursue?"

"No." She slid her hands from beneath his. "I don't know what's wrong with me."

He chuckled softly and raised a hand to count off items on his fingers. "One, you were locked in a cell and nearly starved. Two, our son was taken from you by force. Three, you're here with me when you seem to have a fiancée to deal with. Four, again, you're here with me, your family's enemy, at my family's stronghold. Five, I don't think you've taken in enough energy to have the strength to think rationally about much of anything. Need me to go on?"

"No." He might have been right on all counts, but he didn't have to sound so smug.

The limo drove beneath a huge set of gates, at which point Sean said, "Besides, there'll be enough to fight about in a few minutes."

His comment as they pulled up to the castle sounded more like a warning than anything else, and it confused her already drowning senses. "If you're so certain we'll end up arguing with our next breath, why were you so kind on the plane?"

"I don't like to fly. Why would I willingly step into a tin can with wings, give up control to someone else, when I can move quicker and safer by myself?" He paused to shrug. "It seemed it might be easier to not spend the time aboard the craft fighting."

"I could have flown alone."

"Right. And who would you have called when trouble showed up at the wing?"

"Again, thank you."

"Don't thank me." He waved toward the gathering near the doors. "Thank Cam and Ariel."

The car came to a smooth stop, and Sean opened the door to exit. He stopped and then turned half around to face her. "By the way, Aunt Danielle is already planning our wedding."

"Our what?"

Her expected shout would have been laughable had he not been so serious. Sean stepped out of the car and offered her his hand. She looked at the appendage as if she contemplated removing it from his arm.

"I warned you that we'd be arguing soon."

She took his hand and slid across the backseat. "Arguing?" Caitlin swung her legs around. "There's no sense arguing about something that will never happen."

He pulled her from the car and against his chest to whisper into her ear. "We're in agreement there, but arguing with Danielle Drake will only ensure it happens."

"So we just agree with her instead?"

Sean sidestepped and rested his palm on the small of her back to escort her to the castle doors. "Don't agree to anything. Hedge."

He paused in front of Braeden. "You two have met." His brother nodded.

Caitlin's soft intake of breath let him know she'd noticed Cam. How could she not? Other than the color of their eyes, he and Braeden were identical.

Quickly filling her in on who was who, Sean slipped into her mind. *"You obviously realize the twins are Braeden and Cameron. Braeden's eyes are amethyst, Cam's are sapphire. You might notice that Braeden has just a touch more silver streaks at the temples, but don't mention it, he'll only argue. The older woman with the long black hair is my aunt Danielle Drake—she's not a changeling. The woman with the dark brown hair is Ariel, Cam's wife, and she can only take dragon form when she's pregnant. Braeden's wife, Alexia, is probably upstairs with the children. You'll recognize her by her red hair, and she's not a changeling, either."*

Caitlin sighed, then responded in the same manner, asking, *"And I'm supposed to remember all of that?"*

"Sorry to intrude." Ariel stepped forward. "You'll figure us all out soon enough." She extended her hand to Caitlin in welcome. "You should try to tell the twins apart when they're wearing colored contacts."

"I think I'll pass on that." Caitlin asked, "Were you one of our rescuers?"

Ariel waved off the question as if it was nothing

more than a common, everyday occurrence. "Glad to help."

"I do thank you." Caitlin glanced to Cam. "And you, too."

As talkative as his twin, Cam simply nodded.

And then to Sean's complete surprise, his brother barked like a dog. Just once, but it was enough to make Caitlin flush with embarrassment. She managed to choke out, "I apologize," before looking as if she wished she had the ability to disappear on whim.

Aunt Danielle's eyebrows rose a fraction of an inch before she chastised Cam with a piercing look.

Braeden cleared his throat and motioned to the door. "Let's move this inside."

Once the heavy doors thudded closed behind them, Ariel and Cam wandered off arm in arm with nothing more than a wave over their shoulders. Aunt Danielle hung around until Braeden stared her down and she made her own exit up the curved staircase.

The moment Caitlin parted her lips, Braeden raised a hand. "I have nothing in the way of news. You'd already told us that Nathan holds the child in his castle ruins, but a quick flyby came up empty. I spoke with Baron St. George, and he had nothing new to impart. I have men searching the area but until they return in the morning, there's not much else I can tell you."

Sean felt her pain; it twisted in her gut like the sharp blade of a knife and slammed into her chest with the force of an unseen battering ram. He pulled her to his side, wishing there was a way to spare her the agony she suffered, asking Braeden, "Is my suite ready?"

"Yes." His brother paused a split second then added, "And her bags were just delivered."

"Let's go upstairs." Sean coaxed Caitlin to come with him, fully prepared to carry her if need be.

To his relief, she shook off the utter doom surrounding her long enough to bid Braeden good-night. Then she followed him to the rear of the Great Hall, where an elevator was concealed behind a large tapestry.

They'd made a great many updates to modernize the medieval keep over the last few years. Nearly all of them welcome improvements as far as Sean was concerned.

Caitlin's eyes widened briefly as the elevator door slid open, prompting Sean to offer, "We could use the stairs if you like."

"This is fine." She entered the cab. "Have many improvements been done?"

He hit the button to close the doors. "You mean like running water and electricity? Yes." Leaning against the wall he leveled his gaze on her. "But if you're looking for a dungeon, it's been turned into a gym."

She grimaced, making him wonder why the mention of a dungeon would bother her.

Caitlin asked, "I take it the truce is officially over?"

"Apparently." She had to have known they'd be back to this conversation eventually. There were still too many unanswered questions. Such as what exactly did she think she was going to do with their son— his son—when they got him back? And who was this Baron Derek?

When the elevator bounced to a stop, he led her through the open doors and down the hall to his suite, where he placed his index finger to a touch pad outside the door. After the barely perceptible sound of the lock tumbling into place reached his ears, he pushed the door open. Not having to carry keys, or keep track of a keycard, was just another modernization that made life easier.

He ushered her inside a suite that looked fairly identical to his apartment at Dragon's Lair. Sean checked the bedroom to ensure her luggage had indeed arrived then came back out to the living room.

"Your luggage is in the bedroom. Are you hungry?"

"No. But I'd like to take a shower and change my clothes."

"Feel free." He waved toward the bedroom. "Take your time."

He watched her walk down the hallway and wished for a moment their truce was still in effect. Perhaps then she wouldn't be taking a shower alone.

His wandering thoughts were cut short by the sound of items thumping and clattering onto the kitchen counter.

Sean stared at the items that had suddenly materialized on the kitchen counter. The jewel-encrusted, worn, leather-bound book was the family grimoire. Since it'd been locked away in Braeden's office safe, obviously his brother had sent it to him.

Two dragon pendants, one emerald, the other one sapphire, appeared next to the book. Sean rolled his eyes. Those could only have come from his sisters-in-law, which meant Braeden hadn't wasted a moment getting the rest of the family on board.

He flipped open the grimoire to glance at the first few pages. Sean knew, from his brothers' experiences, that he'd likely see nothing that could help him without Caitlin being present, so he closed the book and then opened the fridge, looking for something to wash the dryness from his mouth. Not finding anything that looked remotely interesting, he closed the door, only to open it again, pull out a pitcher of orange juice and then pour a glass.

He glanced at the clock. Nearly an hour had gone by since they'd entered the suite. What was keeping Caitlin? He'd told her to take her time, but hadn't expected her to avoid him this long.

She couldn't have disappeared. He hadn't detected that ability in her, and he was certain that if she could, she would have when the demon showed up outside the plane. No, she was still in the bedroom, intentionally avoiding him in all likelihood.

Sean placed the glass in the sink and then left the kitchen to stand before the open sliding doors that led out to the balcony. The ever-darkening forest beyond Mirabilus seemed oddly comforting. Lengthening shadows creeping slowly closer to the castle, along with the creaking and moaning of the pines as they swayed against the brisk sea breeze, served to calm his dragon.

Over the passing months Sean had discovered that his beast took comfort from things others considered dark or eerie. Instead of causing tension or putting him on edge, he found himself relaxing, easing peacefully into the crash of thunder, streaks of lightning and the approaching darkness of night.

Howls and growls of beasts in the distance, generally unheard by human ears, set him at ease. Just knowing that nature was performing as it should was enough to lull him into deep, blissful slumber.

At one time the low chuff or growl of a bear would have caused him concern, as would the mournful howl of a wolf. But now, as much beast as he was human, the territorial protests of the forest animals caused him nothing more than a second's notice—a mere heartbeat of recognition before it was swept along with all the other *nonevent* moments of life.

Sean glanced toward the hallway. A *nonevent* kind of moment was what Caitlin should have been. She should have remained an extremely gorgeous woman he walked by on his way out of the bar. Instead, he'd had to meet her, had to mark her, had to spend three days and nights in her bed.

And because of all those *had tos* he was now a father and mated. And his child was stolen, a bargaining chip in a game as old as time.

Being a father wasn't a bad thing. It actually made him feel as if he'd accomplished the miraculous feat alone. And being mated also wasn't exactly a bad thing. Although Sean wished he'd had more say in the matter, more time to decide if this was truly his mate before the beast had up and taken the decision out of his hands. While it was too late now, it would have been nice if the dragon could have chosen someone who actually wanted to be mated to him.

Some type of shared wanting would come in handy for this wedding his aunt was planning. The woman was going to be sadly disappointed when it came to her youngest nephew since he wasn't at all interested in getting married.

But right now he had other, more important things to concern him. Like the little fact that he was essentially lying—withholding the full truth—to Caitlin about something that really wasn't quite so little, after all.

How was he going to tell her that everything she thought she knew about him was a lie, or at least not the whole truth? He wasn't a dragon born. His beast existed because of a curse, and he had no way of knowing what would happen once that curse was broken.

Hell, he didn't know if it could be broken. And even if he discovered a way to rid himself of this curse, did he want to surrender that part of him?

Chapter 5

Sean turned away from the panoramic view and headed down the hall to see what was keeping Caitlin, meeting her as she opened the door, rubbing a towel over her head. "I was coming to get you."

She peeked at him from beneath the bath towel. "You told me to take some time, so I did." She snatched the towel from her head. "I assumed we weren't going out anywhere, but I didn't really bring anything comfy-casual to wear, so I borrowed some things from your dresser. I hope you don't mind."

Sean lowered his gaze from her wet hair. He couldn't remember his T-shirt or sweatpants ever looking quite so beguiling before. Of course she had to choose one of his old, small, thin, white T-shirts that suddenly seemed nearly transparent where it hugged her body. Even though she'd lost far too much weight since he'd last seen her, there was still enough padding beneath her smooth flesh to provide curves worth exploring.

Caitlin shoved the wadded-up, damp towel against his chest. "They're called breasts, and you've seen them before."

Unable to speak through the dryness making his tongue stick to the roof of his mouth, he stood there in silence and watched her sashay down the hallway toward the kitchen. The gray sweatpants—also threadbare and too small even for her—accentuated each and every dip and curve.

Oh, yeah, she'd chosen clothes from the bottom of the these-are-too-small drawer of his dresser on purpose. If she thought to distract him, the tightening of his groin and heavy thudding of his heart proved her effort successful.

Where his instinct was to protect and command, hers was to tease and tempt. And when she wasn't outright exhausted, she did a damn fine job at both. He tossed the towel behind him, not caring if it made it to his bedroom floor or not, and took a deep breath before following the bewitching temptress into the kitchen.

"Are these what I think they are?" Caitlin touched a fingertip to the grimoire before picking up the emerald and sapphire dragon pendants. "What about the box?"

"That's in Danielle's possession. I don't expect to see it tonight."

She frowned and then slid her gaze from the sparkling gems to him. "You're going to let me give the book and pendants to Nathan?"

Sean shook his head. "Hardly."

"Not even in exchange for our son?"

Only if it became absolutely necessary and he had a surefire way to ensure the items stayed safely in Drake possession. But he wasn't going to tell her that. "We'll get our son back."

"Not if we stand here chatting."

It was only natural for her to be upset over the kidnapping, so he wasn't surprised by the coldness in her voice. But her words chipped at his patience. "You didn't think I was coming here just to rush pell-mell into the Learned's stronghold without a plan in place first, did you?"

When she didn't respond, he stared at the flush coloring her cheeks and realized that was exactly what she'd thought. "Just how stupid do you think I am?"

"I never thought you were stupid. Just…"

"Gullible? Easily beguiled? Quickly seduced?" He leaned on the counter next to her. "You thought what? That you'd walk back into my life, surround me with an aura of lust and I'd hand the ransom over to you without question?" Sean dipped his head closer to hers. "What made you think I would do that?"

"He's our son."

"I know that. But the Learned has used every trick conceivable to gain possession of these items. Since the only thing he craves is power, it's apparent that somehow having these items would make him too powerful for anyone to stop. You yourself said that you felt his evilness. That is not someone who should be permitted to live, let alone rule the world."

"So, you will risk our son's life to stop Nathan?"

He would risk his own life to stop the Learned, but not the child's. "We will get the boy back."

"How?" She slapped a hand flat on the countertop. "How are we going to get him back?" Her voice rose with each word until she paused, gasping, then breathlessly asked again, "Will you risk his life to stop Nathan?"

The shakiness of her voice let him know that the

minuscule amount of strength he had given her earlier aboard the plane was fading. Sean moved behind her. She stiffened, but then her body softened, welcoming his warmth, and he pressed against her.

"Caitlin, I know you are frustrated and that everything seems to be taking forever, but I promise you, the child will come to no harm. Nathan may be twisted and brutal, but he is far from stupid. He knows the child's value. He knows full well that if he harms the boy, he'll get nothing. And I assure you, Nathan isn't going to risk coming up empty-handed." He grasped her shoulders and squeezed lightly. "We have a small leeway of time to plan his rescue. So try to unwind a little. We will figure this out."

Once she relaxed slightly, he reached around and opened the grimoire. "This is the history of the Drake family from the Middle Ages until now." He turned the pages slowly, letting her look at each one.

"What do I care about your family's history?"

"This book contains spells that only a dragon and his mate can see. It might have some answers for us."

"Why do you have it, then? You didn't know you had a mate until recently."

"While I waited for you to join me, it just appeared on the counter."

"Simply appeared?"

"Yeah, I'm told it does that on occasion."

"Wonderful."

By her tone of voice, he didn't think she thought it was *wonderful* at all. To ease her concern, and uncertain if it was true or not, he said, "Braeden spelled it here."

He flipped the first two pages and then paused. "That wasn't here before."

"What do you mean, it wasn't there?"

"I just looked at these first few pages while you were in the bedroom, and this one wasn't here. Apparently the history of this book is true."

"In what way?"

Sean turned back a page, then flipped back to the new image. "It seems that part of the book's magic is that it'll paint scenes meant only for us."

"Do you think it will tell us how to get Sean back?"

"We'll have to go through it to find out."

Both of them looked at a picture of two young women kneeling on the floor with a wooden chest between them. He studied the image. It looked as though the women were using two of the dragon pendants as keys to unlock the chest. One pendant was sapphire and now belonged to Cameron's wife, Ariel. The emerald one, which currently belonged to Alexia, wasn't in the picture. He'd never seen or heard anything about the amethyst one the other woman was using on the chest.

He shook his head. This was something he'd have to ask his brothers, or Aunt Dani about, because if the picture was right, there was still one pendant missing. And the wooden box was nothing like the cube Aunt Dani kept close at hand at all times. The one in the grimoire was shaped more like a small chest.

Sean turned to the next page. This picture was still in the Middle Ages and was of an old, white-haired man on a bed, with a crazed-looking younger man leaning over him holding a puzzle box.

This one he understood. He tapped the image of the younger man. "This is Nathan the Learned. Unfortunately, he is a distant relative."

"Is that the box he wants?"

"I'm sure it is. It contains the soul of his uncle Aelthed." He pointed toward the older man. "That must be Aelthed."

At Caitlin's frown, he explained, "In the twelfth century, Nathan conjured a spell to capture his uncle's soul the moment it left his body, and it's been there ever since. He did so because Aelthed killed his own brother, Nathan's father, for committing what amounted to treason against the family and then buried him in an unhallowed grave. At the time, Aelthed was the Druid High Lord and when his death was at hand, he refused to pass the power on to Nathan."

Caitlin brushed a fingertip across the image of the puzzle box. "So even if Nathan wasn't evil from the beginning, he was pushed into it?"

"I don't know for certain. I can only guess that he was evil from the day he was born and Aelthed's actions were the tipping point." Sean turned the pages, letting each flip past in vivid illuminations. Every page propelled them through the decades.

"Stop!" Caitlin grabbed Sean's wrist to stop him from turning over that page. "That's my father." She stared at the picture of a man tied to a tree while a half man, half dragon loomed over him.

She pointed at the sword near the man's side. "That's Ascalon."

He'd seen the dragon slayer's sword somewhere before. An image of it hanging against a dark, forest green wall flitted in and out of his mind. A shiver trickled down Sean's spine. "Isn't that one of the weapons mounted in your bedroom?"

Caitlin nodded. "It's been handed down through the centuries and was passed to me on my twenty-first birthday." She pumped back an elbow into his gut. "It was supposed to keep me safe from dragons."

Sean was fairly certain that had she been in full control of her body and mind, she would have realized who she'd led to her home that night and would have used Ascalon. He tensed against another shiver. Just the name of the weapon made him break out in a sweat. There was no defense against the sword. It was pure magic. One small cut from the blade would leave any dragon changeling defenseless. He had no way of knowing if it would work on a cursed dragon or not and had no desire to find out.

So far his beast's magic had kept him safe through its ability to heal almost instantly. However, if he wasn't immune to the weapon's power and his skin or scales were so much as nicked with Ascalon, the magic would drain from the beast, leaving it and him without the ability to heal. As a man, he would be rendered motionless. In beast form he would be reduced to nothing more than an oversize lizard. In either case, a death blow would then become—fatal.

"Are you afraid, Sean?"

He snapped his attention back to Caitlin. She hadn't moved, and her voice was so soft, so steely, that he wasn't certain she'd actually spoken.

"Are you?" She repeated her question.

He cocked an eyebrow. If nothing else, she bounced back quickly. While he still sensed her anger, the fear had been replaced by a cold, ice-forged steel. "Why would I be afraid?"

"You should be."

The weapon had been hanging on her bedroom wall. Sean frowned then directed his attention to her luggage in his bedroom. One was long enough to carry a broadsword. He tilted his head and extended an arm.

Caitlin jumped at the sound of her heavy bag thudding onto the kitchen floor behind them.

"Did you bring your sword with you?"

She laughed softly. "Would you go into the lion's den unarmed?"

He spun away from her, grabbed the bag before she could react and tugged down the zipper. A length of forest green velvet had been wrapped around the weapon. Carefully reaching inside, Sean lifted the sword out and placed it on the countertop.

"That's mine." Caitlin tried to force by him and reach for the weapon.

Sean easily pushed her out of the way. "Touch it and I swear, Caitlin, you'll regret it."

He jerked on the free end of the fabric, unrolling it until the sword clattered onto the counter. A leather-wrapped, wooden scabbard protected the blade. He traced the cross-bindings, wondering if they were as old as the weapon before sliding the blade free.

His beast screamed in wild-eyed rage and abject fear. Shocked by the depth of the reaction, Sean silently crooned to the agitated dragon until it quieted. At the beast's questioning glare, he promised, *We have the blade. I'll put it someplace safe where it can't harm us.*

Sean was surprised by the lack of ornamentation on the weapon. The hilt was bare save the worn, well-oiled leather wrap, the pommel nothing but a metal ball. He lifted the sword, holding it out to test the swing, and was impressed with the balance. Even though it was impossible, it was as if the blade had been made specifically for him.

Caitlin leaned against the counter. "That's part of its magic. The fulcrum changes with each person who wields the weapon. It will always feel perfectly balanced in the hand of a preternatural."

"You would think that wouldn't be the case if a dragon held it."

She shrugged. "Yeah, well, it was assumed that the St. Georges would rid the world of the beasts, so maybe that wasn't a consideration."

He ignored her to look closer at the etching on the flat shoulder. A rough picture depicting a dragon slayer standing over a dead dragon had been etched from the crossguard and down the spined blade.

"Check this out." Caitlin reached toward the weapon.

Sean jerked back; his beast snarled.

She stopped and extended her index finger. "Just let me touch the blade. I won't try to take it away."

He took a breath and nodded, but stayed on alert for any sudden movement on her part.

When Caitlin placed her fingertip on the tip of the blade, the spine glowed a deep amethyst color. She slowly trailed her touch up the ridged spine. The glowing light pulsed, expanding and contracting, as it followed along behind her finger.

She drew her hand away and the light disappeared. "I think that's the magic."

"Does it do that when you use it?"

"I've never run into a dragon before." She grinned. "We could find out."

Sean slid the blade back into the scabbard, rolled the velvet around the wooden case and then held the bundle up with one hand. "This is going somewhere safe. I'll return it to you…later."

He released the bundle and willed it into the safe in his office. Not only was the strongbox made with a twelve-inch-thick casing and locked with a combination lock, it also had a fingerprint sensor. The digitized print was synced to the ring finger on his left hand. A joke his brothers teased him about all the time—insisting he was married to his safe.

To make the safe even more impenetrable, Sean kept it constantly secured with magic. There would be no way for Caitlin to retrieve her deadly weapon until he was ready to give it back to her.

Once he heard the faint click of the safe's door closing, he willed the dial on the lock to spin and then lowered his arm. "There, now everyone is safe."

He glanced at Caitlin and frowned at her smirk. For some reason she didn't seem too concerned about being separated from her sword. When she arched her eyebrows, he asked, "What?"

She didn't reply. Instead, she extended her right arm and crooked her index finger.

To Sean's shock, Ascalon, minus the scabbard and velvet wrap, flew directly to her hand. She closed her fingers around the hilt and twirled the blade. Only then did she return his stare to ask, "Tell me, Sean, *now* are you afraid?"

His heart pounded at her repetition of the exact same question he'd asked her in his bedroom back at the Lair. The hairs on the nape of his neck rose, a cold sweat beaded on his forehead and his snarling dragon's gaze was riveted on the glowing blade. Fear didn't begin to describe the tumult of emotions making him nauseous.

"You should be." She threw his own warning in his face.

Sean took a step back, wondering if Braeden would be outraged to learn that *yes*, he could be more foolish. Not only had he welcomed the dragon slayer into their lair without giving it a second thought, he now found himself at the pointed end of the one weapon in existence that could easily end his life along with the lives of his brothers and their families.

Caitlin tossed the weapon in the air, sending it spinning end over end before her. She easily caught the sword, rested the blade across her forearm and extended the hilt toward him. "You can return this to your *safe* hiding place."

She didn't need to add the obvious—no matter what he did with the sword it would always answer her summons.

"Who else has that power?"

"As long as I breathe, only me."

The fact that she'd freely given him that information somewhat eased his concern. Sean grasped the sword and willed it back into the safe. Even though it wouldn't protect him from Caitlin, at least it would keep the sword out of anyone else's hands and sight. He didn't know what his brothers would do if they discovered such a dangerous weapon on Mirabilus.

Then, as if nothing had just transpired, Caitlin moved back to the counter and turned to the next page in the grimoire.

The dragon shook off the lingering dread and stared intently at the woman with a new, albeit disconcerting to Sean, gleam in his gaze.

Too many thoughts crowded his mind, making it impossible for Sean to decipher what his beast was thinking.

"Who are they?"

Caitlin's question drew him from his uncertainty. He once again took his place behind her and looked over her shoulder. A picture of two people in a burning car going over the edge of a mountain had caught her attention. "My parents."

He pointed to the dragon hovering just behind the car. "And that is Nathan."

She turned the page. "And these are?"

"Me, Braeden and Cameron, when we were much younger, with our Aunt Danielle."

Caitlin leaned over to get a closer look at the grimoire. The softness of her hips pressing into his groin instantly changed the direction of his focus.

"So, you were raised by your aunt?" She shifted from one foot to the other.

The perspiration running the length of his spine was far from cold and had nothing to do with fear. Sean clamped his hands on either side of her hips to keep her from swaying side to side. "Uh, yes."

Caitlin paused then smiled to herself. So he wasn't as put off by her actions as she'd thought he would be. After she'd brazenly called Ascalon to her hand, she'd thought for certain that Sean wouldn't want anything else to do with her. She was honestly surprised that he hadn't ordered her from the island.

Apparently, his need to be responsible for her welfare was stronger than she'd realized. Regardless of this whole dragon mate connection idea, once her son was rescued from Nathan's clutches, she would prove to Sean how little she needed, or wanted, his protection.

Although, right now, she did want something from him and from the hardness pressing against her, she was fairly certain the only connection he was concerned with at the moment involved naked bodies and moans of pleasure.

From what she remembered, the sex they'd shared had been indescribably mind-blowing. And she knew from the make-out session on the plane that his touch and kiss still had the power to make her heart race and her toes curl. More than that, she still wanted him with a desperation she couldn't explain.

Her natural instinct was to simply take what she wanted. However, they'd never had the opportunity to fully replenish her energy, and the power she'd used to draw her weapon to her hand had just about drained what little life force she had in reserves.

She longed to turn around and tell him exactly what she wanted, what she needed. But Caitlin feared she had already flogged his ego with Ascalon. She desperately needed his help to rescue her son, and while this was so out of the ordinary for her, it would probably be wiser to let him take the initiative—for now.

However, since it wasn't in her nature to let anyone else take the initiative, she found herself unintentionally sighing softly, exhaling just the tiniest hint of lust, before she shifted back to her other foot. At his barely perceptible gasp, she bit her lower lip, determined to remain in control of her desires and let him do all the teasing and leading of this sensual dance. Pointing at the two older boys in the picture, she asked, "The identical twins are Braeden and Cameron, right?"

"Yes." He buried his face against the side of her neck. "Except for their eyes."

She didn't even try resisting the urge to moan at the feel of his hot breath and lips moving against her flesh. Tilting her head to give him easier access, she asked, "Anything different besides their eyes?"

"Not really." He paused beneath her ear. "Do you really care?"

The frustration evident in the tightness of his voice made her quickly swallow a burst of laughter before saying, "No. But you're the one who wanted me to go through this book before we devise a plan to rescue our son. The least you can do to speed this along is answer my questions."

Sean groaned before resting his chin on her shoulder. "You're right. Continue."

She nodded, then turned the page to see an iridescent dragon peering up at her. "That's gorgeous." She reached toward the picture, wanting to see if it felt as detailed as it looked.

"I wouldn't do that."

The dragon's head seemed to morph into three-dimensional life as it rose up from the page and hissed at her.

Caitlin blinked, uncertain that what she'd just witnessed wasn't a figment of her imagination—or something placed there by Sean. To make sure, she tentatively touched the tail.

Before she could withdraw her hand, the tiny beast sunk its teeth into her finger.

"Damn!" She jerked her arm back. Shaking her hand, she asked, "What the hell was that?"

"I warned you." Sean flicked a finger at the blood-thirsty creature, sending it scurrying back down into a one-dimensional painting. He turned her around and grasped her wrist to bring her hand to his mouth, then ran his tongue slowly across her wounded finger.

The temperature in the room increased by at least a hundred degrees. Caitlin struggled to draw in breath. Her stomach turned and tumbled when he once again drew his tongue along her finger. She tried to pull free, but he simply glanced at her and shook his head.

From the gleam in his eyes, he was enjoying her discomfort far too much.

"Sean, that's enough. It's healed." Caitlin closed her eyes. *Could her voice possibly tremble any harder?*

His soft chuckle answered her unspoken question.

Everything about him was a role reversal for her. Even though it had been her intention, she wasn't used to someone else doing the teasing. It was unfamiliar, uncomfortable and she wasn't at all certain she liked not being the one controlling the levels of lust and desire.

Once again she tried to pull free. "Sean, please, don't."

He released her hand then cocked an eyebrow and looked at her. "So, I misread your signals?"

His heated gaze trailed down her body and back up until he pinned her with a hard stare. "The tight-fitting clothes, come-hither pheromones and that shifting from one foot to the other had nothing to do with teasing?"

Caitlin wondered if flames would spark to life from the heat burning her cheeks. Most men wouldn't have called her out. For one thing, other men would have been too far under the spell of her pheromones to be able to form a complete sentence. And for another, they wouldn't have had the guts to question her.

"No, you didn't misread anything. I was leading you on, but I changed my mind." She knew from the more pronounced arch of his brow that he didn't believe her.

"Fine." He reached around her to pick up the grimoire and pendants. "I'm going to finish looking through this in my office. If you want to join me, feel free."

He turned and took a step before stopping to look over his shoulder at her. "I'm not into guessing games. You want something from me, ask for it."

Ask for it? Speechless, she watched him walk away. *Ask?*

Chapter 6

The woman would drive him out of his mind, Sean realized. A succubus who turned down an overture after she'd been the one to start the sensual dance? It wasn't in her nature to blow hot and cold like this.

He realized she was worried about their son and knew that played a huge part in her indecision. Still, something wasn't quite right. Hard as he tried, it seemed as if the answer was just out of his reach, and he couldn't quite grasp it.

Her mother's untimely interruption had been unwelcome, as had his brother's and the demon's, but none of those instances were responsible for this oddness between them. Something else was causing this strain. *What?*

Sean dumped the grimoire on his desk, cringing when the ancient tome landed near the edge, slid halfway off and then teetered. Cursing at himself, he lunged for the book. But his fingertips barely touched the binding as it rushed beyond his reach to hit the floor with a heavy thud.

The pendants he'd closed inside the book skittered out from between the pages to shoot in different directions across the floor. The emerald dragon pendant slid under his desk, while the sapphire one sailed to the other side of the office and smacked into the base of a bookcase before ricocheting back across the room.

A flash of amethyst split between the other two, skipping across the gleaming dark walnut floor like a flat stone flicked across the smooth surface of a pond, coming to a dead stop in the open doorway at Caitlin's feet.

"What is this?" She bent down and picked up the gem.

"I don't know. I've never seen it before." Sean retrieved the grimoire, quickly checked to be sure it was still in one piece and placed it on the center of his desk before scooping up the emerald and sapphire pendants and sliding them into a pocket of his jeans.

He reached for the gem. "Let me see it."

Instead of handing it to him, she just held out her hand. The dragon-shaped amethyst glowed on her palm as if it had a heartbeat.

Sean stared at it.

"Where did it come from?" Caitlin held it closer to her body and stroked a finger down the dragon's back.

Sean shivered as he felt the gentle touch against his own back. Had his brothers not told him about this effect, he might have been caught completely off guard. They'd gone into great detail about their wives teasing them at the most inopportune moments. While his beast and Caitlin seemed to be mated, he wasn't about to give her that kind of power over him. As if nothing was amiss, he waved toward the grimoire. "It came out of the book when it fell."

"That explains the noise I heard." She walked into the office. "But how could it have fallen out of the book if it wasn't there to begin with?"

He resisted the urge to shrug. "How did the dragon picture come to life and bite you? I can't tell you how anything with this grimoire works, except to say by magic."

"That makes sense." She sat in an armchair before the desk.

"I'm glad it does to you." Sean dropped into his chair and rested his arms on the desktop. "Can I see it?"

Caitlin leaned forward slowly as if reluctant to part with the piece of jewelry, then handed it to him.

The instant he touched the pendant, the glowing stopped, leaving it dark and lifeless. He frowned. "Interesting." He held it out to her. "Here, take it back for a minute."

The glowing heartbeat resumed when she held the dragon in her hand. "Do you think it's alive?"

"Yeah, and obviously it likes you better."

She frowned at him then placed it on the desk. "No need to sound so snappish about it."

"I'm sorry." He hadn't intended to sound irritated, only stated the facts as he saw them. "I've never seen it before, so how would I know if it's alive or not?" He picked up the now-dark pendant and held it between his index finger and thumb. "Besides, it is apparent the thing does somehow respond to you."

Caitlin leaned forward, reaching toward the gem. "Well, I can fix that easy enough." She flicked the tiny dragon on the end of its nose as if it was a misbehaving puppy.

An unseen fist slammed into Sean's nose hard enough to bring tears to his eyes. The pendant clattered to the desk as he slapped a hand over his nose. "Damn!"

Staring at him, Caitlin's eyes grew large. "Your nose is bleeding."

He wiped at the warm, sticky blood and fought not to respond to her statement of the obvious. While his brothers had told him about the pendant's ability to transmit sexual desires and wishes, they'd said nothing about this.

She narrowed her eyes, and the beginning of a purely evil smile teased the corners of her mouth. "Did what I think happened, just happen?"

Sean cast a wary gaze between her and the pendant. He never should have given it back to her in the first place. With what he hoped was a fierce frown, he said, "Don't get any ideas."

They both reached for the gem at the same time. He groaned when she nabbed it from beneath his fingers.

Leaning back in the chair, with the pendant securely in her grasp, Caitlin batted her eyelashes. "Why, Sean, I think this little piece of jewelry is charmed especially for you. Just like a little voodoo doll."

He didn't like the lilt in her voice, nor the glint in her eyes. It was one thing for him to know the power contained in the piece of jewelry, but to have her figure it out would be like playing with fire. He needed to get that pendant back in his hands where it, and he, would be safe from mischief.

Sean held out his hand. "Give it to me." As soon as the words were out of his mouth, he knew he'd made a mistake. What was he thinking? It was doubtful she'd interpret that as an order, or command—no, Caitlin would take it as a challenge.

Her slow smile only confirmed his fears. She raised the pendant to her lips, making him shiver with anticipation. Sean took a deep, steadying breath. While she might think she held all the control, she'd soon discover her error. He'd make sure of that after she made the first move.

She paused, her lips barely brushing the spine of the carved gemstone. "Aren't you worried in the slightest?"

He ignored the warmth of her breath against his back and shook his head. "No. You aren't going to hurt me until after our son has been rescued."

"Who said anything about hurting you?" She slowly drew the tip of her tongue along the back of the pendant.

Savoring the heat racing along his spine, he channeled it into the now-wakening beast within then returned her smile. "I hope you receive as well as you give."

She paused, frowning.

Before she could make sense of his warning, he coaxed his beast into daydreaming about Caitlin. It was a simple enough task. Unfortunately, there was no way for him to avoid the desire and lust rippling through the dragon.

Sean relaxed in his chair and watched the play of emotions and desire rush across her features. His dragon chuffed, and her eyes widened momentarily in surprise. When he imagined stroking his fingers along the length of her neck, she tilted her head to give him better access. He sensed her desire, felt it in the echo of his own drumming pulse.

Caitlin sighed. And once again, he sensed that something wasn't quite right. He focused more closely on her response, and while the aura of lust clung in the air around her, he didn't sense any wanting…or any longing for him on her part. She wasn't beckoning him closer.

That lack made him pause. Whether they had sex or not wasn't an issue. This teasing on his part had been nothing more than a warning to let her know that she wasn't the only one who could manipulate desire, just a continuation of the experiment he'd started on the plane to see how far he could go using nothing more than his dragon's lust and his own thoughts.

He reined in his thoughts, ignoring his beast's disgruntled groan, and leaned forward to rest his forearms on the desktop. "What's wrong?"

Caitlin closed her eyes for a moment at his question. Everything was wrong. She shouldn't have come to him for help. Now she was essentially trapped on an island with a man who had the power to manipulate her desires with nothing more than his thoughts. That was her forte, and she'd never expected him, or any man, to have the same sort of power over her. Simply knowing he could set her heart racing and send her desire soaring with nothing more than his thoughts was unsettling, to say the least. Yet a part of her couldn't help but wonder just how far they could go in such a manner.

They would test those limits…someday. But now wasn't the time.

She took a deep breath and then looked at him. To her relief, he didn't appear angry. His frown conveyed more concern than anything else. "I won't deny that I find this experiment rather…enjoyable." After placing the pendant on the desk, she continued, "But maybe this is something we can explore…later."

"After we get our son back."

To her surprise, he'd finished her sentence so easily.

But after all, that was her only reason for being here at Mirabilus.

She nodded and placed a hand over one of his. "I'm sorry, but I can't focus on much else right now."

He laced his fingers between hers and stroked his thumb along the side of her hand. The warmth of his touch, the gentleness of his action, made her heart flutter. "Then let's figure out a way to get him back."

That suggestion sounded good to her, but how? "And what do you propose?"

He released her hand, reached behind him to grab a chair and pulled it beside his. "Join me."

Caitlin narrowed her eyes. Across the desk wouldn't work just as well? "Seriously?"

"Totally." He pulled the grimoire toward him and flipped it open. "We need to be together to finish going through this tome. And with the size of this desk—" he waved a hand at the expanse of mahogany "—it would be easier if we were on the same side while doing so."

With the two of them within touching distance, she could only imagine how this would end. But he had a point. It would be easier than sliding the grimoire back and forth across the desktop. Before she could over-think the idea, she moved to his side of the desk and purposely scooted her chair a few inches away from his then sat down.

"Comfy?"

Since she'd now have to lean over to see the pages clearly, not really. But she wasn't going to admit that. "Yes."

His soft chuckle should have been a warning. But before it completely registered as such, he hooked a foot around the leg of her chair and dragged it against his own. When she leaned away, he slung an arm over her shoulder and drew her close. She was effectively pinned by the arm of her chair on one side, his warm hard body on the other and the desk in front of them.

"Now, isn't that better?"

Strangely enough, she didn't actually feel trapped or imprisoned. With the warmth of his body and arm surrounding her, she felt…safe. And oddly calm and comfortable—something she hadn't enjoyed in what seemed like a lifetime. With her parents, Derek and the council, these last few months had been a living hell. Caitlin stiffened, knowing that this was something she could all too easily come to enjoy.

Craving this comfort, she would be fine with his calming touch, if she had any intention of staying with him. But she didn't. She couldn't. Except for their son, they shared nothing in common. Nothing that would keep them together for what could be a very long time, given neither of them was burdened with a human's short life span.

Besides, they were different species—even enemies as far as her parents and the council were concerned. It wouldn't be fair to him, her or little Sean to even consider sharing a life together. Someone would only end up getting hurt, and she feared that someone would be her, or worse, their son.

Caitlin peered down at the grimoire. The image quickly filling the page took her breath away. She gasped.

Sean drew lazy circles on her shoulder. "What do you see?"

It was like watching an old black-and-white photo being developed. The unadorned concrete floor, ringed by cement block walls, steadily grew clearer. Then light from a single bulb hanging from the ceiling glowed eerily off the empty opening where steel bars had served as a door.

Couldn't he see what the invisible hand drew so accurately? She hesitantly touched the corner of the page. "That's Sean's nursery."

"Looks like a dungeon to me."

Obviously, he did see the pictures on the page.

He leaned closer to her, his breath rushed warm against her ear. "Where is the rocker, the stuffed animals and the night-light? I thought those things were unspoken requirements for a nursery."

Caitlin shrugged. "It actually used to be a dungeon a few centuries ago." Even though it had been updated for her use, it still was a dungeon—a prison cell that had effectively done its job.

He traced the tip of his thumb along her neck. "And what exactly was our son doing there?"

"It's where I lived, so why wouldn't he be there, too?"

The brief tightening of his arm still resting across her shoulders was the only clue to his opinion of her questioning reply.

"St. George's home is so small that there were no other rooms to use as your living quarters or a nursery?"

She didn't know how to answer him. If he didn't like knowing that the nursery was in the dungeon, what would he think if he knew she and their son had been imprisoned there?

More details were etched into the picture. She closed her eyes, suddenly aware that she wouldn't have to tell him anything.

"What is this, Caitlin?" He leaned forward, pulling her toward the desk along with him. He tapped a finger on the page before leaning back, giving her room to breathe. "Are those bars?"

"Yes." Her voice was so soft, she wasn't certain he'd heard her response.

"Beg pardon? I didn't hear you."

She cleared her throat then repeated a little louder, "Yes."

"I've seen you in action. While you can suck the life from a human with little effort, I doubt you pose the same danger to your family or the rest of their kind. So why would you need to be confined behind bars?"

"Because I *can* suck the life from a human."

"Are you telling me that you have no control over yourself whatsoever?"

"Of course I can control myself—under normal circumstances. But there's nothing normal about being pregnant."

He was so close his snort of disbelief ruffled her hair. "You make it sound as if you had some kind of disease."

"We didn't know how I would react, so my parents thought it safer this way."

"You might convince someone else of that, but I'm not buying it."

She tried to pull away. "Let me go."

"No." He curled his fingers into her shoulder, holding her in place. "Look at me."

Caitlin swallowed her groan. If she did as he requested, he would be able to see the doubt in her eyes.

He grasped her chin and turned her head toward his. "Caitlin, tell me again why they locked you up."

She paused, blinking, hoping to give herself time to be certain of her answer. "So I couldn't kill anyone."

One eyebrow winged over his eye. "Whose brilliant idea was that?"

She hesitated before answering, "My parents'."

"You had to think about it?" Sean brushed his thumb along her jawline. "Want to try again?"

He saw through her half truth too easily. Her answer hadn't exactly been a lie. When the High Council convened to determine her fate upon learning of her pregnancy, her parents hadn't come to her defense.

She'd been appalled and hurt by their lack of support, but they'd insisted that since the consequence of her actions with Sean would affect the safety of the entire clan, it was imperative that the matter be decided by a higher authority. Before she could formulate a feasible argument to their unwarranted fear, she'd found herself before the council.

She sighed. "The High Council."

"And how did they expect you to feed? Did they provide any life force for you—other than the baby you carried?"

His suggestion, that she would stoop so low as to harm her own child, made her ill. She jerked away from his touch and stared at him in disbelief that he'd even think such a thing. "What are you insinuating?"

"After seeing this—" he once again tapped the picture "—I'm trying to figure out how much danger your family and their council pose. How can you be certain they aren't working with Nathan?"

Caitlin shoved her chair back, breaking free of his hold to escape his nearness, and rose. Pacing back and forth along the far wall, she said, "That's ridiculous."

Thankfully, he didn't move from his chair, but his gaze seemed to bore into her, making her spine tingle with building worry.

"Really? Is it? They want nothing to do with the baby, nor do they want you to have anything to do with him."

"That's quite a leap, don't you think?" She tried to find a way to get him off this track.

"How so?"

"They were ashamed of what I'd done." That much was true. "They confined me so I wouldn't harm anyone." She'd believed that—at first, but after they'd let Derek visit her, she'd begun to wonder and now she wasn't sure at all. "To jump from that to accusing them of seeking to intentionally harm my baby is one hell of a jump." She could only hope that was true.

What sounded to her like a low-pitched, threatening hiss echoed in the office. She stopped pacing and turned her attention to Sean. The look of disbelief deepened to anger, turning his face into a frightening mask of rage. His narrowed eyes met hers, and when he curled his lips she swore venom dripped from his exposed fangs.

He rose, slowly, and she backed away until her escape was stopped by the wall. His hand trembled as he pointed to the grimoire. "What is this?" Laced somewhere between man and beast, his voice was rough, raspy and filled with hatred.

Caitlin knew what scene had filled the page without having to look at it. That cursed book was showing him Derek's *visit*. A visit that nearly ended her life. She glanced at the safe that secured Ascalon from all but her. Just knowing the weapon was close at hand gave her enough courage to hold her ground.

She said nothing, simply waited for him to figure it out on his own. And it didn't take long.

"I will kill him."

"And I won't stop you." She blinked. From where had that response come? It was heartfelt and honest, but she'd not meant to say it aloud. As far as anyone knew, she was still going to go through with her marriage to

Derek. What they didn't know was that she'd see him dead before she'd exchange any vows with him. There were other uses for the honed sharpness of Ascalon's blade besides slaying dragons.

"This…this is your Baron Derek?"

She nodded, unwilling to give him more than what he'd asked for.

He rubbed a hand across his neck where she'd bit him earlier. "What are you?"

"I was born with fangs. Useless fangs that can tear and rip, but I'm not a vampire. Our son wouldn't permit Derek to change me."

"What do you mean?"

Caitlin swallowed hard; remembering that night wasn't something she wanted to do. Every time she did let that memory invade her thoughts, her stomach twisted at the way she'd been tossed about the cell, before he'd pinned her to the bed. She recalled the abject look of hatred in his eyes the second before he tried to latch his fangs into her neck. "Derek tried to turn me."

"Why?"

Looking at him, she shrugged. "I don't know. To make me a better fit as his wife, I suppose." Because the truth lurking at the back of her mind was still too hard to face, she lied.

"You are mine."

"No. I am not." He really needed to get that idea out of his head. "Had I been yours as you insist, you wouldn't have left the way you did. But I wasn't going to be his, either." She spread her arms, hands out, begging him to understand. "I fought him as best I could. He's a vampire, Sean. He's stronger than I'll ever be, and I couldn't risk letting the baby be harmed."

"He raped you."

"Not physically, but yes, essentially you could say that's what he tried to do. He did force himself on me against my will. But your son wasn't going to permit anything to happen."

Sean looked back down at the grimoire. "You were still pregnant, what could he do?"

A small smile flitted at the corner of her mouth. "Make my blood so vile that the second it touched Derek's lips he turned violently ill."

"And your parents still want you to marry this bastard?"

"The whole thing was probably their idea to begin with. All I know is they were angry afterward. At me. Not him."

She closed her eyes against the memory of the bitter fight she'd had with them after Derek had stormed away. A shiver tracked nearly down to her toes.

With a soft, nervous laugh, she looked at him and admitted, "I was overjoyed that the baby had stepped in, so to speak. It's hard enough being a psychic vampire who requires living energy to survive. I don't ever want to need blood, too."

"And yet you stayed with them."

"What choice did I have? I can't disappear at whim as you can. Those bars held me captive as easily as they would a human. I was never let out of that cell until after Sean was taken."

"And you came straight to me." He leaned on the desk. "I wonder, was it because you wanted to, or because they sent you?"

She debated. Should she tell him the truth or add more lies to the ones she'd already told? With a sigh, she lifted her chin and held his stare. "In a way, both, actually." At his questioning look, she explained, "It was my idea to come to you. If things hadn't played out as they had, I'd have come to you long before the baby's birth."

"And?"

"And yes, it was also my parents' idea. They told me to do what I must to get the items the Learned demanded to save our son."

"Considering they're so willing to give him away, that doesn't sound logical at all. Since he's such a stain on their pristine reputation, I would think the child's death would serve them better." He frowned. "I have to wonder if the baby was anything more to them than bait."

She'd had the feeling that her parents had given in to her plea to come to Sean far too easily, but hadn't yet had time to sort out why. "Bait for what?"

"Me. My brothers. Nathan's goal in life is to see us dead."

"Why would my parents help him?"

He looked at her as if she'd completely lost her mind, before asking, "Why would the dragon slayers want to see the dragons die?"

She couldn't help rolling her eyes at the absurdity of his question. "Sure, maybe a few hundred years ago, but aren't we all a little more civilized now?"

Sean snorted. "If we were human, perhaps. But we aren't. It's ingrained in our DNA to hate each other."

"So you've hated me and my family since the moment you were conceived?"

"Not exactly." His gaze darted away before it returned to her. "But we weren't talking about me, were we?"

So, she wasn't the only one in this office keeping secrets. Did he really think she wasn't going to ask? "What do you mean—*not exactly?*"

"We were talking about you."

She'd expected that answer. "Yes, we were." She slowly walked toward the desk, noting the frown had left his face. Now he looked more...not quite worried. She doubted if he really worried about much; maybe a better description would be...concerned. *Why?* "But since Sean is your son, if there's something I need to know, perhaps now might be a good time to share."

He glanced down and shook his head. Pushing the grimoire toward her, he said, "Looks like I won't need to tell you anything."

She studied the still-forming picture of a dark-haired woman curled into a ball on a planked floor. Bloody stripes crisscrossed her back and trailed across her arms. Nathan stood over the naked woman with a whip in his hand.

Caitlin gasped as the woman's pain surged into her blood, hot and agonizing. The rage beneath the pain was palpable, nearly alive with its intensity. She grasped the edge of the desk to keep from being overwhelmed by the emotions flooding her senses.

Sean touched her shoulder, startling her, to ask, "Are you all right?"

She brushed away his disquiet to study the words forming above the image. Reading aloud, Caitlin re-cited, "Not a dragon born, yet a dragon you shall be. Once this beast has taken form, it will answer only to thee."

She waited for the grimoire to fill in more words, but it seemed to have come to a stop. Sean reached down and turned the page. There, a lone figure, Nathan, had taken shape. A wicked, satanic smile curled his lips into a grimace. Pure evilness shimmered in his eyes. She read the words above his picture. "I am thee."

She shivered as a cold hand of dread seemed to close around her heart. Was this curse meant for Sean? Had his dragon been conjured into being by the Learned?

"Sean…?" Uncertain how to ask him if he was Nathan's minion, she let the question trail off and shifted her attention to the man standing across from her. If his ashen complexion was any indication, she wasn't all too certain he'd known very much about this curse before now.

"Look," Sean whispered, his focus drawn to the facing page.

Once again the woman appeared. But this time she lay facedown on the floor, her body shredded by the whip. Her dying gaze transfixed not on Nathan, but on whoever might be seeing this depiction of her last breath.

"St. George will set you free." The words, a mere breathless whisper, hung on the air surrounding them.

Caitlin glanced quickly around the room. Neither she nor Sean had said anything, and those words were just now coming into sight on the page. So who had spoken?

Then, once again, this time a little louder, the strange voice said, *"St. George will set you free."*

Chapter 7

Strong waves, dark and foreboding, pounded against the rocky cliffs below the castle. The thundering crashes echoed relentlessly through the stone fortress, bringing peace to none within.

High above the roiling waves, Nathan the Learned stared out an open window in the east tower. His attention focused across the wild sea toward Mirabilus.

Very few beings—human or preternatural—have ever seen Mirabilus. The glamour spell the ancients had cast upon it centuries ago held as strongly now as it had that day.

The residents' daily lives had been disrupted only by the actions of Aelthed. He alone had brought humans to the druid island. First it had been the medieval Comte of Gervaise, who had promptly won the heart and undying love of Mirabilus's queen. She had given birth to the first half-bred twins. The idea of a halfling female ascending to the throne of Mirabilus had been so reviling that his own father had tried unsuccessfully to kill both of them.

Between the ineffectiveness of the hawthorn sickle used as a sword of judgment and the utter lack of planning, his father's men had failed in their quest to rid the world of the halfling heirs. Those followers had died at the hand of the second human Aelthed saw fit to guide to Mirabilus—a medieval knight by the name of Faucon.

At least the knight had taken one of the half-bred daughters off the island as his wife. But the other one had remained to become queen. And her husband—Nathan swallowed the bile that churned from his stomach to his throat—her husband had ascended to Dragon Lord of Mirabilus.

A position of power that should have been his.

The door to his chamber creaked open. "My lord?"

Nathan swung away from the window, his heart thudding fast and angry with a long-lived hatred, fueling his eternal thirst for vengeance.

One of the nursemaids trembled in the doorway. The wail of the baby she held broke through the haze of rage and the roar of the crashing waves. Nathan's lips curved up into a sneering smile at her unexpected stroke of luck. Had the babe not been in her arms, he'd have spent his anger on her.

"What do you want?"

"The…baron—"

"Get out of my way." Her words were cut short as a flurry of black pushed by her and stopped in the center of the room. The man swung toward the nursemaid and pointed at the door, his dark cape hanging from his arm like a wing. "Leave us and take that squalling abomination with you."

Nathan nodded toward the woman, giving his permission for her to withdraw, before turning his attention on the baron. "To what do I owe this pleasure?" If the uninvited guest in his castle couldn't read the annoyance beneath his words, the man was denser than what he'd first thought.

"Why is that…thing…still alive?"

It was all Nathan could do not to laugh at the man's obvious distaste. "It is good to see you, too, Baron Hoffel." He shrugged at the baron's lack of response and then moved away from the window. "Had you fulfilled your end of our deal, Derek, all of this would be over, and the child would no longer be here."

"And you know I tried."

A little too hard as far as Nathan was concerned. The idea had not been for Hoffel to kill the child or the mother. That pleasure belonged solely to him. No, the dimwit was supposed to have freed the woman from her cell and brought her here.

"I don't know what else you wanted me to do."

Hoffel's whine threatened to crack the tenuous hold Nathan had forced on his temper. As much as he wanted to relieve the man's head from his body, he might come in handy for a time.

"How was I supposed to know she could poison her own blood?"

Another point of disagreement. Nathan didn't think for one minute that St. George's daughter possessed that type of magic. It was more likely that the unborn dragonette had instinctively protected his own life by turning his mother's blood vile in response to the vampire's attack.

"Besides, what difference does it make? You still have the child."

Yes, but he'd wanted the mother and the child—before the birth.

It had all seemed so simple. Yet every action in his quest to gain supreme power had gone so wrong of late.

The gypsy mage's forced assistance with the curse had worked—the youngest Drake had fully transformed into a dragon, the birth of his offspring was proof of that. However, the beast had failed to follow his master's orders. Nathan had repeatedly ordered him to kill his family, but somehow the Drake had found the strength of will to fight those commands.

When the beast had run away from Dragon's Lair, Nathan had been tempted to kill him for his disobedience. But he'd stopped himself, knowing that the young one's death would serve no purpose. He'd guessed that eventually Drake would return to his family, and he had.

Unfortunately, he'd returned with stronger control over his urges. Nathan knew he'd have to excise more power over the beast to get him to do as ordered, but the strengthening ritual required him to have the beast chained to his altar. The chaining would be the easy part. Getting the man to his castle would be tricky.

He was still trying to devise a plan when he'd learned from his spy on the vampires' *sacred* High Council that Baron St. George was looking for a family to adopt his daughter's bastard half-breed child. Nathan knew he'd found a way to draw the Drake he'd cursed to his castle.

His plan had been to simply kidnap St. George's daughter and bring her here as bait. However, the High Council in all their wisdom—or lack thereof as far as he was concerned—had ordered the baron to lock his daughter away in a cell. He still wondered at that decision. Were they hoping to starve her to death for her betrayal in mating with a dragon?

Nathan gritted his teeth. Violence was one thing and it was oft times required, and while he had no qualms about torture, starvation was the action of someone weak and depraved.

When he achieved supreme power as the Hierophant, the first thing he would do was dissolve the vampires' council. The idea that a sitting group of old vampires should act as an all-powerful judge and jury over their kind was outdated and would be useless under his reign.

That was when he'd decided to use Hoffel. He glanced in the man's direction and bit back a curse at the ineffectiveness of that idea. Nathan had thought that since the Hoffels and St. Georges were working on a betrothal between their two heirs, it would be easy enough for the man to whisk the woman out of her spell-proof cell.

Obviously, while both sets of parents agreed the betrothal was a good thing, the participants didn't. It seemed to Nathan that they hated each other more than anything else.

When that plan fell through, Nathan took matters into his own hands and waited until the baby was born. He didn't need the woman, not when the child would be enough to draw the beast to its aid. No dragon, pure born or curse created, would be able to ignore the need to protect its offspring.

It had taken him a while to come up with a solid plan. He'd had to discover the guards' timetable and then wait for the baron and his wife to be gone from the residence. Finally, once he'd learned the council had called a meeting of the families, Nathan had slipped into the vampire's mansion.

His research had paid off. True to form, the guard waited until the baby and its mother fell asleep for an afternoon nap and then left his post to spend a good twenty minutes in the restroom. Everything had fallen into place exactly as planned. Knocking the fool out and swiping the key to the cell was child's play.

Quietly, Nathan had unlocked the cell and took great pains to give the appearance of Drake's misty dragon when he'd entered. The woman was easy to deal with since he'd caught her off guard, and when she thought to protect her son, he'd slammed her across the room, scooped up the child and issued his demands before he'd left.

Since the baby was in his possession, the only thing he needed to do for now was wait. He knew Drake wouldn't permit St. George to bring the grimoire, pendants and puzzle box. The items were too important to entrust to a nonfamily member. No, he would bring them in person.

Which was the whole idea. Once Drake was here, in Nathan's fortress, he would be powerless to stop what would happen.

And when Nathan finished strengthening his curse over the dragon, he would add one, compelling the beast to kill himself after his family was dead. The only thing Nathan would need to do was sit back and watch as the youngest Drake killed the others. He shivered with excitement at the thought of such a spectacle.

After that nothing would stand in his way of attaining the power he sought.

"What—"

Not willing to listen to the man's whine any longer, Nathan waved a hand toward Hoffel, cutting off the vampire's words and sending him into the cells in St.

George's dungeon. He might have some use for him later, but for now, Nathan had more important matters to attend. For now that the Drake was near, ensconced at Mirabilus, he had an altar to prepare.

Something cold like an ice-chilled finger stroked along Aelthed's neck, startling him from his dreams. He shook off the lingering traces of his slumber and frowned. What had awakened him?

The fine hairs on the back of his neck rose. His breath quickened with the feeling of being watched. Why did it seem that he was no longer alone in his solitary cell?

He inspected his cube, with his eyes and his mind, to ensure that he was indeed still the only soul in residence. Certain that his odd sensation of not being alone was nothing more than his imagination, he closed his eyes and brought the grimoire into view.

A strangled gasp tore from his throat. *No. It wasn't possible.* He and he alone had the power to bring pictures to life in the ancient tome. It mattered not if he was awake or sleeping, a part of his mind was always focused on the grimoire.

Creating the pictures was easy; he had only to get the book into the hands of a dragon and his mate, then he would harvest their thoughts, their fears, their memories, along with his own, to draw scenes that would help them understand what they needed to do, or what they must discover.

But this—he shook his head and once again stared at the picture of a gypsy mage in the throes of her final breath—he hadn't drawn this. How could he? It wasn't a memory from either the youngest dragon or his reluctant mate. And it certainly wasn't any memory of his own making.

So who possessed this type of power?

He raised his arms, spread his fingers and pulled the memory to him, drawing it in, making it a part of himself.

Aelthed trembled at the woman's pain. He wept for the loss she suffered, the days she would never know, the years she would never see. Yet he steeled himself against the pain, hardened his heart to the near unbearable loss and breathed deeply, drawing in more and more of the memory until it was as clear as it had been on the day the event took place.

He opened his eyes and watched the scene unfold before him.

His nephew's rage washed over him, cold and heartless, as he lashed the woman, tormented and threatened her until she spoke the words of the Romani curse that turned the youngest Drake into a changeling.

Even as mortal death closed upon her, she tried to give the changeling a way to save himself. Into the universe she'd whispered his salvation.

Aelthed waved the memory back to the mist from which it'd formed, and he wondered if it had been the gypsy's soul, or the whispered words, that had had the power to add these scenes to the grimoire. Either way, her magic was strong. She'd spoken the words and created a changeling. Perhaps her final words could save the cursed beast.

Unable to stand the heavy silence that had fallen over Sean's office, Caitlin asked, "What does that mean, *St. George will set you free*?"

He dropped down onto his chair. "I know as much as you do. Nothing more."

She hated to ask, she really did; he looked terrible. Ashen would be a good description for the current color of his face. His eyes held a sadness in their depths that turned her cold with worry. But her son's life was at stake, and she needed to know if she'd made a huge mistake in coming to him. Sitting on the edge of his desk facing him, she took a deep breath then in a rush asked, "Do you work for Nathan?"

The harsh stare he focused on her made her slide along the edge of the desk, out of his reach. "What you're really asking is if I'm involved in this kidnapping. So instead of dancing around the subject, just ask."

"Are you?" Why did that two-word question make her feel as if she was betraying him? She didn't know him, not really. Outside of a three-night fling, a lingering thirst for each other and their son, they shared nothing.

"You saw the same thing I did."

"That doesn't answer my question."

"No. I had nothing to do with the kidnapping. Hell, since you didn't see fit to tell me about him, I didn't even know the child existed."

She flinched at his accusation, but said nothing.

"As for working with the Learned, what do you want me to say?" He leaned forward and spread his arms, palms up. "I don't know." He pushed out of the chair, shoving it back so hard that it bounced against the wall. Heading for the door, he added, "If I am, it's not by choice."

She blinked. Seriously? He'd disappeared on her after learning who she was. He'd walked out of the bedroom after the scene with her mother and his brother.

Then he'd walked out of the kitchen when she'd changed her mind. So now he was walking away again? Was this his usual method of coping? "You're just going to walk away again? Is that how you deal with everything?"

He froze in the doorway without turning around. She saw the bunching of muscles in his shoulders and arms and wondered if she'd made a mistake. Now seemed a prudent time to put his oversize desk to use, so she stood up and moved to the other side of it. As an inanimate object, it offered no protection, but at least it made her feel as if there was a solid barrier between them.

"Yes." Slowly, he turned to face her. "That's exactly what I'm going to do." He clenched and unclenched his hands at his sides. "Otherwise, I might do something we'll both regret."

Caitlin shot a quick glance toward the wall safe. "As we both know, I am more than capable of protecting myself from you."

Before she could blink more than once, he was before her. He'd cleared the distance from the door, and around the desk she'd considered a barrier, in a blur of effortless ease. Wrapping his fingers around her arm, he dipped his head to nearly growl against her ear, "If you're so intent on using that damn sword, do it."

His voice was rough, gravelly, and so filled with unexpected anguish that it caught her off guard more than the speed with which he'd moved. Confusion and concern kept any anger or fear at bay.

Caitlin stared up at him and gasped. This was far more than just worry or rage. Without stepping into his mind, she had only her senses to go by and heightening them was easy enough to do. The coldness of his glare, the hard line of his mouth, tenseness of his body and the rapid beating of his heart screamed fear in her mind.

Fear of what? Or who?

She lifted her hand and placed it against his cheek. "Talk to me, tell me what's wrong."

Instead of jerking away from her touch as she'd expected, he pulled her roughly against his chest. "Talking is the last thing I want to do."

She hadn't intended to send out any seduction pheromones, but apparently controlling the level was completely out of her ability when it came to him. There was no denying that, yes, she wanted him as much as he seemed to want her right this second. But not like this, not when anger and unexplained fear permeated the air around them.

Caitlin knew that fighting him would only serve to intensify the dark emotions battling for release, so against all common sense, she relaxed in his hold to hesitantly ask, "Sean, does anything seem out of place or wrong to you?"

He wrapped a hand into the hair at the nape of her neck and pulled her head back. One eyebrow winged up as he answered, "Yes, you're still talking."

Caitlin forced herself not to hiss in frustration at his response. She slipped her hands between them and pushed as hard as possible against his chest. "Stop."

A human would have been sent stumbling backward. But not only did her shove fail to set her free, it earned her a low, guttural growl, too. She looked up at him, and from the elongating pupils knew the sound had come more from the beast than the man it possessed.

Regardless of what she wanted, it was obvious she wasn't going to get the chance to talk reason to the man—not with the beast in control.

After taking a deep breath, Caitlin reached up to stroke the side of his neck. She held his gaze, marveling at the sudden need flowing into her. How had he so easily flamed her desire for him against all of her better judgment?

A throaty rumble answered her unspoken question. The sound took her breath away with its deep intensity. The arm he held around her tightened, pulling her feet from the floor, and swung her onto the desk. He released her long enough to jerk the T-shirt over her head before pushing her down on the cold polished wood.

She gasped as his surging need enveloped her, setting her on fire. She wondered again what caused this unnatural heightened level of desire. But her wandering mind snapped back to focus when he wedged his body between her legs and leaned down to suck the cool tip of one breast into his hot, moist mouth.

Lost in the haze of lust, she grasped at his shoulders, wanting more. Sean caught her wrists and pinned her arms above her head, holding them there with one hand while tugging at the sweatpants she wore with the other.

Caitlin lifted her hips to make his task a little easier. "Let me—"

Her offer of help was met with teeth scraping against her nipple before he lifted his head enough to stare at her. "Stop."

Her breath caught in her throat at his gruff tone, then kicked into short gasps of air as a thin rim of gold shimmered to life around the deep green of his eyes. A part of her mind warned that she should fear the beast. It was stronger than she was and could tear her to shreds with one sharp talon.

But another part, the side that was seriously in need of mental help, coaxed her to let him have his way.

Caitlin closed her eyes, unable to make sense of anything beyond the growing need to be possessed, to have him carry her over the edge of desire into satisfaction.

He came over her, whispering, "You are safe. Trust me." A rush of warm breath against her neck, the tip of his tongue trailing her earlobe and his deep, rumbling voice in her ear promising her safety, made up her mind.

With a soft moan, she surrendered, more than willing to let him take control, to use sex to banish whatever devil seemed to be haunting him, certain she would come out of this encounter physically satiated and whole.

He turned her arms, placing her palms flat against the desk, and curled her fingers over the edge. Not interested in any slow, leisurely lovemaking, Caitlin sighed with relief when he didn't waste time peeling off her sweatpants or his jeans. The instant their clothing vanished, she wrapped her legs around his hips, pulling him closer.

He eased the hard length of his cock into her with agonizing slowness. She wanted to scream at his teasing, torturous motion. He released her hands and grasped her hips, holding her in place, preventing her from pushing up against him.

"Sean." Uncurling her fingers from the edge of the desk, intent on reaching up to pull him closer, Caitlin gasped. Invisible bonds held her arms pinned to the slick smoothness of the desk.

She stared up at him. The gold rim around his emerald eyes shimmered. Yet the heartrending half smile on his lips was all human—and filled with pure male arrogance in his certainty of what he was doing to her.

Caitlin swallowed the whine threatening to escape. She didn't understand what was happening to her. She'd been swept away with lust when they'd first met, but this—this near-unbearable need was unfamiliar, and far from normal in its intensity.

She didn't want to need him like this, didn't want him to have this much power over her. When her son was safely back in her arms, she'd never see this man again, and the last thing she wanted was to miss his touch, ache for his kiss as desperately as she had this last year.

He deepened his thrust, filling her, completing her in a way no one else could. A white light flickered in her mind, shimmering as it grew brighter, feeding her sorely depleted life force.

The ease in which he fed her, the flow of his strength rushing into her, chased away any concerns about the future. The only thing that mattered was right now, this very moment. One way or another, tomorrow would take care of itself.

Chapter 8

Like a pesky gnat, something small and irritating kept teasing at her ear. Caitlin batted a hand toward the irritation.

Her unsuccessful attempt to rid herself of the pest drew a groan from her as she became fully awake. Anxious to escape, she pulled the blankets up and rolled away, intent on falling back into her dreams before the lingering thread beckoning her to return disappeared.

It had been such a long time since she'd found her dreams welcoming. This last year or so they'd been more of the nightmare variety. She didn't appreciate being torn from a pleasant one of her, Sean and their son enjoying a family outing. Since something like that would only ever happen in a dream, having the idyllic situation disturbed was even worse.

The tickling against her ear returned, and she batted at it once again. But this time she made contact with something definitely more solid and much larger than a gnat—it felt more like a face. From the stubble beneath her fingertips, it was a face in dire need of a shave.

She patted the cheek, muttering, "Go away, Sean."

He ignored her suggestion and instead slid beneath the covers to rest against the warmth of her back. "That isn't going to happen. But as much as I would love to spend the rest of the day in this bed with you, we have to get up. My brothers will be waiting for us in Braeden's office soon, if they aren't already."

Caitlin's stomach tightened, and her mind whirled her fully awake. She desperately wanted her son back safely in her arms, yet her gut instinct told her that involving the Drake family would somehow be dangerous.

She frowned at the thought—it was illogical, considering that deed had already been committed the moment she'd come to Sean. Besides, how could it possibly be dangerous when more help in this matter—help from beings far more powerful than she and Sean—would be beneficial, not dangerous?

Regardless of what the Drakes may or may not think about her family, they would combine forces to rescue one of their own. It was natural, instinctual at a basic level for any form of beast to protect their own kind— more so when the being in question was a baby.

A vision formed in her mind, clouding over her rationalizations. A vision so strong that it forced her eyes shut. Dragons—not one, but three—lay bleeding in the agony of their death throes on the stone floor of a ruined castle.

Standing over them laughing, with Ascalon in his hand, was Nathan. Neatly trapped in his free arm, her son wailed.

Caitlin gasped. No. She couldn't—she wouldn't let

them help. Not if it meant leading them to their death. Especially when in the end, her son still wouldn't be free from the demonic wizard holding him.

The warmth of Sean's lips against her neck startled her out of her dire musings. How was she going to do this on her own? As much as she longed to explain, or to discuss this with him, she knew that telling Sean would be a mistake. For one thing, he would never back off. In fact, it would most likely prompt him to act on his own without any assistance from his brothers.

"What's wrong?"

"Nothing." She took a deep breath to calm her riotous emotions before rolling over onto her back to look up at him as he leaned over her.

His eyebrows shot up at her lie. "Are you upset about last night?"

It would be so convenient to use that as an easy excuse to explain away her obvious discomfort. After all, his initial love play had been rather...forceful.

A tremor of desire rippled down her spine. Oh, yes, forceful and very focused on her satisfaction. By the time they'd made it to the bed, she'd been more than just satisfied; her life force had been filled to the brim and then some.

But she didn't want to cover up a lie with another lie. Doing so would only become confusing. Instead, she ignored his question to ask, "Any food in your kitchen?"

"Hungry?"

"Famished." On cue, her stomach growled.

Sean traced a fingertip down the length of her nose then sat up. "It would be rude to let you starve." He patted her leg. "I'll go find us something to eat while you get dressed."

She watched him leave the bedroom without another

word. He'd acquiesced too easily. The tone of his voice
had changed from playful to...noncommittal—flat. He
knew something was up other than her simply being
hungry.

Caitlin threw off the covers with a sigh. It didn't matter. He could think, wonder and suspect all he wanted,
but until she told him of her plan, he wouldn't know for
certain. And since she had no intention of telling him
anything, he'd simply have to keep wondering.

She hadn't figured out how she was going to rescue
her son without help from the Drakes, so it would be a
bit difficult to discuss it with him. Besides, it would be
better this way. Not only would she be sparing his and
his brothers' lives, she could then prevent Sean from
trying to take her son away from her, as well.

That wasn't going to ever happen regardless of what
he thought. She'd never had any intention of letting her
parents or the High Council give her son away, so she
wasn't about to let Sean take him from her, either.

It wasn't going to be easy. But what she needed to
figure out right now was how to get possession of the
items Nathan demanded without Sean or his family
finding out. That wasn't going to be easy, but she knew
where the grimoire and pendants were located.

Sean poured a cup of coffee and sat on a stool at the
kitchen bar. She was up to something; he sensed it in
the change of the air surrounding her. It had flashed
warm when he'd awakened her, then cold as he'd reminded her of the meeting with Braeden and Cameron,
and then hot.

Since she hadn't seemed angry, at least she'd claimed
not to be, and they hadn't been engaged in any sexual
act, he could only surmise that the heat came from racing thoughts.

He should have reached inside her mind to investigate, but he'd decided he was going to gain her trust. After all, she was the mother of his child and his beast's mate. So if they were to have any semblance of a relationship they had to share something more than sex.

He wasn't looking for love, or any declaration of her heart. But they would be partners in raising their son, so some type of shared bond, a friendship maybe, would prove useful. Perhaps learning to trust each other would lead them in that direction.

The only thing he could do now was to see if it was possible to get her to talk to him. His dragon grunted and rolled his eyes. Sean ignored the beast's obvious doubts. One way or another he would see this through.

"Did you find us something to eat?"

At her question, he rose to get her some coffee. "More or less. I normally eat down in the dining room."

She accepted the cup and after a swallow, took a bagel from the plate of pastries he'd offered. "Right now anything is fine, thank you."

He took a seat and pulled out the stool next to him. "Join me."

She did so, asking, "Have either of your brothers called with any news yet?"

"No. But that doesn't mean they don't have any to share. They could just be waiting for us to arrive below."

"How do you think they'll be able to help?" Picking at the bagel, she continued, "I mean, what can they do that we can't?"

Sean leaned closer, his shoulder resting against hers. "What are you thinking, Caitlin?"

"I don't like this waiting. If we just took the items we have to Nathan, maybe it'd be enough. Then this would be over."

"You know, I get it. I can't blame you for being impatient. But if we went to Nathan with less than what he demanded, our son would be left without parents."

She leaned away. "Yes, but if we keep dragging this out, I could be left without my son."

His beast rumbled as her voice rose. Sean took the opportunity of swallowing more coffee to gain control of his dragon and temper his response. Certain both were in check, he set his cup down and took one of her hands between his. "Look, first of all it's our son. *Ours*. You aren't in this alone. Besides, I thought we discussed this yesterday. It's safer to confront Nathan with strength."

"You mean magic."

"It doesn't matter what you call it. The force and power of three beasts will succeed far better than you and I ever could."

She paled at his statement and closed her eyes. Sean slung an arm across her shoulder and pulled her close. "Tell me what's wrong."

Caitlin shook her head, but he could feel her cold fear as it seeped into him, chilling him to the bone. "What are you so afraid of? Tell me, let me help."

She jerked away and moved to the glass doors. Staring out at the mist-shrouded forest, she said, "You can't help."

He remained where he was, ignoring the urge to enfold her in his embrace and protect her from whatever had her so worried. "And why would you say that?"

Not saying a word and not moving away from the door, she shook her head.

This wasn't like her. This odd, discomforting nervousness. At least it wasn't like what he knew of her. Trying to talk to her, to reason with her, was getting him nowhere, and he wanted to know what had frightened her so between last night and this morning.

Uncertain which tactic to use, he fell back on what was familiar to him. He rose and headed toward his office saying, "Don't tell me, then. But it changes nothing. Cameron, Braeden and I will get our son back with or without your input."

Caitlin spun away from the door with a gasp. "No!" When he didn't pause, she followed. "You'll just die in the attempt."

Die? What was she talking about? Why would she suddenly be so certain of that happening?

A shimmer from his desk caught his eye. Sean frowned then stopped in the doorway and turned to face Caitlin. She bumped to a stop against his chest.

He grasped her shoulders and asked, "What did you see?"

She looked away for a heartbeat then turned her attention back to him. Fear etched her features, leaving her looking more pale and drawn than she had upon her arrival at the Lair. "The three of you dead. And Nathan laughing over you as he held Sean."

"He can't kill all of us."

She glanced toward the safe. "With Ascalon he could."

He swallowed a curse before asking, "When had you planned on telling me this?"

"Never."

A kick in the gut wouldn't have taken his breath away as fast. Releasing her, he stepped into his office. "So you were content to let me go on a mission you were convinced would end in my death?"

So much for building any trust with her.

"No. I had planned on going alone."

Now his beast gasped for breath. "Alone? You're convinced that three beasts will fail, yet you believe you would succeed?"

She was either far more brazen that he'd ever assumed, or she'd lost the ability to reason. It had to be one or the other, because nobody in their right mind would think like that.

"What made you believe for one second that I would ever let you do that alone?"

She shrugged. "You couldn't stop me if you didn't know."

"Right. Because I'm completely clueless and wouldn't notice you weren't here."

"I hadn't thought that far ahead yet."

"Obviously." It was impossible to keep the biting tone from his voice.

Was she always this impetuous?

If so, they were going to be in for a rockier road together than he'd ever imagined.

As it was, his beast was already gnashing his teeth at the mere thought of her traipsing off to Nathan's stronghold by herself.

Sean sat down before his desk and waved her to the chair on the other side. "Show me where you saw this warning."

She glanced at the grimoire. "It wasn't in the book. It was more of a mental flash."

For some reason, that just made it worse. She'd planned on risking her own life because of some fleeting thought? "You sure it's not just an overactive imagination?"

"No." Frowning, she shook her head. "It's stronger than that."

His attention was once again captured by the pulsing glow of light coming from the grimoire.

"Apparently, there's something we need to see." He flipped open the ancient tome to the last picture they'd observed then turned the page.

Caitlin sucked in a loud breath and shoved her chair back from the desk. "There." Her hand shook as she pointed at the forming picture. "It isn't just in my mind."

Sure enough, taking form on the page was the scene she'd described.

He and his brothers were on a stone floor, broken and bleeding, the vaporous mist of their life forces flowing into Nathan as he stood over them laughing. In one hand he held Ascalon—blood dripped from the blade. In his free arm he held a crying baby.

Then, as Sean stared at the image, a thick chain began to form. One end was shackled to his ankle, and link by link it stretched across the floor to an altar where that end had been secured.

From the items on the altar—the burning candles, the crystal cauldron, jewel-encrusted chalice, dragon statues of emerald and sapphire, along with a wooden, curved-blade athame—it was obvious that Nathan had been casting spells. Ones that apparently included him.

His dragon screamed. The rage made his hands tremble. Sean curled his fingers, tightening his fists in an attempt to stop the anger threatening to overtake him. He needed to focus on the rest of the still-forming image.

On the floor before the altar was the body of a dead woman with long black hair. Thin, bloody stripes, as if caused by a whip, marked her naked body.

As if sensing his attention, the woman turned her head and stared at him.

"Yet a dragon you shall be."

The words of the curse echoed in his office. Caitlin's eyes grew large, shimmering against the paleness of her face.

His beast ceased to breathe as his own heart raced, pounding hard inside his chest.

Sean pushed away from the desk, unwilling to witness any more that might be shown to them. He didn't need further evidence of why he'd been cursed into a changeling. The task he was to complete for Nathan was obvious to him. He'd been so concerned about his urge to kill his family that he hadn't taken any other scenario into consideration.

He didn't need to kill them; all he had to do was to lure his brothers to Nathan's castle. Unwittingly he would do so under the guise of helping him rescue his son.

Caitlin had been partly right—while he would go to rescue their son, Braeden and Cameron couldn't be permitted to help. He would not be responsible for killing the Dragon Lord and his twin.

"Sean, look!"

He followed Caitlin's wide-eyed gaze back to the page with trepidation. On the facing page, a dual picture formed.

One half of the page was a desolate image of the world with Nathan in supreme control. The other an idyllic setting with him, Caitlin and their son surrounded by his aunt, brothers and their families.

"St. George will set you free."

Once again, the confusing promise filled the air.

He moved back to the desk and turned the page, hoping another picture would form, explaining how he could defeat Nathan.

Caitlin moved behind him. Placing a hand on his

shoulder she asked, "You don't think it'll be that easy, do you?"

Sean reached up and covered her hand with his own, wondering if he should be uncomfortable with the way she'd so easily read his mind. "No. But sometimes it doesn't hurt to hope."

His cell phone vibrated, and he glanced at the screen. "Your brothers?"

He nodded in reply to her question and hit the intercom button on the desk phone, opening a line to the office. When it beeped, he said, "On our way."

Sean rose, scooping the dragon pendants from his desk drawer, and slipped them into a front pocket then grabbed the grimoire. He extended an arm toward the door. "Ready?"

Caitlin paused at the huge metal-studded door that Sean held open for her. She felt as if she were being ushered into a medieval lord's chamber for an audience that would decide her fate. She supposed that in a way, it would. Together would they all be able to come up with a plan to save her son? Or would they spend their time devising a plan that would only get them killed?

Did she want to be a part of that? She glanced at Sean, who raised a questioning eyebrow at her hesitation. Whether she wanted to be a part of this or not wasn't an option. She took a breath and entered the room.

Her feet sank into the plush, dark midnight blue carpet. A thin ray of sunlight filtered into the room through an opening between the drapes. The light shimmered off the jeweled hilt of a sword, one of many weapons mounted on the walls, and bounced off the face of a sapphire dragon perched on a marble pedestal. The flicker of light against the dragon's eyes made it appear as if the gemstone beast was looking at her, watching her, waiting for just the right moment to pounce.

She turned her attention to the two men standing before the desk. Their exchanged greetings were brief since she'd met the men.

Her thoughts drifted to the three pendants—amethyst, sapphire and emerald. She sat in one of the chairs in front of the desk with a glance to each man, once again noting the color of their eyes.

A dragon for each brother—was that by coincidence or design?

The grimoire had shown sisters with eyes the same color as the pendants they'd used. Perhaps these brilliant hues were common in the Drake family. If so, was it possible that the brothers had the wrong pendants?

"Sean?" She thought it worth mentioning. "Do you remember—"

Braeden's rousing curse cut off her question. He rose to glance out one of the many tall, narrow windows of his office. "What is Baron Hoffel doing here?"

Caitlin groaned and sank as far back into her chair as possible, wishing it would just swallow her. "I didn't invite him."

Sean sat down in the chair next to her. "I didn't think you had."

Cameron leaned against the desk and asked, "Someone care to clue me in?"

Before she could explain, Braeden said, "Hoffel is Ms. St. George's betrothed."

"How cozy." Sarcasm dripped from Cameron's voice. "Can anyone explain how he found his way here?" He stared at her as he asked.

"I don't know." Caitlin shook her head. "It's not like I could, or even would, give him directions."

Without another word Cameron left the office. She presumed it was to escort their *guest* to the meeting.

The silence in the room as Braeden and Sean stared at her while waiting for Cam to return with Derek, was thick and heavy with unasked questions. It was all Caitlin could do to draw in breath. She sank her nails into the arms of her chair, hoping the act would lessen her worry.

While hell would freeze over before she married Hoffel, she didn't relish the idea of having to explain his death to the High Council, or her parents—or his own parents for that matter.

Sean placed a hand over hers and leaned closer. "If you don't kill him, he'll leave here whole."

She'd been so caught off guard by Derek's arrival and so worried about how the Drakes would react, that she hadn't even noticed Sean's mental intrusion.

But at the moment that was the least of her concerns. There'd never been any intention of marrying the baron, regardless of what her parents or the council thought. However, her plan had been to string everyone along until her son was safely back in her care. Then she and little Sean would leave—before the marriage and well before anyone else could take him away from her.

But her success with getting away from her parents, Derek and the High Council with all of their antiquated rules and stifling expectations depended on her ability to not become the target of their suspicion.

After Derek's attack in the cell and the subsequent blame laid at her feet for his atrocious behavior, it had been all she could do to retain the appearance of civil-

ity. In reality she wanted nothing more than to slide her
sword through his neck.

"Bloodthirsty, aren't you?"

The voice racing through her head didn't belong to
Sean. Nor did it feel anything like him. She shot a glare
toward Braeden. He raised his eyebrows then silently
added, *"Don't worry, I won't say a word."*

Sean's fingers tightened slightly over her hand. She
drew her attention to him. Apparently, by the way he
glanced from her to his brother, he knew something
was up. And when he tried to force his way into her
thoughts, Caitlin closed her eyes and dropped a solid
wall between both of the men and her mind.

The last thing she needed right now was for Sean to
discover what she planned after they rescued her son.
He'd demand she stay at his side, where he could protect her and little Sean. She didn't need nor want his
protection, and she wasn't about to run away from her
controlling family only to go straight into his arms. For
reasons she couldn't quite pinpoint yet, that idea felt as
if she'd simply be trading one set of chains for another.

A knock at the office door made her heart race. Hoffel was here. Why he'd come to Mirabilus was beyond
comprehension. It was one thing for her to walk into
the beasts' lair—she had a very good reason for doing
so—but for him to follow her defied logic.

Sean briefly tightened his hold over her hand before releasing it and then leaned closer to whisper, "He
can't hurt you."

"I know." She was well aware that Sean's dragon
wouldn't permit Derek to lay one finger on her. But
she wondered what his beast would think, or do, when
he saw her greet another man as if she welcomed his
presence.

Chapter 9

Sean couldn't help but stare at the man who'd entered Braeden's office. It was impossible not to, considering he appeared to be dressed up for Halloween—entirely in black. From the theatrically swirled cape as he strode through the door, to the tailored suit—tie, clip and cuff links included—down to the wing tips, not one speck of color broke the darkness.

He'd seen funeral directors who dressed less somberly than this.

It wasn't just his attire. The man couldn't be more than five and a half feet tall. Which would be fine if he had either the build or the attitude to go along with his stature. But he didn't. His flamboyant entrance made him appear to be more of a low-budget character actor than anything else. And his beady-eyed glare would be more appropriate for a teenager of about sixteen.

His bearing and appearance would make him look like a child standing next to Caitlin. Sean wondered how old Hoffel had been when he'd been turned. Perhaps he hadn't yet been an adult at the time. If so, it would explain quite a bit.

Braeden stepped forward to shake the baron's hand in welcome. "Baron Hoffel, what brings you to Mirabilus?"

"Caitlin shouldn't be alone at a time like this. I came to see that she had the support of her husband-to-be."

His claim on Caitlin, while stated in a thin, reedy voice, couldn't have been made any plainer.

Sean watched silently, curious to see Caitlin's reaction as she rose and went to the baron's side. "Thank you. I'm certain my son's father and his uncles appreciate your added assistance as much as I do. After all, this could turn out to be a bloodbath, and every hand could prove useful."

Obviously, Hoffel wasn't the only one who saw fit to stake their claim. Caitlin had just done a pretty good job of it herself by making it plain that these men were her son's family, not Hoffel. But that wasn't what surprised him the most. It was the baron's reaction that had caught his interest.

Granted, Hoffel was a vampire, and his complexion was on the pale side to begin with, but Sean was positive the man had turned a rather ugly shade of white at Caitlin's words. If ever there was a time when he was torn between outright laughter and pure blood rage, this was it.

For all of Hoffel's theatrics, for his great bravery in abusing a woman, there was nothing alpha about him. In the end, the man was nothing more than a coward and a bully.

Sean had little use for either.

Braeden returned to his desk and waved the others toward the chairs.

With as much restraint as he could muster, Sean let the baron claim the chair closest to Caitlin. It wasn't as if the man could hurt her—if he so much as thought to lift one finger to cause her pain or harm, Sean would basically rip his head from his body and serve it for brunch.

Caitlin looked at him and gasped softly. Sean felt her warm touch brush across his mind. He frowned. How had she done that since he'd been intent on not letting Hoffel in and had put a secure lock on his mind?

Her hand, inside the pocket of the jacket she wore, moved slightly. A slow touch trailed up his spine to linger at the base of his neck.

How in the hell had she gotten a hold of that pendant?

No sooner had he asked himself the question when he'd come up with the answer—before they'd left his suite he'd given her a hug for encouragement. The snitch had obviously pilfered it from his pocket without him even realizing it.

He quickly checked his pocket. Sure enough, only two of the pendants were inside. This meeting could turn out to be more interesting than he'd ever imagined.

Obviously tired of waiting for Braeden to ask, Cam barreled ahead. "Care to tell us how you got here?"

Hoffel shrugged. "Luck, I suppose." He smiled sheepishly, adding, "I became lost and followed a small fishing boat into shore."

Surprised his brother left the brazen lie alone, Sean asked, "And what do you plan to do to help in my son's rescue?"

The baron quickly covered his sneer with a cough

before offering, "I've had the occasion to meet the Learned once or twice. I could be in a position to mediate the boy's release." He reached over and clasped Caitlin's hand in both of his own. "After all, Cait and I need to make sure he arrives at his parents' house safe and sound."

Braeden's eyebrows rose. Cam's eyes widened in shock. Sean leaned forward in his chair. "I can assure you that isn't ever going to happen."

Hoffel placed a light kiss on the back of Caitlin's hand and held Sean's stare. "That isn't up to you, is it?"

Sean resisted the urge to rise and tower over the man. Instead, he forced himself to remain seated, but warned, "If you want to turn this into a pissing match, feel free. But you aren't going to win. That is my son and he will be raised here, by me."

Danielle Drake chose that moment to waltz unannounced into the room. "Gentlemen, let's keep this civil, shall we?"

She breezed past the baron to reach out and take Caitlin's hand. "You and I need to get acquainted. Why don't we let the men have their little discussion and we'll rejoin them soon?"

Without another word, she led Caitlin from the office, but not before issuing a silent order to Sean and he was sure his brothers. *"Get rid of him. I don't care if you toss him in the ocean or kill him. But he's up to no good."*

Caitlin didn't release her breath until they were outside the castle. She hadn't been aware of holding it until she gasped for air.

"Thank you." She studied the other woman then said, "If I remember correctly, you're Sean's aunt Danielle."

"Yes." She laughed. "Guilty as charged." And then she led Caitlin to a stone bench. "Please, take a seat. We really do need to talk."

Once Caitlin was seated, Danielle pulled a wooden cube from the pocket of her brightly colored dress. "And this—" she lifted the cube before her "—is Aelthed."

"The druid from the grimoire?" Caitlin marveled at the concept. "He's real?"

"Yes, and you're the second person to meet him other than me. He met Ariel, Cam's wife, a while back out of necessity."

"What about your nephews?"

"There's been no reason for them to be introduced."

Amazed, Caitlin asked, "Why me?"

Danielle set the cube on the bench between them. "I'll let him answer."

Before Caitlin could question the woman, a voice floated up from the wooden box. *"Because, my dear, you are going to free me and my nephew from our prisons."*

Caitlin stared at the seemingly inanimate object a moment then asked, "How am I going to do that?"

"I'm not quite certain yet, but we'll find a way while you're rescuing the dragonette."

Danielle placed a hand on her leg. "You really aren't going to marry Hoffel, are you?"

Seeing no reason to lie, Caitlin said, "Not in a million years."

"Good." The older woman frowned. "And you aren't giving the child away, either, are you?"

Caitlin smiled and shook her head. "No. It would be easier to tear my heart out with my bare hands."

"Excellent. Then it's settled."

A sinking feeling in the pit of her stomach urged her to hesitantly ask, "What is settled?"

"All of you will figure out a way to rescue the baby and kill Nathan. Then you and Sean will wed—"

"No. No. No." Caitlin raised her hand. "Hold up. I have no intention of marrying your nephew."

"Yes, dear."

Oh, no! She'd forgotten Sean's warning about not arguing with the woman. She was supposed to have hedged. Sean would have to deal with this on his own. Right now her only concern was her son. "If none of you will give me the items the Learned demanded, how am I going to ever get my baby back?"

"What items would those be?"

Was it possible that nobody had told her yet?

Caitlin lightly tapped the cube. "He wants this cube and the grimoire, along with the emerald and sapphire pendants."

Visibly flustered, Danielle Drake waved her hands before her. "No. He can't have those things. It would mean the end of everything. Literally, just everything."

Sean had said something along the same lines, in a less frantic manner, making Caitlin wonder exactly how much magic these items held.

Danielle picked up the cube and held it tightly to her chest. "No. He is not getting Aelthed." Tears shimmered in the woman's eyes.

Had she known the older woman would get this upset she never would have said anything. Caitlin patted the woman's shoulder. "Shhhh. It's okay. I'm sure it won't come to that. Please don't worry."

Now the woman was rocking side to side on the bench. Caitlin's heart fell. What had she done? She glanced over her shoulder toward the castle. "Please, let's go back inside."

"No." Danielle pulled away from her touch. "They'll take him away."

"I won't let them. I promise."

"You can't stop them!" Danielle flapped a hand at her. "Go away. Just leave me be."

Caitlin rose and looked again toward the castle then back at Sean's aunt. "I don't want to leave you alone like this. Come in with me."

"No!"

Seeing as how urging her only made the woman more agitated, Caitlin turned away and headed back to the castle. She'd let Sean and his brothers know what she did as soon as she got back in the office.

"Danielle, beloved, really. Was all that necessary?" Aelthed chided.

Danielle sneaked a peek over her shoulder to ensure Caitlin had indeed gone back inside before she sat up, straightened the skirt of her dress and then put the cube back down on the bench beside her. "I got what we wanted, didn't I?"

"While traumatizing the poor girl."

"She'll get over it. It's not like she's not hiding things, too."

"Did you notice her hesitation when she mentioned the pendants?"

"Yes, I did. Do you think she found another one?"

"No. That would be impossible. Lady Rhian's amethyst one was shattered into a million pieces. By now it would be nothing more than dust and memories."

Danielle sighed. "True. But wouldn't it be wonderful if we could somehow re-create that needed key and set you free once and for all?"

"Perhaps."

"Yes, well, right now I'm relieved to know the woman isn't working with her family, Hoffel or the Learned. At least I don't have to worry she's only here to hand the boys over to Nathan."

"Sean!" Caitlin burst into the office without pausing to see if she was interrupting anything or not.

He immediately came to his feet and met her half-way across the room. "What's wrong?"

"I did something stupid."

He led her over to the chair she'd vacated earlier—the one right next to Hoffel, who to her dismay was still present. "Sit down and tell us what you did."

Catching her breath, she explained in a rush, "I said something to upset your aunt, and no matter what I did she only became more and more flustered. I think she's having some sort of panic attack or something."

All three Drakes stared at her a moment before exchanging an odd look with each other. Finally, Braeden rose and addressed Hoffel as he headed for the door with Sean and Cam on his heels, "We'll have to continue this discussion later. I'll have one of the men show you to a room you can use."

He paused at the door. "Caitlin, come with us, please."

His voice was so stern and commanding that she didn't question him. She simply followed the three men from the room.

Once they walked outside, the three of them ducked around the side of the castle, pulling her along.

Cameron broke into laughter first. Then Sean. While Braeden's only show of amusement was a half smile and shake of his head. At her frown, he explained, "Our aunt has a bad habit of engaging in dramatics. She apparently wanted some information from you, got it and then chased you away."

"You have got to be kidding me!" She would strangle the woman for wasting her time in such a frivolous manner.

"Oh, no, that's Danielle Drake. What did you tell her that *upset* her so?"

"I told her about what was demanded in exchange for my son."

Braeden sighed. "She apparently hadn't believed me when I relayed that information and wanted to hear it directly from the source."

The other two started laughing again.

Caitlin glared at Sean. "I'm glad you're so amused. Perhaps you'll find this just as funny. Our marriage *has* been planned and, oops, I forgot to hedge."

With that, she turned and stormed away.

"What a bunch of jerks." Their amusement grated. Especially Sean's. There was nothing funny about any of this. Her son's life was in danger, and they were guffawing over some prank their aunt played?

Fine. They could laugh and waste all the time they wanted. She, on the other hand, wasn't going to sit here doing nothing any longer.

Tonight, after all of them were in bed sleeping, she was going to make her way over to the Learned's stronghold with that damn grimoire and the pendants. It was doubtful she'd be able to get her hands on the cube, but she could tell him where it was—in Danielle Drake's possession.

She stomped into the elevator and punched the button for the third floor. In the meantime she needed to make sure she could pick the lock to Sean's desk, so she could more easily get the items. And then she would have to find a way across the water—even if she had to steal a boat to do so.

Terror ripped her from the nightmares chasing her. Caitlin reached across the bed, finding only empty air where she'd instinctively thought to find Sean and the comfort just a touch would provide. She gasped at the chilling stab of loss and sat up, hugging her arms about herself in an attempt to dispel the shivers racking her sweat-soaked body.

They'd argued after he had returned to the apartment about his finding so much humor in his aunt's trick. He didn't appear to be taking any of this seriously enough for her satisfaction. His easy manner and mirth had been the last straw of her temper and patience. The rest of the day and evening had been spent in fuming silence on his part, and focused planning on hers. Finally, when she couldn't stand to be in the same room with him any longer, she'd gone to bed. She'd been so certain that sleep would elude her, but it hadn't. She'd quickly fallen into nightmare-laden rest.

Visions of Sean's death circled in her mind with the rotating wildness of a tornado. The same gruesome scene played over and over as she watched helplessly. Her body was frozen in place, unable to go to his aid.

He was naked, chained to Nathan's altar. She heard nothing as if suddenly deaf, but she could see the anger in his furrowed brow and blazing eyes. His lips parted in a soundless shout—a yell of rage that was met with Nathan's vile laugh. The evil, humorless laughter ended as the wizard thrust the tip of Ascalon through Sean's chest.

In distorted, slow-motion frames, Sean fell to the stone floor. His life blood flowing from him along with his soul. A curling fog streamed from his body, and Nathan gleefully pulled the departing energy into himself.

"No." Caitlin threw off the covers. She couldn't let that happen. What she was about to do would enrage Sean, but she'd much rather endure his anger than lose him forever.

Regardless of what he would think, or say later, she knew this was the right thing to do. Hadn't they both witnessed the grimoire drawing the same horrible image of his death? This wasn't the first time she'd had this dream—it had haunted her before his family's book had put her nightmare into pictures.

She had to trust her instinct on this. These images were more than just pictures or vague warnings, and far more than simple worry on her part. They were portents of the future—omens that she could no longer ignore.

Caitlin quickly tossed on the first clothes she grabbed and tied her hair back with a stretchy band. Knowing she would need something to carry everything in, she rooted around in the closet, snagged her long duffel bag and then left the bedroom. As quietly as possible, in case Sean had returned from wherever he'd headed after she'd gone to bed, she stayed against the wall while she crept down the hall and peered around the corner.

Her soft *whoosh* of the breath she'd been holding rushed into the darkness of the empty living room. She approached the door to his office with her fingers crossed. Hopefully, it wouldn't be locked. He'd be angry enough without her breaking into his office.

To her relief, the door opened at her touch. She flipped on the desk lamp and held out a hand, calling

Ascalon to her grip. After sliding the weapon into the bag, Caitlin swept the grimoire on top of the sword.

Since she'd already practiced earlier, picking the lock to his desk was easy enough to accomplish after a couple tries. Once she had possession of the two dragon pendants that Nathan had demanded, she dropped them into the bag, too.

She felt the front pocket of her jeans to ensure the amethyst pendant was still there. Nathan hadn't asked for it, nor did she have any intention of giving it to him, but as far as she was concerned, since it responded to her—it belonged to her.

Now she just needed to get out of this apartment and to the dock where Hoffel waited for her as planned. Earlier in the afternoon, she'd realized that he actually had had a good point about mediating. He *had* met the Learned, and he might prove as useful as he thought he could be, so she'd approached him. Her selling point had mirrored his—rescuing the baby so they could get on with their lives.

And the man had bought it.

Right now she didn't care. She'd willingly use whomever she had to use to get her child back where he belonged.

Once Caitlin exited the apartment, she rushed down the hallway to the stairs where she thought she'd have less of a chance of being caught.

To her relief she encountered no one on the stairs and saw no one when she peered down and out into the Great Hall. After taking a deep breath, she raced across the hall, wincing as her footsteps seemed to echo off the stone of the walls.

But thankfully, her moves had all been well planned

so far because she made it outside into the night air without mishap.

She hugged the castle wall as she skirted around to the side, avoiding the lights before darting out into the open expanse of ground between the castle and the beach area.

Halfway across the open ground she felt rather than heard or saw someone fall into step alongside her.

"Going somewhere?"

The sound of Sean's voice made her heart stutter and stomach turn.

He took the bag from her hand, flung it into the air where it disappeared, then grasped her upper arm and steered her back toward the castle. "I'm afraid your lover's already been detained."

Between gritted teeth she said, "He is *not* my lover."

"Really? You might want to fill him in on that."

She ignored his dig to ask, "What did you do with my bag?"

"Put everything back where it belongs."

"You really didn't expect me to just sit around and do nothing like the rest of you have been, did you?"

When he didn't respond, she continued, "He is my son. My son! I can't just leave him to die at Nathan's hands. Why can't you understand that?"

Again, he kept walking without saying a word.

"Damn you, Drake! What is wrong with you? How can you not care about your own son?"

He came to an abrupt stop, swung her around before him and slapped his hand over her mouth. Standing nose to nose with her, he shouted, "Shut up. Just. Stop. Talking."

Caitlin flinched at the gravelly tone of his voice— more growl than anything. She leaned away from the brilliant emerald shimmer emanating from around his elongated pupils.

Yes, she feared the beast evident in every fiber of Sean's being. But she refused to back down.

She tore her face away from his hand. "No! I will not shut up." She poked a finger into his chest. "Why don't you act like the beast you claim to be and save our son!"

Before she fully knew what was happening, he shifted, quickly—almost instantaneously from man, to misty dragon, to strong, solid beast. An angry, muscular beast, who grasped her by the nape of the neck as if she were nothing more than a piece of paper before taking to the sky.

Caitlin's scream followed them into the nighttime clouds.

Chapter 10

Sean's beast flew low over the choppy waters, letting the icy cold spray cool him and hopefully the woman still clutched securely in his talons. Her screams hadn't lessened, but they were borne of anger, of rage, having nothing to do with fear. She was mad because her plans had been thwarted.

Too bad.

Didn't she realize that her plans would have gotten her killed? He longed to shake some sense into her. But the human part of his mind knew that if he started, he'd be unable to stop, and harming her would serve no purpose.

So for now they would soar until her ire abated enough to hear reason and his anger eased over the fact that in the end, she'd chosen to go to Hoffel. That stung.

It wasn't as if he and Caitlin had a relationship; they didn't. Outside of the child she bore, they shared nothing other than over-the-top sex.

He understood his dragon's rage—the beast was jealous, plain and simple. Somehow he'd have to get over it and learn to live with the fact that he and his mate were never going to share a life.

His own anger confused him—oh, sure, the mere thought of being passed over for that weaselly, snot-nosed bully Hoffel was a huge slap in the face as far as his ego was concerned, and there'd be no getting over that.

But why did it feel like more than just a bruised ego?

He hadn't been sitting around all day doing nothing like she'd suggested. He'd spent most of the day with his brothers and some of Mirabilus's men, devising a way to rescue the child and kill the Learned without the loss of too many lives.

He and Cam had flown at least half a dozen missions, scouting every speck of the Learned's stronghold. They'd charted each and every weakness, while noting in detail the strengths that would prove difficult to overcome.

He'd even seen their son.

The boy was fine. He'd been screaming his lungs out, but he hadn't appeared harmed, just throwing a fine temper—like his mother. The nurse had fretted over him as if she'd actually cared about his distress and was doing everything within her power to ease it.

At one point Sean swore the child looked directly at him. But that must have been wishful thinking because his beast had been nothing more than a sliver of fog weaving in and out of the mist.

It had been all he could do not to slip in through the narrow window opening and take the child from the castle ruins. But how? In solid form he wouldn't have fit through the opening—he was unable to control his size in solid form; he would always be a big, lumbering hulk. And in smoke form, he had no way to physically carry the boy.

He would have told Caitlin all of this. For that matter, she could have helped with the plotting and planning, but she'd been in a snit because she thought they'd laughed at her over Danielle. Had she let him explain, she'd have known that they'd been laughing at Danielle's antics, not Caitlin's gullibility. But she'd stomped off.

And when he'd gone to the suite to talk to her, she'd stormed into the bedroom and slammed the door closed. He could have forced his way in and made her listen, but instead, he'd done his own storming off.

Sean rolled his eyes. Anyone watching them would think they were a couple of hormonal teenagers instead of adults at times.

When he'd gone back up for dinner, the chill in the suite had been too cold to bear for long. So again, he'd left her alone, thinking that was the easiest option.

Finally, when he'd realized that the ignoring routine was getting them nowhere, he'd gone up to talk to her, only to find her, the grimoire, the pendants and Ascalon gone.

While searching for her, Cam had called to inform him that Hoffel was on the beach with a boat, waiting for Caitlin. Sean tracked down Caitlin, leaving his brothers to deal with Hoffel. At least they wouldn't kill the fool.

"Sean, are you in there?"

He shook himself out of his woolgathering and noticed she wasn't screaming anymore. He dipped his head to peer down at her. She was seated on the pad of his…foot with her back resting against one of his curled talons.

"Ah, you do hear me."

Of course he heard her. But his first instinct was to keep ignoring her, even though he knew that would get them nowhere. The problem was that he was in beast form, and he wouldn't be able to keep the dragon's feelings out of any conversation he had with her. And the human side of him feared that in this short amount of time the beast had become far more attached to the woman than was good for either of them.

She stroked her hand down a smooth talon and then leaned over to rest her forehead against it. "I just needed to do something to get our son back. Surely you can understand that, can't you?"

Wonderful. She was going to appeal directly to the dragon. He couldn't allow that. Sean focused his energy on her. He might not be able to speak out loud, but he could still get his thoughts across.

"Leave him alone, Caitlin."

"I'm just explaining myself."

"There's no need. We aren't confused in the least. You chose Hoffel."

The dragon huffed and soared higher.

She wrapped her arms around the talon she'd been leaning against. "Only because you and I weren't speaking."

"Bull."

"You can't seriously believe I'd ever choose the baron for anything, can you? You met him. He's a vicious coward."

Maybe it was time she was confronted with the truth Braeden had discovered about her fiancé and perhaps her family. "He's the Learned's henchman. How do you think he found his way here? It was no accident. So, tell me again how neither you, nor your family, are involved with Nathan."

"What? No."

"Don't play dumb, Caitlin. I know better. Isn't that why you came to me in the first place? So that I'd get myself and my brothers killed trying to save our son?"

"Sean, I swear, I would never do that. I don't believe my family would do such a thing."

He wanted to believe her, but he'd be risking far too much to do so. And he wasn't willing to risk everything for her. "Really? You don't believe your kind, loving, blood-sucking family would ever do anything to harm another person?"

"It's not like they're out there slaughtering the villagers."

"No. They're just out there roasting dragons on a spit."

She sighed. "This is getting us nowhere."

"No kidding. Why don't you just tell me the truth and be done with it?"

"I have told you the truth."

"Your truth has too many holes in it."

He strengthened his focus, determined to discover the truth on his own and reached out to touch her mind. To his surprise, she let him in with little resistance. Sean shivered against the pain he met. This time it wasn't her hunger that threatened to tear him apart—it was the cold, twisting ache of what could only be a mother's loss.

Since her immediate, basic needs had been met—she'd been fed and was no longer starving—her nurturing and maternal needs had rushed in to fill the void.

There existed an ache inside her that could only be soothed by the return of her child.

Yes, he was angry that the Learned had his offspring. He was horrified that the St. Georges had done their best to kill the child before it came into the world. When he'd seen his son, he had been filled with overwhelming awe and a warmth inside like nothing he'd ever felt before. And if the child died, he would be angry, sad, beside himself with grief.

But it would be nothing compared to Caitlin's pain. Hers would be unbearable.

Through no choice of his own, he'd not yet had the chance to imprint with his son. He would mourn the loss of something he never got the chance to know.

Caitlin would mourn the loss of a part of herself.

Sean's beast crooned, soft and low, seeking a way to provide Caitlin with temporary solace. He would never be able to convince the dragon that its efforts were a waste of time. Nothing it did would help. But the animal acted on instinct, and right now its mate was in pain, and it would seek a way to somehow ease that agony.

Sean let him be and pushed deeper, past the pain, reaching for memories that would give him the answers he sought.

He hadn't doubted her claims that her parents had locked her away, leaving her to starve—he'd seen the proof of that—he just hadn't given any thought to the hurt and anguish such a spiteful, unkind act had caused her. She might be an adult, but they were still her parents and they'd sought her death, or at the very least the death of their own grandchild.

Nor had he doubted that Hoffel had attacked her; the grimoire had clearly shown him that.

But neither of those were the memories or thoughts he was looking to find. So he poked around a little more.

And there, the memory he sought came into focus. Yes, just as he'd thought, her parents had directed her to come to him. That whole scene with her mother back in his bedroom at the Lair had been nothing more than one of her mother's orchestrated shows meant to manipulate him so he'd believe that she had come to him on her own.

When in truth they'd ordered her to bring Ascalon with her so that if Nathan didn't succeed in killing him and his brothers, she could.

However, she'd come to him with the firm intention of ignoring their orders. She was set on getting her child back and then leaving—everyone. Caitlin wasn't going back to the St. George family home. She'd lied to her parents, Hoffel and the High Council. She wasn't going to marry Hoffel.

But she wasn't staying with Sean, either, and she wasn't leaving her child behind.

His anger that she would blithely disregard everything he'd told her about being mated and raising the child sparked to life.

Before that spark could flare to a full-blown inferno, he stopped. Could he blame her? After everything she'd been through, could he really fault her for wanting to run away, to disappear? Hadn't he run away for less?

That was most likely why she'd gone to Hoffel tonight. She'd mistakenly believed that with his help, she would get her child back and then she would just disappear without anyone being the wiser.

Little did she know that Hoffel would have delighted in helping the Learned kill her, or at the very least watched the event with glee.

He eased out of her mind and directed the dragon back to Mirabilus.

"Sean."

"No. Just be quiet."

"But—"

"I don't want to hear your explanation. I just want you to be quiet."

The last thing he wanted was for his dragon to discover what she'd planned. It was going to be hard enough to keep the beast out of that part of his mind; he didn't want it to overhear a conversation. They could talk later if she insisted, after his beast was fast asleep and not tuned in to its human part. Until then, she just needed to keep her explanations to herself.

Sean circled the beach, landing alongside an old work shed. He set her down gently, and with the curve of a talon pushed her into the shed before shifting back to human form and then following her inside.

Aelthed shook off the regret and sadness swirling around him. The cursed changeling was upset, but being pure Drake, he wasn't about to give voice to his sense of loss or the confusion he felt because of it.

Stretching out his legs, seated in the corner of his cube, Aelthed could empathize with the changeling. It had taken him a good many months to finally understand his own sense of loss over something he'd never really had.

As a man, a human man—or as close to human as he'd ever been—he was dead. Even if he found a way out of the cube he would exist as nothing more than a disembodied soul. No matter what he did, he would never feel Danielle Drake's arms around him, never taste the sweetness of her kiss, never experience the pain or pure joy of her love.

And he'd grieved over those things for quite a while. In truth, there were still moments when despair threatened to drop him into the agonizing pits of hell.

He wished there was a way for him to help the changeling avoid the same fate, but he knew that wasn't possible. St. George's daughter wasn't ever going to give her heart to the dragon. It didn't matter whether they rescued the child or not; it wasn't in her nature.

Succubus or not, she was the spawn of a vampire. A heartless, soulless creature who cared nothing for the emotions or needs of others. That was the way she'd been raised. And that was how she would raise the dragonette—it's what was familiar and normal to her.

Now that was something Aelthed couldn't permit. To keep a dragon from going rogue, it needed to learn and understand the value in feelings, human feelings. Otherwise, what was to keep it from ruthlessly killing those smaller and weaker than itself?

She would never willingly surrender the child, and since she wasn't going to remain with the changeling, something had to be done; someone would have to intervene.

"Aelthed, love, what are you stewing about?" Danielle's voice broke into his thoughts. "I swear there's smoke streaming from your cube."

"Ah, you've returned." He leaned away from the wall of the cube. "What were you able to learn?"

She dropped down onto the bed and scooped the cube off her nightstand to hold it close to her chest. "Well, Hoffel is a dimwit."

Aelthed chuckled. "I doubt that. It's more likely that

he's playing a dimwit to keep you from discovering anything."

She issued a decisive *hmmphhff* before asking, "Do you actually think the man possesses any level of intelligence?"

"I'm not certain, but the changeling, his mate and I do agree that Hoffel is a vindictive, petty, vicious little man and worth watching."

"That's what Braeden thinks, too. Cameron isn't at all certain the baron is dangerous, but feels that it would be wiser to kill him and not have to worry about it."

"Yes, Cameron would think that."

"Well, he does like to take the direct route to solving problems."

"Are you sure that's really it? I've always thought he just enjoyed ridding the world of bad guys."

Danielle's soft laugh floated against him, leaving him awash with unrequited longing so intense he had to fight off a shiver.

"What's wrong, Aelthed? Something doesn't feel quite right."

The concern in her tone brought a sigh to his lips. She'd been far too perceptive of late. "Nothing you need worry about."

His cube moved slowly. "My love." The warmth of her breath let him know that she held his prison near her lips. "I wish more than anything in the world that I could hold you, too."

Sean waved Caitlin through the open door in the back of the work shed and into the tunnel beyond.

Someone—a worker, or one of his brothers—had lit the torches lining the wall, so at least they weren't walking blindly down the tunnel in the dark.

Caitlin trailed a fingertip along the damp wall. "What is this place?"

"It leads to Aelthed's workroom."

"Aelthed? The druid?"

"That's the only Aelthed I know."

Caitlin wasn't in the mood for answers bordering on sarcasm. She shot him a frown over her shoulder, but before she could say anything, the tunnel opened up into a circular room.

More torches lined the walls, and lit candles had been placed here and there to provide light. She walked slowly around the perimeter of the chamber. A layer of dust and grime coated countless ancient jars and containers on the shelves.

The hard-packed dirt floor was littered with broken shards of pottery, glass and other bits of objects she couldn't identify—and probably didn't want to know what they were.

In the center of the room was a wooden table—likely a casting altar from the items gathered on the worn top. She glanced down at the silver scrying bowl already filled with water.

"Sean, what are we doing here?"

He stood behind the table. "There's something I want to show you."

And he couldn't have done that elsewhere? "It has to be done in a medieval chamber?"

"No, but I like the added atmosphere."

She didn't. It reminded her too much of the High Council and the black magic they called forth on occasion.

"Couldn't we…"

He grasped her wrist and gently tugged her toward him. "Humor me."

She couldn't help roll her eyes, but she joined him, standing between him and the table.

Sean encircled her with his arms, making her feel safe. His hands stretched out over the bowl.

"You do this often?"

"Shhh." He waved his hands over the bowl.

The water started to move. Slowly at first, wavering back and forth until it settled into circular ripples coming out from the center as if a pebble had been dropped onto the surface. Then it rippled faster, before it flattened to the smooth clearness of a mirror.

"Watch."

She saw an image begin to form—faint at first, but then it grew clearer, more defined. Sean moved his hands farther apart, letting her see more of the water's surface and more of the image.

It was like she was flying. Below was the ocean—the white-capped waves rolled toward land, and high on a craggy cliff were the ruins of a castle.

She flew closer and closer until she could make out the cutaways of narrow window openings. Then she slowed and flew lower—keeping out of sight perhaps?

"Was this you?"

"Yes. Keep watching."

The fool had gone to the Learned's stronghold.

A sound rose up from the bowl. High pitched, faint, barely discernable, so she inched higher, nearer to the window. Then she heard it—

The cry of a baby.

Caitlin gripped his forearms and held her breath as she leaned forward, trying to get closer to the image on the water.

In what seemed inch-by-inch increments that took hours to cover, she rose. Finally, just when she thought she'd go mad from anticipation, she was just outside the window.

And there he was—her son.

Screaming down the castle walls. He was displaying a fine temper—one worthy of a dragon.

Caitlin reached toward the water, aching to touch even the reflection of her child, but before she could get close enough to graze his image, Sean stopped her, holding her back, preventing her from getting the tiniest bit of comfort.

She wanted to scream and rage as her child was doing, but the only sound she could make past the thickness in her throat was a ragged whine of despair.

"Just look. If you touch it, the image will dissolve."

She didn't know whether to fight against the strong arms wrapped tightly around her, holding her fast against his chest, or to melt into the safety and comfort they offered.

Her child's cries wiped the question from her mind. She didn't care about the arms around her; the only thing she could focus on was her son. She stared at him, relieved that he appeared unharmed—angry, but whole and sound.

As if he felt his mother's presence, he turned his face to her. The brilliant green, tear-filled eyes looked directly at her. His face was red from his tantrum, making the shock of light blond hair appear even lighter.

The nursemaid holding him turned away from the window, and Caitlin found herself pulling away from the view through no choice of her own.

"No!"

The harder she tried to stay near the window, the faster she seemed to retreat, until the window, the castle, the ocean, vanished from sight.

Her chest tightened until she could no longer draw in air. Her arms ached from the emptiness she didn't think she could bear a moment longer.

The chamber spun into nothing but a cold, empty blackness.

Chapter 11

Sean caught her before she fell to the floor. He reached out to his brother. "Braeden, a little assist, please."

The flames of the torches and candles flickered out at almost the same instant Braeden spelled him and Caitlin to his bedroom.

He laid her on the bed and checked her pulse. The strong and steady beat reassured him that she had fainted, and nothing serious was wrong. Which was what he'd assumed, but he would rather be certain.

Sean brushed her hair from her face, his fingers lingering of their own accord on the silken strands. And when she started to rouse, he spelled her back to sleep. He had things to do. He didn't want her around to argue with him, nor did he want to have to worry about what she was up to.

It would piss her off, but her mood was the least of his concerns.

He closed the door behind him when he left the bed-

room and stood in the middle of the living room, looking around at his possessions. This had been his suite
of rooms, his apartment—his home, on Mirabilus, since
he'd turned eighteen. It would be strange not living in it.

But he wasn't going to share living quarters with
Caitlin anymore. Not even for the few remaining days
she'd be here.

Once their son was back in her arms, she would look
for, and find, some way to escape. He didn't want her to
feel as though she had to *escape*. He'd rather she simply
leave, openly—freely. Perhaps if he didn't fight her on
it, didn't make her feel as if she needed to run away, she
would keep him apprised of her whereabouts.

He couldn't get back the time he'd already missed,
but he'd like to know his son. He wanted to be there
from now on, to see him take his first step, to go off on
his first day of school—he didn't want to miss any of
it, not the good, nor the bad…or the hard.

And he couldn't do any of that if he didn't know
where Caitlin had taken the boy.

There was nothing in the living room or kitchen that
he'd need in another suite. The one he'd chosen for his
temporary use came fully furnished. However, he did
want some of the things from his office.

Sean flipped on the desk lamp and started putting
a pile of things together on the top of his desk. He removed the grimoire and two pendants from her bag, but
left Ascalon in place. The weapon wasn't his, and he
doubted that she'd be using it on anyone here.

Other than his laptop and cell, the only additional
item he wanted with him was the amethyst pendant.
That gem was probably in one of Caitlin's pockets.

A pale, pulsing glow from the desk caught his attention. He walked over and flipped open the grimoire.

The last picture they'd seen had been the one where he and his two brothers had been killed by the Learned. He turned that page over, unwilling to dwell on the implication.

The scene forming now was once again of the two women from the twelfth century. They were fitting their pendants into depressed areas on a wooden box. He leaned down to study the picture closely. It appeared that once they had the gemstones locked in place that they turned them in a specific order, and the top of the box then slid off the base.

Sean didn't know where the box was located. He'd never seen it. Was it, or did it represent, the cube Aunt Danielle kept close at hand—the one that supposedly still trapped the soul of the ancient High Druid Aelthed?

He and his brothers had never witnessed any proof that the druid's soul still did exist in the cube, but they'd had no reason not to believe their aunt.

Sean studied the page again. Apparently, he did still reside there. Why else would the grimoire have drawn the same scene more than once? More apparently, the grimoire wanted the druid freed.

He closed the grimoire and put it, along with the two pendants, into a carryall, shut off the light and left the suite.

The moment he closed and locked the outer door behind him, his beast's eyes opened. Sean sighed then warned, "Don't start."

Thankfully, the dragon's look was curious more than anything else. Even when Sean went into the suite a floor above, the creature remained calm, which actually surprised him.

Maybe the fact that they were still close to Caitlin—only the thickness of her ceiling and his floor separating them—helped keep the dragon from throwing a fit about no longer sharing a suite. Or perhaps realization hadn't fully set into the dragon's mind yet.

Not willing to bring it up, in thoughts or words, Sean dumped his bag in the office and then went into the bedroom.

The sound of light snoring let him know she was there before he turned on the light. He backed quietly out of the room.

Sliding open the glass doors, he stepped out onto the balcony. "What the hell are you doing?"

He was grateful that no one was around to see or hear what would appear to be a one-sided conversation. In his mind, he could see the dragon sit back on his haunches, cock his head and look at him in confusion.

So, he didn't know anything about Caitlin having been moved? How was that possible?

He took a breath and then spilled what was going on. "I left her. We aren't going to stay in the same suite or sleep in the same bed anymore."

The dragon glanced toward the bedroom.

"No kidding. I know she's there. She's not supposed to be. You need to move her back to her suite—our old one."

It was pretty sad when his beast looked at him as if he'd lost his wits. Great. If the dragon didn't spell her to this suite, then who did?

He knew that neither Braeden nor Cam would have done so; they wouldn't interfere like that. And Danielle, even though she wouldn't hesitate to interfere, didn't have the ability. Neither did either of his sisters-in-law.

Sean frowned. No anger, no outrage, no regret from the dragon at the news that he was leaving its mate? Nothing?

Something wasn't right. The creature may not have moved her here, but it was a safe bet it knew who did and wasn't sharing.

"It isn't going to work. She will be leaving and you can't stop her."

The dragon narrowed its emerald eyes.

"If you try to stop her, we'll lose all contact with the boy. Do you understand that? Is that what you want?"

Other than a slight slant, the expression didn't change—it remained focused and narrowed, like it knew something Sean didn't.

How was that possible?

This beast, cursed as it may be, was a part of him. Hell, it was him.

Sean dragged a hand through his hair and spun back inside the apartment. This was not happening. It couldn't be happening. Because if it was, then the only logical explanation was that he'd finally lost his mind.

Grabbing his bag from the office, he left the suite and returned to his own a floor below. Without pausing to do more than toss his bag on the sofa, he strode to the bedroom door and then stopped with his hand on the doorknob. What was he going to do if she was in there?

What could he do?

Nothing other than go sleep in his office.

He cracked open the door just a hair and felt his shoulders slump as the sound of Caitlin's steady breaths brushed across his ears.

Aelthed scratched at his beard. It didn't make any sense. How was the succubus materializing from room to room? Who was responsible for the spell?

It wasn't the cursed changeling; he'd sensed no such power in him. He could move objects—a bag, a sword,

or things like that, but not a person. Nor was it the other
two changelings; they were each in bed with their wife.
Danielle was fast asleep.

So who?

And how did the cursed dragon know?

He agreed with the changeling; that shouldn't be possible. The man and the beast were one. Aelthed rubbed
his temples and revised that thought. The man and the
beast were supposed to be one. In normal changeling-
beast combinations they shared a mind. Each knew the
thoughts of the other.

But there was nothing normal about this combination.

"St. George will set you free."

He spun around in the center of his cube. There was
no one there, so from where had the voice come?

A glimmering image flickered in and out of view.

Aelthed stared hard at the image. It was the gypsy
mage—the one who'd spoken the curse. And the one
who had the power to write in his grimoire.

He fisted his hands at his sides, shouting, *"What do
you want?"*

Laughter filled his cell. A tinkling, soft laugh, followed by the swish of skirts and jingle of tiny bells.

"Trying...to help...old man." Her words faded in and
out, as did her form.

Aelthed snorted. For all the power she had, she certainly wasn't able to hold her form very well.

A silken caress, a scarf perhaps, brushed across his
face, followed by another laugh. He jerked away from
the touch. He'd not felt contact with another being in
over eight hundred years, and he didn't welcome the
intrusion.

The air swirled around him as the still-glimmering image moved closer. She extended an arm, and he leaned away.

"I thank you to keep your hands to yourself."

This time her laugh raced against his ear, and her fingertips stroked his beard.

"Stop that!"

"Aelthed, who are you fighting with in there?"

Danielle's voice was filled with concern.

"That blasted gypsy."

"Oh!"

He closed his eyes at the shocked dismay in her exclamation. Before he could explain, he felt his cube thud down onto a hard surface and bounce once before coming to a teetering stop.

"Dan—"

The slamming of a door cut off his words.

Aelthed glared at the half-formed gypsy. *"So much for helping this old man."*

"Sorry."

At least she didn't laugh.

"I don't need your help, so why don't you go actually help the abomination you created instead of just playing with him."

To his relief, the glimmery image faded, leaving him alone to figure out how to make peace with a woman he could only talk to through wooden walls.

Sean stared at the grimoire open on the desk before him. The newly forming picture of a cube—like Aunt Dani's prized possession—appeared slowly on the page. But this time, instead of just a plain box, there was a cutaway allowing him to see into the cube. He wasn't too surprised to see that it wasn't empty. But it was odd to see an actual man trapped inside.

The cube his aunt possessed wasn't large enough to contain a person. At least not a living person.

Did the image of the man represent ashes, maybe? Were the ashes of this old man inside there?

The man in the scene shook a fist at him.

Sean leaned slightly away. Apparently, not ashes.

The dragon leaned closer and sniffed then, seemingly unconcerned, yawned and finally went back to sleep.

So…did the beast somehow know this man?

"Something new?" Caitlin asked from the office door, holding two cups of coffee.

He motioned her in. "Check this out."

She set one cup on the desk and took a seat next to him. Curling her legs up in the chair, she held her own cup close. Bending her head side to side, she said, "I feel like I must have tossed and turned all night."

Sean's eyes widened briefly, but he wasn't going to explain why she felt that way. Instead, he pulled her attention to the grimoire. "There's the cube the Learned wants."

"Is that the one your aunt has?"

"Yes. But look inside."

She leaned forward slightly, glanced at the image then calmly sat back in her chair. "I still think he looks older than he sounds."

"Older than he sounds?" Sean turned in his chair to stare at her. "Care to explain that?"

Caitlin squinted for a moment before opening her eyes. "That's right, I forgot. The three of you haven't met him."

"And you have?"

"Yes. When your aunt took me outside yesterday, she introduced us."

Sean slammed the grimoire closed. "You didn't think that worth mentioning?"

"You didn't ask. Oh, that's right, you were too busy being amused because she'd duped me."

"We're going to do this again?"

"We could gather everything up and go get our son."

"We aren't gathering anything up to give to the Learned."

"So we're going to sit here another day doing nothing?"

Sean wondered how she spoke so clearly through clenched teeth. "That's exactly what we're going to do."

Her coffee cup hit the desk so hard that coffee sloshed over the edge. "You just don't care, do you?"

"You saw him for yourself. Did he appear to be in any danger?"

"No. But you don't know when that could change."

He placed a hand on her arm, hoping to calm her and himself. "Caitlin, the Learned isn't going to do anything to harm his only guarantee. We plan on moving tomorrow."

"What's wrong with today? What difference will another day make?"

He could ask the same thing, but he knew the answer—she was anxious. "We are taking our time because we can and we must. Men are probably going to die. There's no helping it. Braeden wanted everyone to have today to see to their families and for us to go over every detail once more."

Caitlin shook her head, a confused expression on her face. "Wait a minute. You would rather have people die in a rescue attempt that may not work, instead of just giving him what he wants in exchange for a certain release?"

In an attempt to blow off some of his own agitation, Sean rose and paced. "Certain release? The only thing you can be certain of with the Learned is death. You've seen the things he's done, what he's capable of. How can you not see how much more dangerous he would be with those items in his possession?"

"I want my son!"

He walked toward her. "Caitlin, please understand."

She held up her arms, palms out, to stop his approach. "Stay away. Don't touch me."

Sean spun about and walked out of the office. She wasn't going to see reason, and he had no words to convince her that he and his brothers were doing the right thing.

He heard her crying and felt as if his own heart was going to break. There was no way he could just leave her like this, so he went back to the office and came to a rocking stop in the doorway.

She was still seated in the chair, head bowed, crying, with a glowing Ascalon held out before her.

"Do you want me to leave?"

She nodded and waved the sword at him.

Sean bypassed the elevator for the stairs, hoping the jog down them would provide some of the release he needed.

It didn't, so he kept up the pace and slammed out of the castle. He had no idea where he was going; he just knew he had to get out of there.

By the time he made it to the beach, he was moving at a dead run and saw no point in slowing. The instant his toes hit the water, he shifted to a smoky dragon and lifted into the sky.

He circled the island, flying in and out of clouds. It was too bad he couldn't just keep going higher and higher until he hit the moon, or Mars, but he knew that was a foolish wish since even dragons needed air to breathe.

What was he going to do with her? His brothers' wives were bullheaded, but Caitlin took demanding to another level. When she wanted something her way, she wanted it that way now. Not tomorrow, not when it was the right time, but now.

Had she always been this way?

His dragon snuffed at him. Yes, yes, he was being unfair. She was upset about the baby. He knew that. But he was doing everything he could within reason.

What did she expect?

Suddenly, the warmth of the sun above the clouds grew cold. The blood running through his veins chilled. Something was wrong. By the rapid beating of his heart he could tell that even his beast felt that something was off—not quite right.

He couldn't have been gone half an hour. Both Braeden and Cam were at the castle. What could have happened in so short a time? And why hadn't either of them contacted him?

When he started to direct his flight back to the castle, the dragon intervened and headed west, toward the Learned's castle. Sean's breath caught in his chest. Was something wrong with their son?

He focused his full attention on getting to the Learned's quickly, lending speed to the dragon's flight.

They didn't slow until they were right up against the castle wall. Sean directed them up to the window where he'd seen his son and then he heard it—not the cry of a child in distress, but of a terrified woman—his woman.

Chapter 12

Nathan waved a palm slowly before the highly polished mirror hanging on the wall behind his altar. The blank surface wavered and then filled with a swirling smoke before the vision he wanted came into view.

He'd been keeping an eye on the cursed beast since his arrival on Mirabilus. Waiting, plotting, tamping down his impatience because he knew that eventually, this moment would come.

A quick study of his altar assured him that all was ready.

Now he simply needed to bring the beast here.

Which wouldn't be too terribly difficult since the dragon was a juvenile and unlike his older siblings, who relied more on reason and forethought, still let emotions overrule his better judgment, especially when it came to his mate.

"Let me go!"

Nathan paid little heed to the woman chained to a pillar at the far side of the chamber. She was nothing more than a necessity—needed bait. A mortal who, in her soon to be realized death, wouldn't provide enough energy to lift his arm.

Without turning around, he snapped his fingers over his shoulder at her and smiled at the easiness of the spell.

She screamed again. "Let me— What did you do?"

Her voice changed midscream. Instead of the high-pitched, accented voice she'd used her entire life, it was now lower, the voice of a certain succubus.

He focused on the image before him. It was all he could do not to shout in triumph. No, not yet. True, the beast was now headed to what he thought would be his mate's rescue, but he wasn't yet caught fast in spells and chains.

Soon. Mere moments left.

Nathan waved his hand again, wiping away the image in the mirror and then he moved into the shadows.

Sean's throat tightened. *The Learned had Caitlin!*

No. That wasn't possible.

His heart threatened to pound out of his chest. The beast shook its head in dismay and anger. Possible or not, there was no time for planning or plotting. He wasn't leaving her in Nathan's hands one millisecond longer than necessary.

Aiming for the window, Sean entered the stronghold like a smoky arrow.

The second he cleared the window, she cried out, "Help me!"

Keeping his sense alert for Nathan, he followed the

sound, through the chamber he'd entered, out into the hallway and down the curved staircase.

There, at the other side of the Great Hall, he spotted a woman chained to a pillar. Sean's beast reared back, slowing them, giving him time to shift into solid dragon form—a form that would provide him with more strength and speed than that of a human.

Once shifted, he lunged forward to get to the woman, only to slam face-first down on the cold, stone floor. He lifted his head to see a chain secured around his ankle and Nathan walking out from the shadows laughing as he threw a spell toward him and then at Caitlin.

Sean tried to shift to human form as a blazing ball of light blinded him momentarily before the heat of it washed over him. Unable to shift, the beast raged. Intent on getting to Caitlin he turned away from the wizard and reached toward her. She was no longer screaming, no longer upright. She'd fallen to the floor in a pool of blood.

Sean dragged himself as far as the chain would allow, afraid to touch her, afraid of what he would find. But he had to know. He stretched out, straining against the metal bond holding him, hooked the tip of a talon into the hem of her blouse and dragged her to him.

The dragon buried his nose in the sweat-dampened hair bunched on the back of her neck. Caitlin's scent was absent. The only things he detected were the scents of blood and death.

Unable to contain his emotions, Sean let the gut-wrenching pain of loss wash over him, sobbing as the beast's keening cry filled the chamber. He pulled Caitlin's body into his embrace then held her against his chest.

He longed to feel his fingertips against her skin, his

lips—human lips—pressed to hers one more time. But he'd been denied that by the vile cretin who'd killed her.

The beast loosened his hold enough to bring her away from his chest. Even if he couldn't kiss her, he could at least gaze on her.

He took a shuddering breath before turning his gaze down to the sight he knew would shred his heart.

As realization that the woman in his hold was not Caitlin set in, Nathan's cruel laugh rang loud in the chamber, bouncing off the unadorned stone walls.

The dragon placed the woman on the floor, drew to his full height and then growling, it turned to tear the wizard apart with his talons. As he lunged for the Learned, a puff of smoke coated his face, filled his nostrils, and he swayed on his feet as a sudden dizziness claimed him.

Sean cursed as his beast once again hit the floor and succumbed to the blackness of sleep, leaving him alert, contained within the dragon, unable to defend himself or his beast against whatever Nathan had in store.

The wizard walked behind his altar to light the candles. "Now, my beloved creation, you will learn obedience."

He picked up his curved-blade athame and approached the dragon. He drew the tip of the small weapon along the beast's chest until blood coated the blade, which he let drip into a shallow bowl back on the altar.

Sean fought against the all too familiar anger, hatred and bloodlust seeping into him. He focused his thoughts on Caitlin, their child—anything other than the dark hunger threatening to fill his soul.

Again, Nathan laughed, then chanted words Sean couldn't decipher. When the wizard finished his chants, he threw ashes over the dragon. "I wash you in death and in a hatred that only the blood of this human's kin will quell."

He walked back to the altar and then returned with a small vial. He poured the contents along the beast's spine. "Heed me in this, or your spawn and mate will die while you watch."

He then circled the altar three times, doused the candles then returned yet again. After releasing the chain on the dragon's ankle, he patted the beast's forehead and spoke to Sean, "Fear not, changeling, you won't remember a thing until it's far too late."

A darkness washed over Sean as Nathan left the Great Hall. He wanted to fight it, tried to struggle free from the descending sense of doom, but the more he fought, the stronger it became.

"Shh, beastie, rest."

A woman with long, flowing black hair bent over him, whispering—the gypsy mage from his dreams. She sat beside him on the floor, stroking the scales on his chest.

"You are my boy, my big, brave boy, and I tell you true, St. George will set you free."

Sean relaxed, no longer fighting the darkness washing over him. He gladly sank into its cold embrace.

Aelthed knew she was nearby. He could feel her in the room. Tired of this curtain of silence she'd thrown over him, he asked, *"Danielle, are you going to keep ignoring me?"*

"That depends."

When she didn't say anything further, he prompted, *"On?"*

"On whether you're alone, or with someone. I certainly wouldn't want to interrupt you if you have company."

"Woman, have you gone daft?" When he caught his breath, Aelthed said, *"I invited no one into my cube—it's not as if I can. The gypsy was here to explain what was going on with the grimoire and the cursed changeling's mate."*

"So, she wasn't here for you?"

"No."

"I'm sorry. You are perfectly within your rights to entertain anytime you so desire. I shouldn't have said anything."

Aelthed shook his head. Had she been listening to him at all? Apparently, she'd missed the part about not being able to invite anyone inside his cube. He changed tactics. *"Danielle Drake, I wish to* entertain *only one woman—you. I would take you as my wife if possible. I would think you knew this without being told."*

His cube bounced as she sat heavily down on the bed, sending him stumbling to the floor. Her sweet warmth invaded his space as she lifted the wooden box to her cheek.

"Oh, Aelthed, I know a great many things, my love, but that was not one of them. I'd hoped and wished that someday you could come to feel for me, but I'd not known that you had."

"Well, I do. Now stop your nonsense."

She sighed, then asked, "So, what is going on with the grimoire and Caitlin?"

An icy chill swept over him. He turned his head, hoping to better deduce what was happening.

"Aelthed?"

"Shh." He hushed her, adding more gently, *"Give me just a minute."*

He spread out his arms and waved the cold to life. It wavered, gathered and then cleared, giving him a vision that horrified him. The cursed changeling was chained on the floor of Nathan's stronghold. Aelthed's breath caught in his throat. He moved his arm to spin the vision slightly. The sight of the Learned behind his altar casting a spell upon the beast froze his heart.

"Danielle! Get me to the Dragon Lord, now!"

She jumped up from the bed, clutching his cube tightly as she raced for the door to her suite. "What's going on?"

"Just hurry. Nathan captured the youngest Drake."

"No!" She came to a dead stop. "Is he alive?"

"I think so. Hurry! I'll tell you what I can as we go."

Braeden slammed the phone receiver down onto the base. "I don't know where the hell he is."

Cam tapped off his cell. "He's not answering his cell, either."

"I said eight, right?" Braeden glanced at his watch. "It's almost nine."

"Maybe we should call Dan—"

The door to Braeden's office slammed open, cutting off Cam's suggestion. Danielle half ran, half staggered into the room, dropping breathlessly onto a chair. "He's been taken!"

Cam sat down next to her and took her hand in his. "Calm down. Who's been taken?"

"Sean."

She lifted the cube. "Aelthed saw it."

Braeden didn't know whether to swear or to raise the hounds of hell. "Did Aelthed say what happened?"

She placed the cube on the desk. "Tell them."

"Hang on a second." Holding his arm outstretched,

Braeden called Caitlin to the office. She materialized—
holding what could only be Ascalon in her hand.

"Son of a—"

He dropped back down onto his chair. This was turning out to be a great start to the day.

Cam looked at the sword, then at Caitlin, then back
at the sword. "Is that…"

She nodded slowly and sank down onto a chair at
the back of the office. "I… I…" Taking a deep breath,
she placed the weapon on the floor at her feet. "I was
cleaning it."

Braeden raised an eyebrow, asking, "For anything
in particular?"

The sword disappeared. Caitlin jumped to her feet,
shouting, "Hey!"

A voice rose up from the cube on Braeden's desk.
*"I put it back in its scabbard. Can we get to the task
at hand?"*

"Is something happening I should know about?"
Caitlin looked around the office. "Where is Sean?"

Danielle motioned her closer. "That's what this is
about, dear."

Caitlin took the empty chair by Danielle. "It's about
Sean?"

Braeden answered her, "Yes." He then directed his
attention to the cube. "Aelthed, if you please."

*"After their argument this morning, Sean took
flight."*

Caitlin studied the ceiling, while Danielle patted her
hand. Braeden and Cam rolled their eyes.

*"It seems that he and his beast sensed something
wrong at the Learned's stronghold and went to investigate. When they got there, they heard the dragon's mate
crying for help and went in to rescue her."*

Caitlin gripped the arms of the chair, blinking. "I never left our suite. What are you saying?"

"I'm saying that he thought he was coming to your aid and instead was captured by Nathan."

"No!" She jumped to her feet and slapped her hands flat on the desk near the cube. "No. Not Sean, too."

Cam rubbed his temples. "What was he thinking?"

"That his mate needed to be saved immediately."

Caitlin stumbled back onto the chair. "This is my fault."

Braeden lowered the hand he'd been running down his face and stared at her. "How is this *your* fault?"

"Are you working with Nathan?" Cam leaned forward to peer around Danielle at her.

"No, I don't work with Nathan. It's my fault because it was my voice he heard."

"Did you supply that voice?"

"No!"

Braeden stretched his forearms on top of the desk and folded his hands together. "Then, again, how is this your fault?"

"He was out there because we'd been arguing."

Cam leaned back into his chair. "Oh, yes, arguing with a partner is a rare thing, indeed. Especially when said partner is a dragon."

"Don't tease the girl, Cameron." Danielle chided her nephew.

Caitlin wanted to know, "What are we going to do?" Her voice was barely above a whisper. It sounded as lifeless as she looked. "We can't just leave him there."

Braeden opened his mouth, but Aelthed cut him off. *"Nothing."*

"What do you mean, *nothing*?" Her pitch rose with each word.

"He's on his way back."

Both Braeden and Cam checked their watches. Braeden said, "He was there about what—almost two hours?"

Aelthed answered, *"The best I can guess, yes."*

Danielle fidgeted with her hands. "What do you think was done to him?"

"If he's on his way back, he's alive."

"It appeared as if Nathan was casting a spell on him. So he's probably dangerous," warned Aelthed.

Braeden spread his hands in agreement. "My thought, too."

Caitlin asked again, "So, what are we going to do?"

"I hate to kill him outright."

Caitlin stared at Braeden, her eyes wide. "I wouldn't suggest trying that."

Cam's humorless laugh broke his brother's stunned silence at being threatened by the succubus. "And why is that?"

Caitlin raised her hand and before anyone in the room could so much as blink, her sword appeared in her grasp. "I will defend my son's father. Against anyone."

"Enough!" Danielle rose to shoot a glare at each of them. She pointed at Ascalon. "Put that thing away. You won't need it."

Caitlin shook it at Braeden. "Remember, it just takes a nick."

He nodded in acknowledgment, and she lowered the weapon. Turning to Danielle, she asked, "So what do you suggest?"

"We give him a chance to explain."

Caitlin disagreed. "No. If he returns under Nathan's control, he isn't going to explain anything."

"I'm not about to let him waltz in here and threaten

my family." Cam was adamant. "I won't give him that chance."

"Nor do I think you should. We need to keep an eye on him—at all times." Caitlin frowned and then added, "I'm the best one to do that. However, if anything would happen, or if I'd need help, I can't communicate with any of you if you aren't within sight."

"Take me with you. I can call for help if need be," Aelthed suggested.

Caitlin and Danielle both stared at the cube. Caitlin grimaced. "Uhhh, I don't know if that's a good idea."

Aelthed laughed, then he explained, *"The temptation won't be too great since you can't run off to the Learned's with me. You can't take me anywhere I don't want to go. So there's no fear on that score."*

Braeden didn't appear too happy with the idea, but he agreed. "I can go along with this for right now. But if we discover that he's possessed..."

Caitlin leaned on the desk. "Then we unpossess him."

Cam rose and stared her down. "I'll agree on one condition. If he's possessed, you get him the hell off this island immediately and I won't kill him."

"And he doesn't return until he's completely free. Is that understood?" Braeden added.

Caitlin nodded. "I have no problem with that, except for one thing." She paused to look at each brother. "I want my son."

"Agreed." Braeden shrugged. "But we're going to have to rework our plan. I'm not going to battle Nathan with Sean at my back."

Danielle picked up Aelthed's cube and handed it to Caitlin, ordering, "Keep him safe, or you'll rue the day you set foot on Mirabilus."

Caitlin nodded then faced Braeden while she pointed up. "Could you...?"

He waved a hand, and she found herself sitting in Sean's office.

Aelthed whispered, *"Hide me somewhere. Anywhere."*

She looked around the office then headed to the hall-way with the box. "Linen closet?"

"That's fine. Just open the door and I'll bury myself up top."

Caitlin pulled the door open and held out her hand. The box disappeared, and the door to the closet closed by itself.

She went back to the office to put Ascalon away before Sean returned. To make certain she'd be heard, she thought...*can you hear me?*

Of course I can. Aelthed's reply came through loud and clear in her mind.

Caitlin felt him enter the suite before she saw his misty form flow into the office. She rose, and the mist swirled around her. Desperation, fear and need seeped into her blood, making her shiver with cold dread at what Nathan had done to him.

"Sean." She raised an arm to gently run her fingers through the mist. "What's wrong?"

He enveloped her until she stood within the twirl-ing form of the mist and smoke dragon. Yet she wasn't afraid of the beast surrounding her, towering over her, thrashing his head back and forth while crying out in a pain so great it made her ache.

What had the Learned done to him? What terrified him so?

"Shh, Sean, I'm here. Come, let me help you."

She reached into her pocket to retrieve the amethyst

pendant and held it tightly against her chest, over her heart, hoping that somehow her warmth and concern would flow through the gemstone beast into the one in such torment.

A faint amethyst glow filled the air around them. It pulsed in time with her heartbeat and chased away the cold dread.

The instant the dragon calmed, Sean shifted back to human and pulled her roughly into his arms.

When she reached up to stroke his cheek, he turned his head away, but not before her fingertips felt the hot dampness of tears.

She buried her face against his shoulder and held on to him as tight as she could, trying to force her heat into his shivering body. "What happened?"

He shook his head, not answering.

If he didn't want to discuss it yet, that was fine. But she needed to find a way to warm him, to make him feel safe, and she knew of only one sure way.

Caitlin lifted her head and rested her lips against his cheek, gently exhaling enough pheromones to call to him through whatever terrors were chasing him.

He took them easily to the carpeted floor of his office and then tore the clothes from their bodies.

There was nothing gentle about his lovemaking, no foreplay, no kissing, nothing that turned having sex into making love. That wasn't what bothered her, since she could give as good as she could get. What concerned her was that he wouldn't look at her, and she didn't sense his dragon anywhere. There had to be a way to reach them both.

She took the initiative and pushed him over onto his back, rolling with him. When he reached up to pull her down in order to reverse positions, she pushed his hands away, mimicking the act of pinning his wrists to the floor. "No. Let me."

She stretched her spine, running her hands up her sides then over her head, relishing the feel of being the one in control, the one setting the pace. She shivered with pleasure and then reminded herself of the reason she was here.

It wasn't to take, it was to give.

Caitlin cupped Sean's cheek and leaned down to kiss him. Knowing she had plenty of energy to spare, she exhaled her life force and silently crooned to the beast, using what she hoped was the same tone, the same emotion he'd used on her in the work shed. She wanted to soothe him, to coax him out of hiding and to make his fears disappear.

Oh, please hear me. Come to me. Be with me. We need you.

Soon, to her relief, Sean's arms came around her. He reached up over her shoulder to draw her hair back, and she felt his eyelashes flutter open. She broke her kiss to rise up slightly and look down at him.

Caitlin stared down into the gold-rimmed emerald gaze of the dragon. She smiled and trailed her fingertips along his cheek. "Welcome back."

His return smile was seductive enough to curl her toes. But when she moved to rest atop his chest, he pushed her upright and held her thighs in place.

Any teasing play she'd missed before, he more than made up for now. His touch was like liquid fire igniting not only her skin, but flowing into her blood, her heart and her soul, too. It filled her with an emotion so intense, so bright, that she feared giving it a name.

Something was happening between them that she didn't understand. Every time they came together it was as if he became more a part of her. Each time she accepted his energy, he didn't just strengthen her life force, he added his own to it.

Nothing like this had ever happened before. She couldn't explain it, didn't know if she wanted to. On one level it frightened her. Would he eventually replace her energy, her essence, with his? Or was the same thing happening to him? Were the two of them—or the three of them including the beast—becoming one?

Her ragged breath hitched with the onslaught of fulfillment. She swore the dragon took her soaring. The earth fell away beneath them as they flew above the clouds and then spiraled toward the ground at a recklessly breakneck speed that left her heart pounding.

She fell atop Sean's chest gasping for breath and laughing. "Well, that was…just…well."

They lay there until their breathing evened out. Sean wrapped his arms around her and softly said, "We need to talk."

Caitlin groaned softly. "I know. I just don't want to move yet."

His arm shifted slightly, then a warm quilt covered them. She sighed. "That's nice."

"Nathan captured me."

She cleared her mind of the conversation with his brothers, aunt and Aelthed. She wanted Sean to tell her what had happened in his own words. "How?"

"He tricked me into thinking he had somehow captured you and had you chained up in his stronghold."

That statement spun around in her mind for a moment. He cared so much about her that he'd risk his own life for hers? "And you went in to save me?"

"Of course."

She propped her chin on his chest and gazed up at him. "Why?"

"What do you mean, *why*?"

In her mind she could see the dragon looking at her as if she'd lost the ability to think. "It's not like we're married, or we've declared anything for each other. So, yeah, why?"

He lifted his head to peer down at her. "Are you hedging for a ring or something?"

"Good grief, no. I'm just curious."

"You're the mother of my child. Regardless of your thoughts on the topic, you are my beast's mate. He would have gone in of his own accord whether I wanted to or not."

He would end up getting himself killed for her. The thought of him not being here made her ill.

"I can't decide if that makes me feel safer, or more fearful for you." She drew a fingertip along his chin then asked, "What happened there?"

Sean pulled away from her touch, slid her off his chest and sat up with his back to her. With his arms wrapped around his bent knees, he said, "It's not clear. It's as if he did something to make me not remember, but bits and pieces keep coming back."

Caitlin trailed her hand down his back, running her fingers along his spine and shoulder blades. "How do you feel?"

"Like there's something I'm supposed to do."

She got the impression he didn't want to say the words, so she said them for him. "Kill your family? It's something the Learned would want, isn't it? Since you failed in that task before, it only makes sense that he do something to force your hand."

"What if I can't stop myself this time?"

"You aren't some weak-minded fool unable to control yourself or the dragon."

"He scared the crap out of the beast. When we watched you die, I thought he was going to roll over and give up." He glanced over his shoulder at her. "What will he do if that happens for real?"

Sitting up, Caitlin rested her cheek against his back and wrapped her arms around him. "I didn't die. It wasn't me. He tricked you and the beast."

"At the time it didn't feel like a trick."

His ragged voice drew a frown from her. "What do you fear the most? Losing me? Killing your brothers? Dying yourself?"

He shook his head but remained silent.

"Get him to talk."

Caitlin rolled her eyes at Aelthed's intrusion. As if she needed the wizard or anyone else to tell her that.

"Sean, everyone knows the Learned took you captive. You need to talk to me. You have to figure this all out before confronting the rest of your family."

"And if I can't?"

She bit her lower lip and bowed her head, resting her forehead against his back. "If I can't get you away from here, they will kill you."

Chapter 13

Sean reached up and patted her shoulder before he rose and headed for the office door. "I'm going to take a shower. Give me a few minutes then feel free to join me if you want."

He walked past the linen closet and shook his head. Did they think he was so dense that he wouldn't eventually figure out he was being watched?

He didn't care. The moment he'd been fully aware of his surroundings, he'd pulled a secure curtain over his mind. The wizard wasn't going to know what he was thinking.

Actually, having the cube close at hand suited his purposes. Right now, however, a minute or two alone suited his purposes better. He needed to get a grip on the emotions playing havoc with his head—and heart.

After adjusting the shower spray, he turned on the hot water and stepped in. His muscles relaxed. That was what he needed, a good pelting-hot shower. Something to wash away the stench of Nathan's stronghold.

His dragon stretched under the water and sighed with relief before curling down for a well-earned nap.

He'd been confused when he'd first left the Learned's. Confused and so terrified that his dragon had hidden away.

But he'd come straight back to Caitlin. Instinct had driven him here. A certain knowledge that she above anyone else had the ability to touch his soul. And she had.

He wasn't certain how that made him feel. At times it seemed the two of them were getting far too close.

While he wanted her to stay, because of their son— or so he told himself—he didn't ever want to need her, or anyone, as desperately as he just had.

He shook his head and wiped the water from his face. It had been a moment of weakness, brought on by the spells Nathan had cast. Surely he could set it aside.

He forced his thoughts back to the Learned's stronghold.

The gypsy mage hadn't been a dream; she was essentially his beast's mother, its maker. The Learned may have waved his hands, combined the potions and performed the motions, but she had spoken the curse that had given him life. Nor had she been wrong. St. George did have the power to set him free.

Even from Nathan.

That psychopath was in for a rude awakening.

However, his first task was deciding what to do with Caitlin. He didn't know if it was Caitlin herself who had freed his beast from the terror that had chased him into hiding, or if was her use of the amethyst pendant—or some combination of both.

It didn't matter. What did matter was that through her he was free. He had no driving need to kill his family. No fear of what Nathan might or might not do.

But he didn't want her or his family to know that.

Not until he killed the Learned and brought his son home.

He didn't want his brothers or Caitlin to go into battle with him. It wasn't their fight. It was his alone.

The Learned had killed *his* creator and had sought to control him more than once now. He had taken *his* son, captured *his* dragon and would die by his hand.

And it mattered little what happened to him. As long as his son was freed and the Learned was dead, Sean wasn't afraid of perishing in the battle.

What about Caitlin? He wanted his son raised by beings who would understand him, who could train him, teach him and see to his needs. And he wanted her safe and cared for, too.

But she had no intention of staying, and he'd already decided he wasn't going to force her. So how could he convince her that her best chance for a decent future was here with his family?

She already knew it wasn't with her family, not if she had their son in tow. He knew without a single worry that she'd never relinquish the child into their care.

Aunt Dani seemed to get along with her. At least there wasn't the strife that there had been between Danielle and Alexia or Ariel. For that he was grateful.

He hadn't yet talked to his brothers or their wives about her. They knew as little as possible, which was something he needed to change.

She needed to feel safe here, or at the Lair, and needed to feel useful and wanted. While he wasn't planning to die in this coming battle, he wanted everything seen to beforehand, just in case. Since he wasn't putting off this war with the Learned, he needed to see to those things immediately.

The door to the shower opened. "Want company?"

Sean enveloped her in a wet embrace, laughing at her squeak and pulling her beneath the water with him. "Since you're wet, you may as well stay now."

"I needed a shower, anyways." She drew circles on his chest. "Did you see our son?"

He heard the hesitation and fear in her voice. "Yes, I did, and he was fine. He was sleeping instead of screaming."

"So, what now?"

He didn't want to talk about it here. It would require more concentration than he was capable of maintaining right now. "It's something we'll discuss after our shower, okay?"

"Sure."

She slowly ran her hands up and down his side, his stomach, his thighs, before he caught her hands. "What are you doing?"

"Playing?"

"No, you aren't. You're looking for injuries."

The added flush on her cheeks wasn't from the hot water. "Are there any?"

"I think there might be a bruise on my ankle."

She eased her hands from his and started to bend over.

"Caitlin."

Standing upright, she leaned against him, her cheek against his chest. "Are there any injuries?"

"No. I'm fine."

She pressed her ear over his heart. "You're sure?"

"Very."

He felt her expression change against his skin. She stood up straight and looked at him. "You *are* fine."

Sean nodded. "Yes. I said I was, and I am."

"No, I mean fine-fine."

"Ah." If he had to guess, he'd bet that somehow his dragon let her know. Should he lie? Or should he tell her the truth and then figure out how to get her to keep her mouth shut? Finally, he said, "No, I'm terribly possessed. I'm planning on killing everyone around me."

"Hmmm." She walked her fingertips up his chest and tapped his chin. "And when do you plan on holding this slaughter?"

His stomach growled, so he used the obvious answer. "After I get something to eat. I'm famished."

"Uh-huh. I would think this coming slaughter would provide you with plenty of food."

He poured a glob of shampoo on her head and started running his fingers through the building foam. "I like my food fresh, but that's a little too fresh." He turned her around.

"Am I on the list of those to be slaughtered?"

After rinsing out the shampoo, he dumped on some conditioner and started working that through her hair. "I haven't quite decided yet. If I kill you, I'm going to have to deal with our son alone. That might cramp my style with the ladies."

"The ladies?"

"Well, yeah, I'd have to go find him another mother."

She lifted her foot and stomped back on his toes.

"Or perhaps I could let you live. Then you could take care of him while I go do...my thing."

"Your thing?"

"You know, my thing."

"If I'm at home caring for little Sean, you aren't

going to be out taking care of any *thing*. Besides, you're avoiding the conversation."

After pouring bodywash on his hands, he washed her arms, shoulders and back before sliding down to run his hands along her legs. Then he turned her back around to face him.

Caitlin hiked one eyebrow. "Now you're just trying to distract me."

"Is it working?"

Her other eyebrow joined the first.

He sighed. "No, I'm not possessed, but I don't want anyone to know."

At least she had the decency to look guilty when she turned her face away. "Well, I'm afraid it's too late for that."

He ran his soapy hands around her breasts. "Oh, you mean Aelthed? He can't hear us in here."

"You knew."

"That he was supposedly hiding in the linen closet? Yes, I knew. My power is a dragon, remember? He can sense an ant walking into the suite—by scent and sound. So, yes, we knew someone was here and since there was no scent, it had to be the wizard in the cube. This isn't my first go round with otherworldly baby-sitters. Why do you think this shower's been… Drake proofed? I needed somewhere to go where I could talk to my dragon without being overheard."

"How?"

"Tell me what I'm thinking. You're close enough."

She looked at him and tipped her head. Then she frowned and put her hands to her ears.

Sean lowered her hands. "Just stop trying to read my mind. The buzzing will go away."

She shook her head. "What was that?"

He tapped the shower wall. "It's a special white noise system installed inside these shower walls. Whenever the water comes on, so does the sound. If you aren't trying to focus on anything, you don't notice it. But if you go silent and focus, you hear the buzz."

She finished. "And that overrides what you're trying to hear."

"That's it."

"Do the rest of them know?"

"Oh, they know there's something in here. They just don't know what."

"One day they'll figure it out."

"And the next day I'll devise something else." He rested his hands on her shoulders. "I don't like having my space invaded any more than you do. And I'd appreciate keeping this between us."

"Hadn't planned on advertising it anywhere." Caitlin shivered. "There's one small problem with this system."

He pulled her tight against him and rubbed his hands up and down her arms. "Just another bug to work out. Are you up for a little flying?"

"Flying?"

"Yeah. I'll meet you on the beach and we'll talk while we soar."

Her eyes widened. "Oh. That would work."

"Good. I'll exit from the bedroom balcony. You get dressed and meet me on the beach."

She pursed her lips then asked, "And how do I keep Aelthed or anyone else from mining for information?"

Sean laughed. "That's easy. I'll give you something to *remember* that will give them something to think about."

Caitlin groaned. "This is going to give me nightmares, isn't it?"

"It could." He ran a finger across her lower lip, before giving her a quick kiss. "But if it does, I'll be there to chase them away."

"Fine." She closed her eyes tightly. "I'm ready."

He kissed her forehead then the tip of her nose before covering her lips with his. The false memory he gave her had nothing to do with nightmares—at least not for the two of them. But it would certainly make everyone else think twice before delving back into her mind, giving her time to make her escape.

She curled her fingernails into his shoulders, clinging to him, and it was all he could do not to take her down to the shower floor and savage each other like they were in this new *memory*.

The second his dragon started to wake up and take an interest, he broke their kiss. Caitlin leaned against him trembling.

"That was...interesting." She looked up at him and batted her eyelashes. "You like my fangs that much, do you?"

He laughed. "Only as much as you like mine."

She pushed him away. "Get out of here before we accidentally test your sick fantasy."

"Just keep that on your mind and hurry up before it loses its edge." He reached to turn off the water. "Ready?"

She took a deep breath and said, "Yeah. I'll focus on fangs and blood and talk without thinking. Got it. Ready."

He turned off the water and stepped out of the shower, pausing to hook a finger around her wrist, saying softly, "Wear something warm."

She watched his long legs carry him away. He

stopped at the glass sliding doors to the balcony long enough to smirk at her over his shoulder.

No doubt she'd been busted ogling him.

Sean flexed his already tight ass muscles and then dissolved into a plume of smoke.

Caitlin laughed. Really, that was the only image she needed to focus on. He didn't have to create some gross zombie-vampire-dragon sex scene that she'd never be able to wipe from her mind.

Hopefully, he didn't actually think it would give her nightmares. It was so over-the-top that it made her want to laugh until she cried.

She dried off and pulled some sweats out of his dresser. They'd be a little big, but at least they'd be warm. She dressed quickly and left the bedroom, getting as far as the linen closet before Aelthed stopped her.

"What did you discover?"

"Nothing much. He isn't very talkative yet. He's obviously been through a lot and needs some air, so we're going for a walk. I'll let you know what he—"

Aelthed's gasp cut off her sentence.

She felt him poking around inside her head. He'd happened upon the memory at the forefront of her mind, and she did nothing to hide it from him.

Aelthed cleared his throat and asked in a rush, *"Are you all right?"*

She responded with a weak wave. "I will be. Don't worry, I heal quickly."

"Uh...are you sure?"

When he started to prod for more memories, she held her focus tightly and headed down the hallway, answering, "Yes. Very."

Caitlin managed to get out of the suite before sighing. Sean was right; the scene of gore and sex was enough to distract them long enough for her to make a clean escape.

However, she didn't know how long she'd be able to hold this *memory* without laughing, so she hit the stairs at a faster pace.

Danielle Drake met her at the bottom of the stairs. She frowned while studying her then turned a pasty shade of white.

Caitlin shook her head, silently signaling that it was too much to talk about right now. She lightly touched Danielle's shoulder in passing and mumbled, "Please, later."

To her relief she made it out of the castle without seeing anyone else, but she could imagine the conversation that would soon be held in Braeden's office. Eventually, she was going to owe Sean's family one hell of an apology.

Once outside, she ran for the beach.

Out of seemingly nowhere, a huge claw, talons extended, reached for her, cupping her securely in its grasp and lifted her from the ground.

"You are terrible." Caitlin burst into laughter. "Your family is horrified."

"Maybe they'll think twice before intruding next time."

Caitlin's laughter faded away at the tone of his voice. She had noticed before, but never quite as acutely, that when he was in dragon shape, the deep, husky, gravelly tone bordered on harsh.

Yet it didn't frighten her. Quite the opposite, actually. It was so laced with sensual tension and emotion that it gave her shivers having nothing to do with the cold.

He flexed his foot, closing the talons more securely

around her and bringing her nearer his body. "Is that better?"

"I wasn't cold."

He didn't reply, so she let her explanation for shivering fall to the wayside; it wasn't important.

Caitlin relaxed on her perch. She was comfortable, and with his body shielding her from most of the wind, plenty warm enough. "Yes, I'm fine. The view is spectacular."

Turning her attention to the reason they were out here, she asked, "So, what do you have planned?"

"You've seen the pictures in the grimoire. I can't let Braeden and Cameron go to the Learned's."

"But you can't go alone."

"I have no intention of going alone. But I also don't intend to supply him with all three Drakes on a silver platter at once."

"You don't think showing up as a...pack would take him off guard?"

"No. The *clan* showing up at one time is what he wants."

"So if you aren't going to take a force large enough to defeat him, what will you do?"

"Give him what he wants."

"What?" Shock brought her up to her knees. She tipped her head, trying to look up at him through the separation between his talons. "You aren't serious. You can't be."

"Very."

"You were the one who told me—more than once I might add—that giving him those items was a mistake. It would give him enough power to rule everything."

"It would be a mistake for *you* to give him what he wants."

"But not you?" How exactly had the Learned damaged Sean's ability to think rationally?

"Not for me and my partner."

"Partner? *One* other person? And somehow you believe that the two of you can hand over the items he wants then walk out of there with our son and all will be well with the world?"

"Not exactly."

She sat back down and tried to read his mind. But he wouldn't let her in far enough to make sense of his plan. All she could see was a mishmash of random thoughts.

Caitlin gave up. "You need to explain this to me, because I must be missing something."

"I don't have to explain anything to you. I just wanted you to know that you will have our son back soon."

"And I'm supposed to be fine with getting little Sean back knowing you'll most likely end up dead?"

"You're going to leave as soon as he's returned, so what difference will it make?"

Caitlin narrowed her eyes. While this had been her plan all along, she didn't remember saying that to him. "I never told you that."

"You didn't need to tell me. We've exchanged enough life force the last few days that we've become bonded to each other. There isn't much I don't know. And what I don't know for certain, I can sense."

"So how does that work for you, but not for me?"

"You have the ability. You just don't access it."

What did that mean? "How are you going to walk back into the Learned's castle without killing your family first?"

Sean's laugh was far too evil for her comfort. "Simple. I'll kill them."

"What?" The longer she listened to him, the more worried she became about his mental health.

"Think, Caitlin. Mirabilus has a strong glamour spell over it. A spell that's never been broken."

"Wait." She interrupted him to ask, "What about Hoffel?"

"He doesn't count. Nathan captured one of the villagers while he was off the island doing business and forced him to bring Hoffel here."

"But Nathan was born on Mirabilus." She'd seen that in the grimoire. "So why doesn't he just come here and do his dirty deeds on his own?"

"My grandfather added a boost to the glamour spell that gets reinforced yearly. It prevents Nathan from being able to perform magic on the island. Which means he can't see what is or what isn't going on over here. He has no choice but to believe what I tell him."

"Right." She swallowed her sarcasm. "And he's not going to see through your lies?"

"By the time he figures it out, it'll be too late."

"Too late for who?" Her head was starting to ache from trying to make sense of his plans.

"For him. Once I give him the items he demands, he'll be too busy, too engrossed with them to pay much attention to anything else. I only need a minute, if that long, to put an end to his madness."

Now that did make sense. The Learned's ego would be so overinflated with the items in his possession that he would think himself immediately invincible.

However, there were other concerns. "What about Aelthed? You can't just hand him over to Nathan."

"I don't plan on it. Before leaving, I stole a potion from the Learned's stash that'll put Aelthed to sleep."

"He left you alone long enough for you to steal things?"

Sean snickered. "He thought I was so far under his spell that he left the chamber without giving it a second thought."

"Mighty full of himself, isn't he?"

"Yes. To his own detriment."

"Once you put Aelthed to sleep, how are you going to get him out of that cube?"

"The dragon figured it out. The pendants are keys. It'll just take the right combination to unlock the puzzle."

"Oh. So the picture in the grimoire of the two women opening the chest is the same way it'll work for the cube?"

"The dragon seems certain of it."

In her opinion, he was putting an awful lot of faith in the beast. "That'll make your aunt happy."

"Why?"

"Oh, please." Hadn't he figured it out? "She's in love with the old wizard."

"Well, I don't know if she'll be happy or not. I have no idea what's going to happen to Aelthed once his spirit is released. He may just disappear."

"Or be like my mother—dead, but still here."

"I suppose that's possible."

"With Aelthed's spirit removed from the box, won't the Learned know that it's empty?"

"I never said it'd be empty."

"Who or what are you going to put in there?"

"Haven't decided yet."

The certainty in his tone didn't sound undecided. It sounded more to her as if he just wasn't going to tell her. Did she care? Not really, as long as she wasn't stuffed inside.

"You aren't going to try killing the Learned while

little Sean is still there, are you?" Caitlin shivered. Her son could get fatally injured in the melee.

"No. I'm going to bring him back to Mirabilus first."

"And then go back?"

"Something like that."

Again, he was withholding information. And again, did she care?

No.

He had a plan to rescue their son, and he seemed confident he would succeed. While it was her place to worry, was it her responsibility to question or point out every flaw until he doubted himself? That would ensure nothing but possible failure.

Even though it went against her better judgment, she needed to trust him to do what he thought was right. So he could keep his secrets, as long as he came back with their son.

"When do you plan on putting this plan into action?"

"Soon. I need some time to put things into motion."

"Anything I can do to help?"

"Don't panic when you hear Braeden and Cameron are dead. I need to spread enough rumors just in case Nathan has someone here doing his bidding."

"I can do that." Caitlin offered, "I can even be upset over it if that'll help."

"That's up to you. But right before I get ready to go, I could use your help gathering together everything I'll need."

"The pendants, grimoire and cube?"

"And Ascalon."

Certain she'd misheard, she asked, "I beg your pardon?"

"He wants Ascalon."

"For what?" It'd be a cold day in hell before she'd turn over her weapon.

"But it's fine if I turn over all my family's charms?"

She would never get used to having her thoughts read—invaded—so easily.

"Then shut me out."

"I've tried. It doesn't work anymore."

She wasn't sure if his dragon snorted or if he did. What she did know was that they were now dropping beneath the clouds. Except for a tiny speck of green below, only the sea was visible for as far as she could see.

"Where are we?"

"You'll see."

He was headed straight for the speck of green in the middle of nowhere. Once they got closer, she could see that the island wasn't as small as she'd first thought. It wasn't as large as Mirabilus, but she wouldn't feel like she was on a desolate rock in the middle of the ocean, either.

There was no shore to speak of, just rocky cliffs that dropped off to the water. Only evergreen trees and other fir-type bushes covered the ground, so they hadn't flown south. But she hadn't noticed any distinct drop in temperature, so they hadn't gone too far north.

Sean touched down in a small clearing where he released her and changed into his misty form. "There's a cabin right at the end of the path."

Caitlin followed his foggy trail. He led her along a flagstone path that wound through a stand of trees and bushes that were probably mistletoe.

To her surprise there was a cabin in the next clearing. A very nice log cabin with a huge porch that looked as if it probably went all the way around. The swing near the front door looked inviting enough to sleep on comfortably.

The door opened, and he drifted inside. By the time she entered, he had shifted to human form, dressed, and was tucking a shirt into a pair of jeans.

She looked around, wondering if the owners were nearby. "Where are we?"

"This is mine." He walked over to the fireplace to get a fire going.

He owned an island? She shook her head. Of course he did. His brothers were into property, so why wouldn't he carry on the tradition?

"Why are we here?"

"It's time you learn how to be a Drake."

Chapter 14

Sean didn't have to turn around to see her face to know what she thought of that statement. Her shocked disagreement threatened to burn the back of his neck. He was surprised that it took her a few seconds before she finally sputtered a reply.

"I am not a Drake. I am not going to be a Drake. So there's no reason for me to learn how to be one."

He silently finished building a fire then rose and turned around. She was still staring at him. Displeasure furrowed her brow, and her lips were drawn into a flat line.

"If you plan on raising one, you should know how to be one." It made sense to him, even if she didn't see it. While she mulled that over, he went and retrieved a tray of supplies to make coffee. It would only be instant since he didn't have any utilities here yet. But it would be warm, so it would do.

"What exactly is this going to entail?"

He glanced at her, wondering why she sounded so wary of the idea. "It's not like I'm going to teach you how to change into a dragon or anything."

After hanging the kettle of water from the tripod over the fire, he sat down on the cedar-frame cushioned sofa and patted the space next to him. "Sit down."

She dropped down onto the chair across the coffee table from him. "I'm quite capable of raising my son. I didn't have any problem taking care of him before."

"I noticed." If he remembered correctly, *their* son was in her care when the Learned kidnapped him.

"You can't blame me for what happened."

"For the record, he's our son, not yours. And I don't blame you for what happened, but yes, actually, I can. If you had known how to defend yourself, or protect Sean against Nathan, this never would have happened, would it?"

She didn't say anything, just looked away. But he caught a glimpse of firelight shimmering off the suspicious moisture in her eyes. "Don't you dare start crying, Caitlin."

The last thing he needed or wanted was for her to get emotional, because that would only make his dragon go goofy on him. He needed everyone to remain calm and focused.

"I'm not blaming you. I never have. I simply stated a fact. You need to know how to protect yourself and our son when I'm not around."

She took a deep breath then looked back at him. "Where do we start?"

Instead of saying anything, Sean had his dragon croon to her. It was obvious she heard the beast, because she visibly relaxed. The frown softened, her lips grew less tight and the tears that had been building in her eyes disappeared.

"That's better." He suggested, "How about we start right there?"

Caitlin nodded in agreement.

"Do you have the pendant?"

She lifted the chain from around her neck. Firelight danced off the amethyst dragon. "Always."

"Good, because that's your key to Drakedom."

Although she tried, Caitlin was unable to maintain a straight face and burst out laughing.

As simple as it was, or as it should be, he liked her laugh, her smile. The way her eyes sparkled like gemstones and the dimples alongside her mouth. Those were little things that she should do often.

Focus, he was supposed to be focusing. In his mind, he asked her, *"Can you hear me?"*

"Yes." She answered in the same manner. *"But I'm sitting right across from you, so of course I can."*

"That's fine. Now try to stop me from entering your thoughts. Nod when you're ready."

"I was able to block you easily enough before."

"You've concentrated so much on hearing me lately, that it's not as easy anymore." He added, "And since we've bonded more, my getting access to your thoughts is like breathing for me."

"You do realize this is how I live, right?"

"You're a succubus, not an empath. You should choose who and what enters your mind and body."

Thankfully, she didn't argue. She took a few moments to collect herself and then nodded.

He started with simple things like images of food, places and animals. Detecting no response, Sean moved on to images of their families.

Again he sensed nothing but a blank wall. He got up, walked around the room, made coffee for both of them while sending her visions of little Sean, the Learned, Hoffel and scenes from the grimoire. When he recreated the scene of Hoffel attacking her, she flinched.

He sat back down and handed her a cup of coffee. "You've got the pendant, use it."

"Use it how?"

"Caitlin, you used it to call to my dragon when you couldn't reach him. I knew then it was your talisman, your charm."

"I thought it was responding to you."

"What about in my office?"

She shrugged one shoulder. "Again, I thought it was letting me use it to respond to you."

"No. I don't think so." He reminded her, "It doesn't glow for me. When I hold it, it's just a stone."

She turned it over in her hand. The more attention she paid to it, the brighter the pendant glowed. "How much power do you think it has?"

"One way to find out." Without warning, he picked up a spoon and tossed it at her, only to have it bounce off an unseen wall, sending it right back toward him.

Caitlin's eyes grew wide. "I'll be damned."

"Don't say that, even in jest."

"I wonder if it would let me defeat Nathan."

"I doubt if it makes you invincible. So I wouldn't advise jumping off a cliff to test it or anything." He slammed her mind with an unexpected vision of the Learned taking their son.

"No!" She dropped the pendant and covered her face with her hands.

Sean cursed his own bungling stupidity and pulled her from the chair over to the couch, scooping up the pendant at the same time. He slung an arm around her trembling shoulder to hold her against his chest.

"That was callous. I'm sorry."

Putting the amethyst dragon in her palm, he closed her fingers around it. "Let your mind think of this."

"Why are you doing this?"

What would be the harm in just telling her the truth? It wouldn't sway her either way, nor would it change anything. "The dragon and I want nothing more than for you to stay so we can take care of you and the baby."

She lifted her head and gave him a strained look filled with pain. "Sean…"

"Shhh." He put a finger over her lips to stop her words then brushed the hair from her face. "I know you're going to take our son and leave. I'm not going to stop you, but I need to know you'll both be okay. Is it too much to ask that you show us you can take care of yourself and a dragon changeling?"

"I was doing fine until I met you."

"Yeah, you did handle those thugs pretty well. But they were human. I'm not concerned about your dealings with humans."

"Seems to me the only other preternatural besides the Learned who I have any trouble dealing with is you."

If she was trying to get a rise out of his temper, it was working. And he'd sworn that wasn't going to happen. He took a minute then asked, "And why do you think that is?"

"Haven't you noticed? Something has been…off… since the day we met. In the alley that night, when I drained the one thug, he was so unhealthy that I knew I'd be sick. But it hit me instantly, completely catching me off guard, and that had never happened before. And for me—me of all people—to wake up, not able to remember taking you to my home and spending three days in bed with you? How does that happen?"

She immediately answered her own question. "It doesn't. Ever." Then she added, "And to end up pregnant? By someone not of my own kind?" She took a breath. "And now it's like we're either ready to jump down each other's throat or fall into bed. There's nothing in between. It's hate or lust with us, no middle ground whatsoever. You can't tell me that's normal."

"Define *normal*. You're a succubus. I'm a dragon changeling—a cursed dragon changeling. How does *normal* even work into our vocabulary?"

"You know what I mean. Normal for us. Yes, I'm a succubus and there's nothing I enjoy more than sex. It feeds me, it gives me energy the fastest way possible and I don't deny I love a man's body. But I can't get enough of you. No matter what we do, it's not enough. You can fill me to the brim, give me life for months in one night's romp and I still want more."

He was supposed to have a problem with that?

She rolled her eyes. Either she'd read his thought, or correctly interpreted his expression. "Never before have I wanted anything else from a man than just sex."

"And that scares you?"

"Scares me? No! It outrages me. I need to be in control of my life. Me. Not my desires or some craving I can't define. Me."

"I haven't tried to control you." The instant the words left his mouth he knew them for a lie.

And she proved that by leaning away to look at him as if he'd just tried to tell her the grass was purple. "No, not at all."

"The dragon and I were in shock from learning I had

a son." He tried to defend his actions upon her arrival at Dragon's Lair.

"Oh, is that what you're going to call that whole bit about mating for life, not seeing my son crap?"

"It wasn't crap. Letting you leave with our son goes against every instinct I have."

"*Letting* me leave? *Letting* me? You don't own me."

This was not going well at all. "That isn't what I meant."

She scooted away from him on the couch. "Then explain what you did mean."

"I meant that I'd realized it would be a mistake to try forcing you to stay, so I wasn't going to fight you on it."

"That's generous of you. Especially considering it's not your decision to make. At all."

Sean stood up to poke absently at the fire. If he kept up at this rate he'd never see her or his son again. "One day, Caitlin, you're going to want someone so badly that you need them. Are you going to walk away because being alone is far more important than anything else?"

"Being alone? No, it's about being independent. People have had control of me and my life since the day I was conceived. Even now they're telling me who to marry, where to live, whether or not I can keep my child. No more. Once little Sean is back in my arms, nobody is going to tell me anything. I'm done following orders. Done having anyone else tell me how to live my life."

Why did it feel as though she'd just kicked him in the gut? Why was his dragon's heart beating so hard and fast? He didn't understand what was going on inside him. If he didn't know better, he'd say that he and dragon were in love. But they hadn't known her long enough for any lasting attachment to have formed. Yes, they were mated, but so what? Throughout the history of man, couples had married without having any feelings for each other. Besides, he was certain that love wasn't this difficult or painful.

Without turning around, Sean asked, "And it doesn't matter what you do to anyone else?"

"Such as who?"

"Our son, for one." *Me, for another.* But he wasn't about to tell her that. It was an admission he wasn't ready to put into words.

"He'll be with me, so it's not like I'm going to be causing him pain or strife."

"Are you going to teach him how to be a dragon changeling? Will you be able to explain the wild emotions rushing through him and how to control them? Or help him cope with the pain during the first few shifts?"

She placed a hand on his shoulder, and it was all he could do not to jump in surprise. "Sean, I'm not going to keep you from our son. I understand that you need to imprint with him so that he'll trust you when the time comes to teach him what he needs to know. If that time ever comes. We don't even know if he's a changeling or not. I promise that you'll have plenty of visits."

Visits. He clenched his jaw. He didn't want visits. He wanted more. He wanted to be a full-time father. His stomach churned. They needed to get off this topic. This was not the reason he brought her here.

He placed the poker back in the bucket on the hearth, turned around to grasp her wrist and headed for the door. "Do you have your pendant?"

"Yes, but why?"

She sounded confused at the abrupt change in the conversation. Right now he didn't much care. "Let's see how powerful it is."

Once outside he said, "Go stand at the other side of the clearing and focus on that pendant."

As she walked away he heard her mutter, "This should be loads of fun."

For him, maybe.

Sean collected a pile of good-sized rocks then shouted, "If this doesn't work, it's going to hurt."

The amethyst dragon hanging around her neck glowed. She shouted back, "Bring it."

He threw the rocks, one right after another, as hard as he could. To his relief the magic surrounding her held fast. The rocks bounced off the invisible shield, protecting her from danger.

Quickly, before he could change his mind, he shifted to solid dragon form. The beast drew in a large breath and let it out as a stream of fire aimed at her.

Caitlin's eyes grew large, but the pendant around her neck glowed brighter.

His breath expelled, he started to draw in another, only to notice she held a fireball in her hand. Smiling at him, she arched an eyebrow right before she threw the fiery ball at him.

To his surprise, not only did the ball make it all the way across the clearing, but her aim was also accurate enough that he had to lean to one side to avoid getting hit. Thankfully, he wasn't standing directly in front of the cabin. Otherwise it'd be a pile of charcoal.

He shifted back to human form. "Not bad. Hang on a second." Sean went back into the cabin and came out with two swords.

"Up for a little swordplay?" He motioned her forward.

Halfway across the clearing, she held out her hand.

Ascalon slammed into her ready palm. The spine already glowed, ready for battling a dragon.

"No." Sean stopped and shook his head. "Not on your life."

"Afraid?"

"No." He wasn't. However, his trembling beast felt sick. "I'm just not that stupid."

"You don't trust me." She gave him a mock pout.

"I wouldn't trust anyone with that weapon." He pointed to the ground. "Put it down."

She tossed the sword in the air and it disappeared. Then she reached out to take the blade he offered her. "Fine. Be that way. We'll play with your toys."

They faced off. Back and forth across the clearing, neither of them getting the better of the other. Although Sean quickly realized that she was quite a bit more experienced than he was. The only way he kept up with her faster pace was to have a stronger swing. He essentially wore her down by making her fight with all of her strength to hold back his blade.

"Damn." He swore after mistakenly taking his eyes off her for a split second. She'd lunged in, nicking his arm. Had that been Ascalon, he'd be dead in minutes.

She backed off, gasping. "I'm sorry, I'm sorry."

Sean motioned her to continue, laughing. "I've cut myself worse with a razor."

When she didn't come back at him, he lunged forward and slapped her hip with the side of his blade. "Don't just stand there."

The next thing he knew, Caitlin screamed and raised her sword toward his face. He flinched and then heard the sound of another blade slamming against hers before it bounced away onto the ground.

He looked down to see Ascalon.

She tossed aside the blade she'd been using to see to her sword then sent it back to Mirabilus, before throwing herself against his chest. "I am so sorry. I didn't know it would do that. It could have killed you."

"It's all right, I'm fine. Don't worry about it." Although he wasn't certain his dragon hadn't fainted.

"No, it's not all right."

He put his arms around her to stop her from shaking. "Caitlin, it's okay. I'm alive thanks to your speed."

She rested her forehead against his shoulder and shook her head. "Are we done with this training stuff now?"

"Yeah, I'm pretty sure we can call it quits for the day." He dropped a kiss on the top of her head. "I've got a couple things I need to see to. Why don't you go inside and relax for a while. When I get back we'll see if we can rustle up something to eat."

He watched her walk back into the cabin and close the door before taking off for the other side of the island.

"Where do you think they went?" Braeden looked out the windows of his office for what had to be the hundredth time before turning back to Cam and their aunt.

Danielle set Aelthed's box on the desk. "I don't know. He took off in beast form carrying her with him."

Aelthed offered, *"For all the blood and rough handling, she actually didn't seem too afraid of him."*

"Why would she be? She's not a Drake, so she's probably not on his hit list."

Danielle shook her head at Cam's statement. "You didn't see what he did to her. That poor girl."

Braeden rolled his eyes. "You don't know if what you read in her mind was real or something she made up. I don't see Sean being capable of abusing a woman like that."

What his aunt had described to him earlier was essentially a horrific rape scene. He highly doubted if it was real. Somehow Sean, Caitlin, or the two of them together had put that in her mind to throw them off. And it had worked. They had no clue what Sean was planning.

"What I want to know is why that scene was in her mind."

"We don't know if it's real or not." Cam leaned forward. "Nor do we know how far Sean is under the Learned's spell."

Braeden shrugged. "I'm sure we'll know soon enough."

"So we just sit around and wait until he kills one or more of us?"

"I am not going to kill him without having a solid reason to do so." Braeden stared at his twin. "Neither are you."

"I hadn't planned on it. But he shouldn't be allowed to run free until we know one way or another."

Danielle laughed weakly. "If you have a way of capturing and holding him, perhaps you'll share it with us?"

"That's the problem with smoke dragons. The beasts are nearly impossible to contain." Aelthed sighed. *"Although, something like this cube would probably work, if someone could cast the spell."*

"You don't think he'd know what we were up to as soon as he saw the cube?" Braeden asked.

"And then what? We just hold him like that for an eternity?" Cam shook his head and leaned back in his chair. "It'd be more humane to kill him."

Aelthed and his cube disappeared. Danielle looked

from one brother to the other. "That was a bit heartless, don't you think?"

Braeden winced. "We were talking about Sean, not Aelthed."

"I know that. But he's been trapped in the cube for over eight hundred years. Should he have simply been put to death instead?"

Cam cleared his throat then reminded her, "Aunt Dani, you do remember that he's already dead, right? It's just his spirit in that box, not the man himself."

Braeden shot Cam a glare as their aunt rose and without another word marched stiffly out of his office.

"Smooth."

"Well, it's the truth, and one day she's going to have to face it."

"Don't you think we have enough to deal with right now?"

Cam shrugged. "Speaking of dealing with things, what are we going to do with Hoffel?"

Braeden sighed. He wasn't certain what to do with the baron. They'd questioned him. Which wasn't as easy as he'd first thought it would be. Hoffel was a coward and a bully, but as a vampire, the man was already dead, so the threat of death held no weight. And the baron was well aware that they weren't going to destroy him. Doing so would only garner the wrath of the council and while neither he nor Cam were afraid of them, they had to think of Lexi, Ariel and the kids.

They had learned that he was working with—or for—the Learned. He'd been the one who had told Nathan about Caitlin being pregnant with Sean's child, which had started this whole mess.

"Once we have Sean's child, we could give the baron to Caitlin along with the information we learned."

Cam laughed. "That would serve him right."

While the High Council might be angry at his death, they might not seek retaliation from a St. George.

"One thing at a time." Braeden tapped his desk. "First, Sean. We need to find him and see what's going on."

"You're worried about him."

"Of course."

"He's not a kid anymore, Braeden. He hasn't been for a long time."

"But his dragon is. There's no telling what crazy plan the two of them will come up with."

Caitlin paced the cold floor of the cabin. What was he doing? More important, was he coming back?

She couldn't blame Sean if he didn't. Not after what had happened.

Ascalon had never come to her defense like that before. Then again, she'd never been in a match like that before—not sword against sword.

It amazed her that she'd even seen the weapon before it was too late. Thankfully, the flash of amethyst caught her eye just in time for her to throw her blade in its path.

She peered out the window again, searching the clearing for any sign of Sean. The sun was already below the line of trees. Soon it would be too dark to see anything out there. Would he be back by then? Letting the curtain fall back into place, she sighed with disappointment.

Caitlin laughed softly at herself. Just mere hours ago, she'd claimed to neither want nor need anyone. She'd convinced him of her determination to be independent.

Yet here she was anxiously awaiting his return.

Was she simply on edge because she was in a strange

place, and night was getting ready to fall, or was she lying to herself about what she felt for him?

She wasn't sure.

It didn't make sense. They hadn't known each other long enough for her to be so attached to him. And she hadn't lied; their emotions did run either hot or cold. Except today, when he'd been forcing her to learn how to use the pendant.

At first she'd been ticked off about it. But not as outraged as she'd tried to pretend. And then it had been sort of…exciting…fun to see how much power she could channel with the amethyst dragon.

Their time at the cabin could actually be considered the most extended period of *normal* time they'd had together since they'd first met. And it wasn't all that bad.

A swarm of butterflies fluttered in her stomach. She looked out the window again and saw him coming across the clearing.

He looked tired, nearly exhausted.

Caitlin quickly ran into the bedroom and slipped out of her clothes then tossed on an oversize T-shirt before racing back to the cabin door and pulling it open.

Chapter 15

Sean's expression was priceless. From the widening of his eyes and the half smile twitching at his lips, his surprise was evident. Desire flared to life, lacing the heat surrounding him with want and lust.

She backed away, inviting him in with what she hoped was a smile of welcome, and not the goofy grin of a raving lunatic. "I wasn't sure you were coming back."

He kicked the door closed behind him and kept walking toward her. His seductive half smile deepening to the focused hooded gaze of a beast stalking its prey. Her heart beat faster.

"I'm fairly certain I said I would be back."

Caitlin swallowed a groan at the deep, husky tone of man-beast. She reached behind her to make sure she wasn't going to run into anything as she angled toward the bedroom, still walking backward.

She teased him, staying just out of his reach. When

he lengthened his stride, she moved quicker, luring him with pheromones she didn't need judging from the shimmer of his eyes, but couldn't stop producing.

"But you were gone so long that I started to worry." Her own voice had dropped an octave. The lower, whispery tone surprised her.

"Were you afraid I'd left you on the island alone?"

Caitlin shrugged a shoulder, tilted her head and looked up at him from beneath half lowered eyelashes. *Good grief, I'm flirting with him.*

Flirting? She never resorted to such childish games. She either took what she wanted or sent out enough pheromones that the other party did the chasing—or at least they thought they did.

Truth be told, this silly game actually made her feel sort of…giddy. And the fact that he was playing along made her want him that much more.

She backed into the doorjamb. Readjusting her path, she entered the bedroom, with him just inches away.

"You look tired."

"Exhausted."

She motioned to the bed. "Perhaps I should go and let you get some sleep."

Sean shrugged. "If that's what you want."

Caitlin stopped. What had she done? He was actually going to let her leave so he could sleep?

He swept her into his embrace with a low growl, pulling her against his chest and backing her up until her legs hit the edge of the bed, then dropped her onto the mattress, still in his arms.

She sighed. "I thought—"

"Shut up." His tongue slid along her lips, stopping her words. "No talking."

Parting her lips, she didn't think to disagree with

him. They'd already proven earlier that talking did nothing but get them in trouble.

"Can you hear me?"

His voice drifted into her mind. The tone rumbling inside her added more fuel to the fire already burning. She answered in the same manner, *"You said no talking."*

"Talking. I said nothing about any other form of communicating."

"Ah." But they'd already been communicating without words.

"If all goes well, and I'm certain it will, this is our last night together. Tell me what you want."

She moaned softly, arching her body beneath him, straining to get impossibly closer. He couldn't tell what she wanted?

Sean slid his mouth from hers, turning her moan of growing desire into a whine of loss. *"Come on, darlin'."* He edged down her body, tugging her shirt up as he inched lower.

The chilly air of the bedroom brought a shiver to her body, chasing gooseflesh along her belly.

"Do you want a fast, hard fuck that'll leave us fighting for breath?"

He closed his teeth around her pebbled nipple hard enough to send a jolt of electricity to curl her toes and drawing a gasp of shock from her lips.

"Or do you want it slow and easy, taking time to savor every inch of our bodies?"

His tongue slowly lathed her still-tingling nipple before he closed his lips over it, sucking gently until she moaned.

He stopped his teasing torment to gaze up at her, asking, *"Well?"*

Caitlin's heart thudded hard enough inside her chest that she was certain he could feel it. It was hard to fathom never sharing a bed with him again, never feeling his hands on her body, his lips against hers. She drew a hand through his hair, caressing the side of his head. *"Sean, if this is our last night together, I want to remember it and you forever."*

His eyes gleamed as he nodded before moving off her to stretch out alongside and pull her into a warm embrace made warmer still by the return of his lips to hers.

Their kiss was slow, languid, the easy movement of his tongue across hers, brushing the roof of her mouth as tentatively as a first kiss—or perhaps a last one meant to savor the moment.

His taste, his touch so sweet, she wanted to cry at the thought of never again sharing such an exquisite caress.

"Shhh, baby." His whisper raced softly against her mind. *"Focus on now, this moment. Let tomorrow go."*

He trailed his lips against her chin, along the side of her face, until he settled on the soft spot beneath her ear. Her toes curled from the attention he paid to that small spot of skin.

How could such light, barely perceptible teasing make her nearly swoon with such longing?

Sean released her long enough to pull his shirt off and toss it to the floor. In the next instant it was joined by hers.

He rolled her over in his arms and eased her back tightly against his chest. One arm slid beneath her head, the bend of his arm forming a pillow. The other he slung around her, his hand resting on her belly.

For a moment or two he didn't move, and she was fine with that, welcomed the chance to savor his warmth against her back. In the silence of the bedroom she could hear his heartbeat as it pulsed strong and steady behind her.

The dragon crooned in the darkness. A soft, sad lament of longing and farewell. The sound, and the emotion it held, touched her deeply, making her long to throw her arms around the beast and promise to never leave him. What was she doing? How could she go? What was she thinking? Her throat tightened with unshed tears, and she parted her lips.

"No." Sean silently stopped her vow. *"Leave him be, Caitlin. Make no promises in a moment of lust. It wouldn't be fair to any of us."*

She choked back a sob, fighting to gain control of her jumbled emotions and thoughts as she forced herself to focus on his hand sweeping up to caress her breast.

That was all she needed to concentrate on—the mind-stealing feel of his fingertips stroking, teasing, building the desire to a fevered pitch. And on his mouth, pressed against her flesh where her neck met her shoulder, nipping lightly, sucking, making a mark that would still be there in the morning.

He slid a denim-encased leg between her naked ones, parting her legs, giving him room to rest his wandering hand.

She held her breath in anticipation. Her thighs quivered, waiting, expecting his oh, so expert touch. Her stomach tightened in preparation for the closest thing she would ever come to flying.

She waited, her heart thudding heavy in her chest. And waited…

Caitlin frowned at his hesitation. He didn't move. He

barely breathed. Surely he hadn't fallen asleep, had he? Disappointment flooded her, slowing her racing heart, evening out her breathing.

A soft chuckle vibrated against her shoulder. Before she could think of the words to berate him for teasing her so mercilessly, the touch she'd anticipated took her breath away.

While his fingers danced against her heat, hers curled into the covers beneath them, seeking something more substantial to touch.

He tugged at the gold chain around her neck with his teeth, reminding her of the power at her beck and call.

Caitlin reached up to clasp the brilliant amethyst in her hand and brought his body into view in her mind. He stood before her in all his naked glory, that devastatingly sexy half smile playing at his lips.

She ran her palms across his chest and shoulders, memorizing the feel of his hard muscles beneath his smooth flesh. Her fingertips trailed over the bulge of biceps that he flexed for her benefit, making her smile at his silliness.

That was yet another thing she would miss. Yes, they fought and argued almost constantly. But his patience in the bedroom was beyond comparison to anyone.

He didn't complain about her leisurely exploration of his body. Like now, as she traced the line of muscle protecting his ribs. There wasn't a spare ounce of fat anywhere. He was built as perfectly as the beast who possessed him—lean and strong, every limb, each muscle, created for power, endurance and survival.

Her attention slipped as his touch slid deeper between the folds of her flesh. The roughness of denim brushed against her thighs, parting her legs farther, giving him more room to torment and tease, to slide a seeking finger inside.

Caitlin forced her thoughts back to the pendant, and the man it brought to life in her mind. Unable to stand on shaking legs, she dropped to her knees before him and slid her mouth over the hard length of his cock.

The velvety softness of the skin covering the hardness never failed to amaze her. It was a contradiction she found fascinating. And his ragged groan as she grazed her teeth lightly over the ridge was like a sensual touch against her own skin.

He ran his fingers through her hair, caressing her head. His thumb tracing the rim of her ear sent a shiver zinging down her spine.

Before she could send her mind further along the fantasy she was creating in her mind, he grasped her shoulders and hauled her to her feet, spun her around and pulled her back against his chest.

The sharp bite of teeth on her shoulder jolted her out of the mental fantasy. She dropped the pendant, letting it dangle from her neck. She'd been so lost in the love play of her own making that she hadn't realized he had literally rolled her onto her knees, stripped off his jeans and was now leaning over her, his knees between hers, his teeth sinking into the sensitive flesh of her shoulder.

She sensed the awakening of his dragon. Even if she hadn't, the near-brutal grasp he had on her wrists and the controlling bite would have been enough to enlighten her.

Through no intentional effort, her own fangs, useless as they were, pushed against her lips as they lengthened. She swung her head side to side, trying to break free of the beast's hold.

Drawing in a deep breath, Caitlin forced herself to

relax. He wasn't going to hurt her. Once the dragon knew he was completely in charge, he would gentle. She arched her back, supporting his weight, and swayed her hips against him.

The sharp hold on her shoulder lessened until he lathed the area with his tongue, easing the sting of his bite. Her fangs retracted, and he released her wrists to thread his fingers between hers.

His lips were against her ear. "Don't make me wait." His rough whisper, breaking his own request for no talking, sent an unexpected thrill shooting through her. He wanted her so desperately that he'd break his own rules.

"Fuck me." She knew her response was crude, but the words she never said at any other time were the only ones she could think of in the heat of this moment.

He entered her fast and hard, in one steady stroke, drawing a gasp then a moan of pleasure from her. Nothing—absolutely nothing—felt as wonderful or complete as him filling her.

Together like this they were one—her, Sean and yes, even the beast, became one entity without individual beginning or ending. And together they built the magic that carried them higher, breaking the bonds holding them to the earth.

His fingers tightened around hers, she felt him strain against her, his climax building as hers raced to catch up.

Their hearts pounding, their ragged breaths mingling in the otherwise silent room, they reached the pinnacle at the same time and fell onto the bed laughing weakly, fighting to catch their breath.

To her horror, for no reason whatsoever, Caitlin burst

into tears. She buried her face in the pillow, not wanting him to see the weakness she wouldn't be able to explain.

Sean rose up enough to turn her onto her back then rested on his forearms atop her. He gazed down at her and slung his arms beneath her shoulders to cradle her head in his hands. "Shh. Caitlin, it's okay."

He kissed her tears away. "Listen to me. You know where to find me. I'm not going anywhere. Take your time, do whatever it is you have to do. But if you need me, for anything, I'm here." He stretched his thumb down and hooked it through the chain of her pendant. "You know how to call me."

All she could think of was how unfair that was. He was going to sit at Dragon's Lair waiting for her? What if she discovered that once she'd taken the time to mourn a relationship that never was, she didn't need him? What then? As determined as she was to explore her own independence, even she wasn't that selfish. Guilt flowed into her, cold and ugly.

He shook his head. "You've nothing to be guilty for. I will wait for you until the day I die. It's not a decision. It's just the way it is. This dragon has chosen his mate, plain and simple. But that doesn't mean I'm not going to live, or that I'm going to live like a monk. I may be a mated beast, but I'm also still a man with my own wants and needs."

Instead of making her feel better, or at least not as guilty, it felt as if someone reached inside her chest and tore her heart free. Caitlin swallowed hard, trying desperately to stop the tears from flowing all over again.

What was wrong with her? Why was she suddenly so emotional?

He covered her lips with his own, sweeping his tongue along hers as he settled between her thighs and entered her, making slow, sweet love to her. Giving her something more to remember and much more to miss.

Danielle unlocked the door to Sean's suite of rooms, knocking as she pushed the door open. "Sean?"

No sound answered her in return, so she walked in, closing the door behind her. "Aelthed?"

When he and his cube had disappeared from Braeden's office, she'd looked for him in her suite, but he hadn't been there.

"Aelthed, please answer me."

"In here."

She followed the sound of his voice into Sean's office and picked the wooden box up from the desk.

"You know that Cam just spoke out of turn, right? He didn't mean anything by it."

"Perhaps. But he was correct. I am already dead. It's something I seem to forget at times."

"Don't say that." Danielle sat down behind the desk, holding the cube against her chest. "You are as real to me as the air I breathe."

"Real or not, I have no physical body. I am nothing more than a voice to you."

"That isn't true." Danielle frowned. How was she going to explain something to him that she'd yet figured out how to explain to herself?

"Aelthed, I don't care what you are or aren't. You've provided me with more companionship, more advice, comfort and understanding than any human or preternatural I've ever known. I love you dearly. Deeply, with all of my heart. And if it were possible, I would spend eternity in that cube with you."

"Oh, Danielle, as much as I cherish your words and your love, you deserve someone who can hold you

tightly in his arms. Someone made of flesh and bone who can steal your mind away with kisses and drive you wild with touches."

She smiled at what he'd just unknowingly given away. "So you've thought of these things, too?"

"Of course I have, woman. What I wouldn't give to run my fingers through your raven tresses, or to hold you naked in my arms, or to wipe that smug smile from your face with a kiss you'd not soon forget."

Danielle laughed. "Someday, Aelthed, I'll no longer be on this physical plane of existence, and you'll be forced to prove whether those words are true or not. I wonder what you'll do then."

"You need not fear that I'll run like some frightened boy. I was quite the ladies' man in my day."

"Hmm. That would have been the twelfth century? Did you ogle them from afar or write songs about their beauty? Or perhaps place chaste kisses on their hand? Things have changed a little since then, my dear."

His laughter filled her mind. *"Trust me, some things have not changed as much as you seem to think they have."*

She found his chortle of amusement interesting. But decided not to delve into the topic any further. Instead, she asked, "Have you discovered where Sean might be hiding?"

"Coward." He cleared his throat then answered her question. *"No. He's found himself someplace unknown to us, obviously, and taken the girl with him."*

"What do you think of what we saw in Caitlin's mind?"

Aelthed's snort echoed her own thoughts. *"I think she, or they, figured out how to show us an outright lie."*

"So do I. Which leaves me wondering how I can trust anything I see in either of their minds."

"You can't."

"So how are we ever going to know if Sean is under Nathan's control or not?"

"We aren't, at least not by mining their thoughts. We're all going to have to watch him carefully and guard our backs. If it were up to me, I'd send you, the other women and the children to Dragon's Lair. I certainly wouldn't leave them within such easy reach."

Danielle nodded. "I agree with sending Alexia, Ariel and the children, but I'm not going anywhere. The boys can use my help with keeping an eye—or a mind—turned on Sean and Caitlin."

"That just places you in danger."

"Afraid I'll join you sooner rather than later?"

"Don't talk like that, woman."

He only called her *woman* when she'd irritated him or he was worried. Danielle relented. "Sorry. I actually don't think Sean is under Nathan's control. I think he and Caitlin have hidden themselves away somewhere to plan the child's rescue, and that frightens me."

"Why?"

"He shouldn't go alone. It's too dangerous. He should be making his plans with his brothers."

"To some degree, you're right. However, have you thought about putting all of them in danger at once? Isn't that what they'd be doing if all three of them went to the Learned's stronghold at once?"

Danielle pursed her lips then said, "I actually hadn't thought about that. I wonder if Braeden has."

"I'm sure the Dragon Lord has considered all angles. He isn't foolish, nor is he stupid."

"True."

Danielle rose and carried the cube to the linen closet. She opened the door and waited until he levitated his box to the top shelf before closing it. Placing a hand on the door, she whispered, "Be safe, my love."

Chapter 16

Sean opened his eyes to complete darkness. They'd fallen asleep, which hadn't been his intention, since he'd wanted to fly to the Learned's stronghold and back to Mirabilus before the sun rose. But what was done was done. It wasn't as if he could turn back time.

The warm bundle pressed against his chest sighed in her sleep. He tightened the arm he'd wrapped over her and she groaned in protest, clinging tighter to his forearm.

His other arm was beneath her head, the bend at the elbow acting as her pillow. He wiggled his foot free from between her ankles and stretched his leg out against hers.

Soon he needed to wake her up. There were things to be done tonight. But not yet. Right now he just wanted to stay right here, like this, not moving, savoring the feel of their combined warmth.

How long would it take her to realize her independence was like a shiny new toy that would dull with age? How many months or years would pass before she came to understand that sharing a life with someone didn't necessarily mean she'd have to give up any part of herself?

And how many days or weeks would pass before she discovered she was carrying not just one more child, but twins?

Two more dragonettes were growing in her womb. Two more Drakes. Two more offspring for him and his dragon to watch over.

He wasn't going to change his mind about her leaving. She could go. But he didn't have to like it, and he'd be damned if she or their children were ever going to be out of his sight.

He hadn't quite formulated a plan to pull that off, but he would. It wasn't as though she left him much choice.

After this event with Nathan, he wasn't about to risk another kidnapping. Especially when there would soon be three little ones to keep safe.

How had Braeden and Cameron convinced their mates to stay? Stupid question when he knew the answer without giving it much thought.

Braeden and Alexia were easy enough to understand since they had still been married when she came to Braeden for help. They cared enough about each other to work through their misunderstanding and to take another chance with their marriage. So far, whatever they were doing seemed to be working for them.

Cameron and Ariel were an interesting couple. She'd been blackmailed into working for the Learned and came to both Mirabilus and the Dragon's Lair essentially as an enemy. But they'd come to trust each other.

While the two of them still got into massive arguments, it was obvious to everyone that they loved each other deeply.

How could he attempt to clear up any misunderstanding or begin to build any trust with Caitlin when she wasn't going to be around?

Sean frowned. This line of thought was just going to fan his anger over the entire situation. He didn't want to spend their last hours together arguing.

He closed his eyes and dragged his chin across her shoulder.

She shrugged, trying to escape the stubble scraping across her skin.

"Caitlin, it's time to get going."

Instead of pulling free of the lingering threads of sleep, she tugged on his forearm, snuggling it beneath her chin.

He once again dragged his chin across her shoulder. His efforts gained him two sets of fingernails seeking to embed themselves in the flesh of his arm. Yeah, she was awake.

Sean flicked his fingers toward the oil lamp, setting it alight.

Caitlin buried her face in the bed. "That's just mean."

He pulled his arms free and sat up. "Get up."

"No."

He ran a hand over her hip, lingering, and then caressed one padded cheek.

She came up on her elbow to look at him over her shoulder. "Don't even think about it."

"I'm pretty sure one sharp slap would have you on your feet in short order."

"You're probably right. But I don't think you really want to go there."

"Someday, I might." He patted her hip, sighing with fake regret. "Just not right now."

She sat up, swinging her legs over the side of the bed. "It's time, isn't it?"

"Yes."

"I should be excited. Relieved that Sean will be back in my arms." She turned to look at him. "But I'm terrified something will go wrong."

"I have every step planned out. A little faith in me would go far." He looked away, not wanting to admit his own doubts about this rescue.

Sean rolled out of the bed. His feet hit the ice-cold floor, making him want nothing more than to burrow back in the warmth of the bed.

Caitlin tossed him his clothes then asked, "I haven't seen a bathroom."

"There's an outhouse of sorts round back." He reached in the nightstand drawer and pulled out a flashlight that he tossed on the bed. "Use this. It'll be dark."

She stared at him a few seconds before picking up the flashlight. "Ohhhkay. Not exactly an upscale resort."

"Nope. I built it for myself."

She slowly looked around the bedroom. "You built this?"

The shock in her voice was evident. "What surprises you more—that the little rich boy used his hands for manual labor, or that the computer geek can use a saw and hammer?"

"With you? Neither. I'm surprised there's no ultra-modern bath."

He didn't follow her comment and just looked at her.

Caitlin shrugged then explained. "You have callouses on your hands, so it's obvious you don't shy away from manual labor. However, your suites—both the one at the Lair and the one at Mirabilus, while sparsely furnished, are done so with no thought given to expense. Everything is quality. And your showers?" She paused to sigh loudly. "They rate such a huge OMG that I want to take one of them with me when I go. I mean, seriously, Sean, six shower bars with eight adjustable nozzles on each one? An unsuspecting bather could drown from just turning the water on."

"I think in the shower, so I may as well have a good one."

"Good? I'd go with magnificent myself." She headed toward the door. "I'll meet you out front?"

Since he didn't want to take the time to dress when they got back to Mirabilus, he did so now. That was one thing he hadn't been able to figure out—when he shifted, where did his clothes go? If he left human form dressed, he returned dressed. It wasn't that important, so he hadn't made it an issue. It was just odd.

After making certain the oil lamp and the embers in the fireplace were both fully out, he walked out of the cabin. Making the bed could wait until he returned tomorrow or the day after. After making sure Caitlin and their son were safely back at the Lair, he knew he wasn't going to be in any mood to deal with his family, so he'd come here to make his plans for keeping an eye on her without appearing to be some crazed stalker.

The night air was cold. If he wasn't careful, she would freeze on the trip back to Mirabilus.

Caitlin put the flashlight back inside the cabin then joined him. "I'm ready." She brushed her hands up and down her arms. "This isn't going to be pleasant, is it?"

"It'll be fine." He reached out to take her hand as they crossed the clearing. "I'll keep you warm enough."

Once they arrived at the clearing near the cliffs, he

turned to her. "When you climb onto my foot, lie down so I can hold you next to my chest without squishing you."

"Ew, I'd hate to get dragon squished." She laughed softly before kissing his cheek. "I'm ready. Let's go."

Caitlin stood back and held her breath. Watching Sean change from man to smoke and then to dragon amazed her. She wondered how it felt. Did it hurt? If so, he didn't give evidence of any pain. Did it just feel... strange?

When he held out his foot, she did as he'd asked and stretched out on the pad. She suffered a moment of panic when he lifted her toward his chest, and the image of being crushed flitted across her mind. Thankfully, her panic subsided as quickly as it had formed.

In fact, between the firm padding of his foot beneath her and the warmth of his chest, she found herself fighting sleep. It was so comfortable and cozy her eyelids kept drifting closed. She couldn't imagine a more pleasant flight.

"Caitlin, wake up."

A blast of cold air rushed across her body, dragging her from sleep. She opened her eyes, startled to find they had already landed on the beach at Mirabilus. A puff of warm air blew her hair across her face, and she looked up into the beast's nostrils.

She patted his nose before rolling up to her knees to climb off his foot. "I'm going, I'm going."

Once he changed back into human form, he took her hand and headed for the castle. "We need to make sure I have everything I need before I head to the Learned's. And you need to get your story of my brothers' deaths set in your mind."

She slowed her steps, hanging back, trying to slow him down. "I'm not so sure this is a wise idea."

"Doesn't matter what you think. I'm going."

"But—"

He stopped and swung around so fast that she ran into him, literally bouncing off his chest.

"I am not going to argue this with you. So you can shut up and either lend me a hand or not. Doesn't matter to me."

"Please don't go there alone." Her legs shook. "I'm afraid."

The anger etched on his face lessened. "You came to me for help. I swore to you that I would get our son back. That vow was from me. I made no promises for my brothers." He grasped her chin and lifted it so she had no choice but to look at him. "Caitlin, this is my battle, not theirs. I am doing this my way. I will not fail you."

She knew she wasn't going to be able to sway him from his path. Grabbing the front of his shirt, she pulled him closer. "If you get yourself killed, I swear to you I will make your afterlife miserable."

That damn sexy, mind-stealing half smile made her wonder if she should kiss him or smack him.

He took the choice away. Lowering his head, he whispered, "Darlin', you do that."

And then kissed away any comment she might have made had she had any control over her ability to think.

Before she could regain any intelligence, they were in his suite. He stood in the living room frowning then dragged her to the bathroom and turned on the shower. "Can you light up that pendant?"

She pulled it free from beneath her sweatshirt and held it in her hand, willing it to come alive. When it shimmered with an amethyst light, she held it up. "Now what?"

"We need to combine our energy to put a shield around this suite. Once I release Aelthed, I can't have him escaping."

"Afraid he'll go blabbing your plan?"

"Yes."

That wouldn't be such a bad thing from her point of view, but it also probably wouldn't change anything. "What do you want me to do?"

"Instead of trying to secure the entire suite, pick a room to confine him to while I'm gone."

"How about the bedroom? It's small enough to secure, yet it should be large enough for him to roam around in considering he's been trapped in a six-inch cube for so long."

Sean nodded. "All right, now focus on the bedroom and envision a shield around it. An unbreakable barrier for Aelthed."

She closed her eyes and focused. Bringing the bedroom into view wasn't hard, but when she added the shield, the whole thing kept changing color. Caitlin swore silently then looked at Sean to ask, "Any specific color for this shield?"

He shrugged. "I'd go with amethyst."

She rolled her eyes at her own lack of forethought. Of course the obvious would be just out of her reach. Closing her eyes again, she brought the vision of the bedroom into her mind, this time surrounded with an amethyst light shield. That color held steady. Since she had no clue what he really looked like, she pictured Aelthed as an old man in medieval robes trapped in the room. She sent him to the door to ensure he was unable to open it or to go through it if anyone else opened it.

And did the same thing with the sliding glass doors to the balcony and the door to the bathroom, just in case.

She inspected every inch, every nook and cranny of the room, making sure there was no escape and that the shield covered everything completely.

Sean turned off the shower. "That should do it."

Caitlin opened her eyes asking, "How do you know if… Never mind." The shimmer of amethyst light seeping in beneath the bathroom door answered her unasked question. Their spell had worked.

"I'm going to go get the grimoire and the other two pendants. You collect the cube and bring him in the bedroom. And, I know you don't like the idea, but I'm going to need your sword."

No, she didn't like the idea, but she also didn't think it would be too big of a threat to him, because if she wasn't using it, the magic wouldn't be there. She held out her hand and called the weapon to her.

Handing it to Sean, she warned, "If it thinks I need it, nothing you do will keep it with you."

"Got it." He placed it on the bed and headed out of the bedroom.

She followed him out the door and while he went to the office, she opened the linen closet and felt around on the top shelf until she was able to wrap her hand around the small box.

"What are you doing?"

Caitlin bit her lip to keep from saying anything. Instead, she quickly pulled the box down from the shelf and rushed into the bedroom before Aelthed could levitate himself out of their reach.

Sean was right behind her, and after quickly closing the door, he put his items on the bed, motioning her to do the same. "Now, from what the beast and I could figure, this is going to take two of us."

He picked up the sapphire pendant that currently belonged to Ariel. "We need to put this pendant and yours on opposite sides of the box at the same time."

She sat down on the edge of the bed, holding her dragon pendant, and studied the box. "I don't see any place for them to fit into."

"Humor me." He pulled a piece of chalk from his jeans and sat near her on the bed. "Since this might take a few tries, I'm going to number the sides."

After he'd jotted a number on each of the six sides, he said, "I'll count to three and on three just press your pendant against the center of side two."

They did that three times, with her using the even-numbered sides. Then switched with her using the odd-numbered sides.

On the second try—with her pendant in the center of side three and his in the center of side four—the flat surface mutated. The indented shape of a dragon, the exact size of the pendants, appeared on those sides of the box.

Sean smiled. "I was right. Okay, now, again on three, turn your dragon clockwise."

Nothing happened.

They removed the pendants from the box, and the indentations disappeared. Then they repeated placing and turning, but this time counterclockwise.

Caitlin gasped as they heard a distinct click, immediately followed by tiny pieces of the box shifting, moving like a 3D puzzle working itself, until the top opened and a stream of fog escaped. Sean motioned her to remove her pendant, and she watched as the pieces once again shifted and moved back into a flat-sided cube.

The stream took shape, and to her satisfaction the shape was of an old man, with a long white beard and hair, wearing medieval-style robes.

Sean rose. "You must be Aelthed."

"What have you done?" The wizard appeared horrified, but his eyes blazed with anger.

"A thank-you will suffice."

"I'll not thank you for using black magic to free me."

"Black magic?" Caitlin broke into the men's conversation. "Wasn't it a dark power that put you there in the first place?"

Aelthed turned a look of disdain in her direction. "You know nothing."

She picked her pendant up from the bed, letting it dangle from the chain. "If its power is dark, then you've no one to blame but yourself, since this came from your own creation."

His eyes widened. He reached out to touch a fingertip to the amethyst. "Where did you get this?"

Sean said, "It fell out of the grimoire."

"That's not possible. This gemstone beast was shattered into dust."

Caitlin blew a warm breath over the small dragon, bringing it to shimmering life. "Doesn't look like any dust I've ever seen."

The old wizard stepped back, his wary gaze on Caitlin. "Be careful with that."

Sean took the pendant from her. "I've wasted enough time." He then gathered up Ascalon, the grimoire, the other two pendants and the now-empty cube.

He stepped closer to the wizard. "Not even a thank-you? Fine. But you owe me."

"What do you want?"

"You stay right here, in this room. When I call, you bring me back here. Got it?"

Caitlin frowned. Why wouldn't he be able to bring himself back here?

Aelthed muttered to himself then said, "You're going to the Learned's."

"Yes, I am. And when I return, I'll have my son."

"A lot of good that'll do once Nathan has everything in his possession."

Adding to Caitlin's confusion, Sean smiled as he headed for the balcony while slipping the gold chain holding her pendant over his head. "He'll be too dead to use any of them."

Chapter 17

Sean landed on a ledge outside one of the windows lining the Great Hall at the Learned's stronghold and shifted from dragon to human form. He leaned tightly against the wall, widening his stance to ensure he had a good purchase on the ledge, then took a deep steadying breath and removed the pack from his back, setting it on the ledge next to him.

"Ready, buddy? It's time."

Gritting his teeth, he and his beast concentrated, each focusing on their own individual form. Sean clenched his jaw harder to keep from crying out as his dragon tore free of its human bond. The separation felt as if his flesh and muscle were being ripped apart as his body mutated. The burning pain seared through him, leaving him shaking and gasping for breath.

They'd only practiced this twice, and each time it had worked. The painful process wasn't anything he wanted to experience too often, but worse than the pain was the emptiness—a cold, sickly hollowness deep inside that drained him of energy and light. His heart and soul became dark, depressing entities that threatened to consume him.

Once the beast was free and Sean had regained the ability to stand without trembling and gasping for air, he handed the dragon Caitlin's amethyst pendant, while he took the sapphire one from the pocket of the backpack.

The two of them worked in unison just as he and Caitlin had done to open the box. Once the top opened, the beast changed into smoke and quickly streamed into the box before it closed up again.

Sean grinned. Wouldn't Nathan be surprised when he opened the cube expecting to find his uncle inside?

Once the exchange was made and he left the stronghold, it would be up to the beast to ensure the Learned's death. He didn't doubt his dragon's bravery or strength; what worried him was Nathan's trickery.

Hopefully, he and his dragon managed to outtrick the wizard this time.

Ascalon hung securely from its scabbard at his side. He slipped the small sapphire beast back into the pocket of the backpack along with the emerald one and opened the pack to retrieve a small scrap of leather. After wrapping the amethyst pendant securely in the leather, he slid it into the pocket of his jeans. Hopefully, if for whatever reason, the thing decided to shimmer and glow, the leather would keep the light contained. He didn't want Nathan to know there was a third dragon pendant.

Holding the cube in one hand and the straps to the pack in the other, Sean climbed into the stronghold through the window and jumped down to the floor of the Great Hall. He flicked his fingers toward the torches, setting them afire. Elongated flickers of light danced across the stone floor and up the walls, casting eerie shadows that seemed to reach out for him like the evil, clawing fingers of a demon.

Sean shook off the image and crossed to the altar at the far side of the hall. The castle was quiet—far too quiet. Not even the sound of mice scurrying across the floor broke the silence. The lack of noise put him on edge. Not a bad thing considering what or who he was up against. He wiped those thoughts from his mind. He had to remember not to think of anything. The Learned would pick up on the slightest thread of a misplaced thought and easily deduce something foul was afoot.

The candles on the altar flickered to life, warning him that the Learned was near.

"Well, well. A Drake who appears to be able to follow orders…eventually. You simply needed a booster of sorts."

Nathan materialized behind the altar. He caught sight of the cube in Sean's grasp and clapped his hands. "The rest?"

Sean placed the cube and backpack on top of the altar. He unstrapped Ascalon from around his waist and placed that next to the other items.

"My son?"

"I beg your pardon?" Nathan sneered. "Is that how you speak to your lord?"

Against every fiber of his being, Sean calmed his churning ego, bowed his head and moderated his tone. "May I have my son, my lord?"

"Not quite yet." Nathan pulled the grimoire from the pack and swept clean a place for it to rest. He opened the family book.

Sean glanced up enough to see that the pages of the

grimoire were blank. That wasn't anything he could control. He didn't have the power to create scenes on the pages.

A guttural curse echoed in the hall before Nathan slammed the ancient tome closed. He glared at Sean before pulling the two pendants out of the pack's pocket.

After inspecting the gemstone dragons closely, he placed them next to their respective dragon statues on the altar. To Sean's surprise both pendants glowed, and a warmth grew against his thigh. The amethyst pendant in his pocket was radiating heat through the leather wrap. Resisting the urge to look down at his pocket to see if the light showed, and giving away its existence to Nathan, Sean focused on the flicking candles atop the altar.

"Ah," Nathan said, turning his attention to the weapon. "This must be the fabled sword of the dragon slayer."

He pulled Ascalon from its scabbard and held it up before him. With an evil smirk, he pointed it toward Sean. "Your brothers?"

"Both dead."

Sean let the image of him using Ascalon to stab Braeden and then Cam form in his mind. He shifted the vision to Alexia and Ariel sobbing and screaming over the two beasts writhing on the floor of Braeden's office in their final death throes. He let the scenes drag out, wanting Nathan to savor every moment of his victory.

"Very good. You make an excellent pet." Nathan raised and lowered the blade a couple times before placing it back on the altar. "I might have a use for you in the future."

The wizard then raised an arm and snapped his fingers. "Take your spawn and go. I will beckon you soon."

He pinned Sean with a narrowed eye stare. "And you will answer."

Sean tipped his head forward, nodding once to show he understood. At the sound of a baby's crying, he turned to see a woman carry the child into the hall.

As calmly and emotionless as possible, he met the woman halfway across the chamber and took his son into his arms for the first time. The boy ceased his cries and stared up at him with eyes the color of emeralds. The searching, curious gaze threatened to destroy Sean's air of calm.

He unbuttoned his shirt and pulled it around the baby to keep him warm then stepped up onto the window ledge and out into the cold night.

"Caitlin, bring us home."

Caitlin swung away from the sliding glass doors. "Now! Bring him back, now."

Aelthed grumbled but waved his hands before him, chanting in a language she didn't understand.

Within a matter of seconds, Sean materialized in the bedroom.

She held her breath. His back was to her so it was impossible to tell if he had their son or if he'd been injured.

Taking a hesitant step toward him, she reached out, whispering in a voice that shook as much as her hand, "Sean?"

He turned to face her, unbuttoning his shirt as he did so.

Relief, joy and a surge of love overwhelmed her, leaving her lightheaded and trembling. She took another step forward and dropped to her knees.

"Shh, Caitlin, he is safe." Sean knelt in front of her. He held the baby between them. "See, he's fine."

He *was* fine. He was more than fine—he was here. Caitlin brushed her thumb across a soft, plump cheek and leaned closer to kiss his forehead. "Oh, sweetheart, Mommy has missed you."

He turned to look at her with eyes so like his father's and reached up to tangle his little fingers in her hair.

Sean untangled the grasping fingers from her hair. "He's missed you, too."

Little Sean turned his head to peer up at his father and wrapped his fingers around the chain hanging from Sean's neck then promptly stuck it in his mouth.

Caitlin smiled. "I don't think I mentioned that he's at the hand-to-mouth stage."

She looked up at Sean. Something was...wrong... missing...not quite right. She touched his arm. "Are you all right?"

"Fine."

She scooted around to sit on the floor with her back against the bed. "How did it go?"

He handed her the baby then did the same, sitting next to her. "Easier than I thought. Time will tell."

Caitlin held her son close. "Time will tell what?"

"Excuse me." Aelthed interrupted them. "Is it possible that I might leave now?"

Sean pulled the chain over his head and handed the dragon pendant to Caitlin. "I suppose we can let him go now."

Between the two of them they removed the amethyst shield confining the old wizard to the room.

The instant the glow dissipated, the door to the bedroom opened then slammed closed. Caitlin snorted. "How do you like that? Not even a farewell."

"Oh, I'm sure he'll be back."

"With your family in tow, I suppose."

Sean nodded in agreement.

"So, what did you mean *time will tell*?"

"You never can tell with Nathan."

He was doing it again—holding an odd conversation that left her with more questions than answers.

She drew her brows together and glared at him. "Was he dead or alive when you left?"

"Alive…for a time."

Caitlin clenched her jaw. Her son picked up on her tenseness and started to fuss. She forced herself to relax and bent her legs. Placing the baby along her thighs, she bounced her heels on the floor, quieting him down almost instantly.

"Did he know Aelthed wasn't in the box anymore?"

Sean chuckled. "Nope."

"Why is that amusing? He's going to be livid when he finds out."

"Doubtful."

"Sean."

He leaned his shoulder against hers. "I promise to explain everything in the morning. Right now I am exhausted. Could we maybe make use of the bed?"

"You promise you're going to tell me what happened?"

He stroked the baby's foot. "I vowed to rescue our son and did so, didn't I?"

"Yes."

"Then I'm fairly certain you can believe me now."

She looked closer at him, realizing what was different—what was missing. How foolish of her. He'd needed help getting back here to Mirabilus. She asked, "Where's your dragon?"

Sean rose. "Tomorrow."

He helped her up from the floor.

"You didn't leave him at Nathan's?"

"I said, tomorrow."

She swung the baby over to one hip and grabbed Sean's arm. "Where is he?"

He jerked free of her hold. "Look, I'm exhausted and—"

"Exhausted? You're only half alive. Of course you're exhausted. What the hell did you do?" No wonder he refused to tell her all of his plans. He knew damn well she never would have agreed to this. Never. She would have gone to his brothers in a heartbeat.

He stepped closer and glared down at her. "Our son is safe. I would have done anything to make that happen. Anything for you and the baby. Do you understand me?"

Their son picked that moment to start throwing a fit. He jerked and twisted around in Caitlin's arms, screaming until his tear-streaked face was red.

She was so angry nothing she did soothed him. She wanted to kick Sean for being so foolish and for upsetting her and their son.

He took the baby from her arms, held him close to his chest and paced at the end of the bed. "I'm sorry, little one, hush. It's okay."

Faster than she thought possible, the cries turned to whimpers then to the sound of soft breathing as he fell asleep against his father's chest.

Caitlin stared at the two of them, torn between relief and shock, with a twinge of jealousy and this odd urge to cry from a heart brimming with the warmth of what she knew was love.

Was that all it took to fall in love? The sight of her son resting so comfortably at ease against Sean's chest?

No. There had to be more to it than that. She was just upset and it had her emotions all jumbled.

"We need a crib." Sean's softly spoken statement broke into her thoughts. "Ask one of my brothers."

The last thing she wanted to do right now was to ask another Drake male for anything. She focused instead on Braeden's wife, Alexia. Within a matter of minutes a fully furnished nursery appeared in their bedroom. Complete with a rocking chair that would never get used.

Sean shook his head. "I said a crib."

"So did I."

He laid the baby in the crib then came to stand before her. "Caitlin, I will always do what I think best for my family. We'll talk about it in the morning, when I'm back to my full self. Right now I feel ready to fall on my face."

She pushed him gently toward the bed. "Go to sleep."

Sean hooked two fingers around her wrist. "Are you coming?"

"In a minute or two."

While he got ready for bed and slipped beneath the covers, she stood at the side of the crib, staring down at their son.

Unshed tears burned her eyes. Fear as cold and deadly as a vampire's death bite wrapped around her heart.

This sacrifice of his could all have been for nothing. If his dragon was unable to vanquish the Learned, they would all soon die.

She knew his beast was strong and brave. But he was young, so very young, and Nathan had Ascalon.

She could do nothing except hope for the best. Caitlin choked back a sob, fearing the worst.

Nathan chortled with glee and ran his hands lovingly over the items on his altar. The dragon pendants glowed as brightly as they had centuries ago when they'd been created. And while only blank pages filled the grimoire, he knew that once Aelthed was gone from this plane, the book would work its magic for him.

He reached out to touch the sword. Ascalon. The only weapon he would ever again require. Nathan lifted his arms toward the ceiling and chanted over the sword, taking the spell from the dragon slayer and gifting it to himself. He stopped only when the raised spine running the length of the blade glowed with an amethyst light.

Now he had everything he needed to rid the world of the remaining Drakes—the wives and their spawns along with that aunt of theirs. Then his way would be clear to assume complete control of all. Both the human and preternatural worlds would belong to him alone.

Finally, he would rule in the manner to which he'd been destined—as supreme Hierophant. No other ruler, not a king, emperor or president, would hold as much power as he. His word would be law over them all. Any rights granted would be by his hand alone. All would bow to his whim.

He fought the urge to sob with exquisite joy. How long had he worked for this very moment? How many endless nights had he dreamed of this success?

And how many lives had been lost in order for him to realize his goal?

Drakes and his own sons alike had suffered and in the end he had won, not the Drakes.

Nathan picked up the wooden puzzle cube he'd manifested so many centuries ago. He held it up to eye level, admiring his handiwork.

"Well, dearest uncle, the time has finally come for you to go free and be on your way." He laughed before adding, "Right after I exhume any bit of energy you might have left."

With trembling fingers, Nathan worked the cube, moving unseen pieces into place, twisting and flipping bits here, then there, until finally he heard the distinct click of the lock.

He set the wooden box atop his altar and pressed lightly on the top. "Come, greet me, Uncle Aelthed."

The instant he raised his finger, the top sprung up, opening the box to the daylight.

Nathan stepped back and waved one hand over the now-open box. "Come."

A stream of smoke rose from the box. Nathan frowned at the unexpected display. "My, my, Uncle. It seems you have plenty of energy left to provide me."

The smoke swirled then took shape.

Nathan's legs began to tremble; his heart pounded heavy in his chest. Something wasn't right. This was not the shape of a man.

It was the shape of a dragon.

He blindly reached out to retrieve Ascalon.

The beast towered over him. Thrashing in rage it knocked down walls. Pillars supporting the floor above crashed to the ground at their feet.

Roars of anger shook the remaining walls, sending centuries-old stones and bricks crashing down around him, smashing onto the altar, destroying it and all it held.

Oil and torch material from the wall sconces collided with the lit candles. Flames leaped to ancient wall hangings and rugs, fanning the inferno higher and hotter.

In one still partially standing corner of the castle, the ghost of the gypsy mage laughed uproariously.

She shouted over the maelstrom, asking, *"Is this the power you sought, wizard?"*

A chunk of stone, large enough to kill a mortal man, tumbled from the ceiling, knocking Nathan down onto the rubble. He reached out to catch himself, releasing Ascalon in his haste.

The sword clattered across the Great Hall, skipping over cracks in the floor and bouncing over broken hunks of masonry.

Scrambling for purchase on the shattered floor, he lunged for the sword. It was the only weapon that could defeat the beast threatening his life.

It wouldn't require great strength or skill, just one small cut from the blade to bring the dragon down. But first Nathan had to get his hands on the sword.

He crawled on his hands and knees, but he could already feel the beast's hot breath rushing against his back.

One talon hooked into the flesh of his leg, ripping through skin and muscle. A scream tore from Nathan's throat.

The instinct to survive pushed him forward. Dragging his useless bloody limb behind, he bolted over a broken statue and wrapped one hand around the hilt of the sword.

Quickly, before he lost all courage and his life, he flipped over onto his back.

The dragon clawed at his chest, sharp talons outstretched, intent on nothing less than ending his life.

Nathan screamed again as the instrument of his certain death found its mark, crushing and tearing the life from his body.

With his final breath, Nathan the Learned raised the sword, nicking a single scale on the beast's chest.

The sword fell from the dead hand holding it and clattered to the floor.

"Oh, beastie, this is not what I envisioned for you." The gypsy mage floated out of the shadows, coming to rest before the now-calm dragon.

She placed her hand on his side, and he looked down at her, a frown of confusion furrowing his brow. Stroking the injured scale, she coaxed, *"Come rest with me a while. I'll not leave you."*

When he fell heavily to the floor, she sat beside him to offer comfort and encouragement in his final moments. "You were brave and strong, my pet."

Chapter 18

"No!"

Caitlin struggled to awaken from the nightmare that held her fast in its grip. She knew it was a nightmare, just a dream, but it was like a movie playing over and over in her head that would never end.

She knelt over Sean lying among the rubble at what could only be the Learned's castle. He was dead. Killed by her own sword.

Nathan stood on the other side of the ruined room holding Ascalon. The weapon glowed with a bright line of amethyst, and he laughed.

His maniacal laugh threatened to drive her mad. Couldn't he see what he'd done? Didn't it matter that he'd killed her mate, or that their son was now left without a father?

Stupid questions. Of course it didn't matter. That had been his intention all along. He'd only wanted the items he needed to become all powerful.

Well, now he had them.

She turned back to Sean's body and stroked his cheek. He was so pale, so cold.

Caitlin bowed her head over him and gasped for breath. The pain was unbearable. It was a struggle to breathe, an insurmountable effort to focus, to even think.

"Wake up, wake up. Not real. Just a dream."

The sound of a baby crying dragged her from the clutches of the nightmare. Bolting upright on the bed, Caitlin fumbled around on the nightstand for the bed-side lamp. A pale glow lit the room, enabling her to see Sean sleeping next to her on the bed.

She heaved a sigh of relief then rose to see what was troubling their son. He was dry, and she'd fed him just a few hours earlier, so it wasn't yet time to eat again. But from the sound of his broken sobs, he was upset about something.

Caitlin held him close, his warm body plastered to hers, crooning to him in that odd singsong dragon cry. The beast had used it on her, she had used it on Sean and now she sang the song to their son. True to past experience, it performed the same magic.

Perhaps he'd had a nightmare, too. Or something had frightened him. Regardless, the crooning calmed him, and that was all that mattered. He rested his head against her shoulder, stuck his thumb in his mouth and soon his body went slack in her arms. He'd fallen back to sleep.

She put him back in his crib and stared down at him. He'd been gone less than two weeks, but it had felt like a lifetime to her. Unable to resist, she traced a finger along his petal-soft cheek. Sometimes she had to touch him to remind herself that he was indeed back where he belonged.

Gratitude and relief didn't begin to describe what she still felt about his return. It was more like an overwhelming rush of warmth, of love that wrapped around her when she held him or gently touched him.

She couldn't help but wonder if her parents had ever felt this way about her. Had they, at any time in her life, felt any warmth for her?

"Don't be silly, child. Of course we did."

"Mother?"

"Right here."

Caitlin felt a breeze brush against her arm.

"What are you doing here?"

"Watching you. Realizing how wrong I'd been."

"About what?" Her mother had been wrong about a lot of things. Which one was she talking about?

"This child. It would be against nature to take him away from you."

"It's not like I was going to let you."

"Rest easy, Caitlin Anna Marie St. George, that is not why I've come."

She rolled her eyes at her mother's use of her full given name. It was such a time-honored, foolproof way of getting someone's attention. "Then why have you?"

Her mother slowly materialized beside her. "I've come here to try making amends. I know you aren't going to spread your arms and welcome me, but I do not like us being estranged. You are my daughter, and I miss you."

"All I ever wanted was my son."

"And not to be married to Hoffel."

Caitlin laughed softly so as not to awaken Sean or

little Sean. "Well, that's not even a consideration any-more. I understand he met with an...accident yesterday."

"Yes, we know. The Dragon Lord called to explain."

That was nice, especially since no one had yet taken the time to explain what had happened to her. Not that it really mattered; it wasn't as if his death bothered her in the least. She was mostly just curious. "It was his own fault for working with the Learned."

Her mother rested a hand on her arm. "I don't dis-agree with you. Neither does your father."

"So who does he have in store for me now?"

"I couldn't tell you." Her mother turned her head to cast a brief glance toward the bed. "But I'd say that de-cision is out of his hands, wouldn't you?"

Caitlin shrugged. "We aren't married."

"I see."

She doubted if her mother saw anything. But it wasn't a point she wanted to argue. "What do you mean, you couldn't tell me?"

"Your father and I..." Her mother shrugged and looked away. "We aren't...he's moved on."

"Oh, is that how that works?"

"Well, darling, I am dead."

Really? Her mother was going to split hairs over the degree of *dead* between a ghost and a vampire? The day had been far too long for this conversation to happen. So Caitlin simply pointed out, "So is he."

"Yes, but he has a solid form." The woman waved a hand down her body. "And I no longer do."

Caitlin rubbed her temples.

"You've had a long day. I just wanted to see if you were willing to allow me to make amends—or at least try."

"Yes, Mother, of course I'm willing." What was she

going to do? Say no? She was angry at what her parents had done, but as insane as it was, she didn't hate them. Would never trust them again, but they were her parents.

"Good. Thank you. I'll leave you to your sleep."

Caitlin waved goodbye then went and sat on the edge of the bed to hold her throbbing head in her hands. She'd thought the sudden pounding was due to her mother's conversation, but now she wasn't so certain.

Her head was threatening to kill her. She was strangely dizzy and sick to her stomach. Something was wrong.

She reached behind her to pat the bed. "Sean?"

When he didn't respond, she leaned back groaning at the stabbing pain in her head and grasped his leg to shake it. She opened her eyes and ran her hand down his leg then spun around.

"Sean?"

He was cold—an inhuman sort of cold—more like a corpse than a cold body.

She scrambled across the bed to his side and shook him. "Sean!"

This couldn't be happening.

"Mother!"

Instantly, her mother was back at her side. "What's wrong?"

"I can't wake him."

Her mother looked around the room then closed her eyes for a brief second. "He isn't dead."

Caitlin put her ear to his chest and the palm of her hand in front of his lips. "His heart is barely beating, and his breathing isn't much better." Worse, his dragon hadn't yet returned. Without the beast's strength, whatever ailed him could kill him.

At that moment her son awoke and started crying. She climbed off the bed to pick up little Sean and waved one hand at her mother. "Get the Dragon Lord. Get someone, now."

After the longest few minutes of her life, Braeden, followed by Cameron and their Aunt Danielle, appeared in the bedroom. Her mother was close behind.

"What's going on?" Braeden bent over Sean, doing the same things she'd just done.

The look on his face when he stood up took her breath away. She slid the baby to one hip and grasped the front of Braeden's shirt with her free hand. "What is happening?"

Braeden shook his head. "I'm not sure."

Another form appeared in the crowd around Sean's bed. "I think I might know."

The Drakes all stared at the newcomer in shock, except for little Sean, who reached out in delight toward Aelthed's long white beard.

The old wizard smiled at the child, asking, "May I?"

Caitlin handed him the baby.

Danielle kept poking Aelthed's arm. "How did this happen? When did this happen?"

Cameron cleared his throat. "Focus, please."

"I believe the younger Drake and the dragon figured out a way to separate."

Caitlin had already figured that much out, but she kept her mouth shut.

Braeden groaned. "Not a wise idea."

Aelthed nodded in agreement. "Wise or not, it's the best possible explanation." He nodded toward Caitlin. "She and Sean released me from my cube. Then he left with it."

Before she could get him to shut up, he added, "Along with the dragon pendants, the grimoire and Ascalon."

Everyone stared at her.

"He told me not to say anything. He was certain his plan would work."

Braeden fisted his hands at his sides. "And what exactly was his plan?"

"I don't know all of it. From what I could gather, he gave Nathan the items he'd demanded, rescuing our son, and at some point the dragon inhabited the cube, intending to kill Nathan."

Her mother vanished, only to return right away. "That much of it obviously succeeded. Nathan is dead."

"And the dragon?"

She put a hand on Caitlin's shoulder. "I'm sorry, child, but I don't think he'll survive. It was Ascalon."

Caitlin slowly sank down onto the edge of the bed. At once, everyone started closing in, offering condolences, telling her how sorry they were and how they'd find someone to help Sean.

Her head hurt so bad she could barely see. But their noise—their clanging din of noise would drive her insane. "Stop!"

She reached up to touch the dragon pendant hanging around her neck, rose and took little Sean from Aelthed then turned to Braeden. "Get us there."

"But—"

She glared at him and repeated, "Get us there."

He nodded, but added, "You aren't going alone."

"I don't care."

In the next instant, she was standing in the rubble that used to be the Learned's stronghold, next to the prone body of Sean's beast. He was still alive; she could see the rise and fall of his chest.

With her foot she cleared the rubble from a space near his head and sat down, holding her son on her lap. She rested a hand on the beast's snout. Stroking gently, she crooned to him. The dragon opened his eyes slightly and stared at her then the child.

Little Sean's eyes were huge, but he didn't cry. Fearlessly, he reached out his little hands and patted the dragon's nose.

The soft rumble started low and soft in the beast's chest, but Caitlin heard it, and the sweetness of the dragon's song was enough to make her sob.

Her son wouldn't understand, nor would he remember, but she scooted closer to the dragon and said, "This is your father's beast. This is the bravest and strongest part of him."

She removed her pendant and draped the fine chain around one of his ears. The amethyst sparkled in the light from the torch Braeden had lit and perched in the crack of a boulder. "We will remember you always, and little Sean here will know of you, I promise you that."

Caitlin shuddered then said, "Thank you for saving us all. We can never repay you for so great a sacrifice except with our love." She leaned over and kissed him between the eyes. "Oh, I will miss you so."

The dragon's song faded away. His chest rose and fell one last time. Caitlin rested her head against his larger one and cried.

She heard Braeden approach. He leaned down to take the baby, whispering, "Come on, buddy, give your mother a minute or two."

When her arms were free, she wrapped them around the beast. "You brave fool. We could have found another way."

A few minutes later Braeden cleared his throat, and

she knew it was time to get back to Mirabilus. She had to see to Sean, hoping that she didn't have to go through this same thing again with him. She didn't know if she could bear it.

She dropped one last kiss on the dragon's head and turned away. Braeden handed her little Sean, picked up a backpack and pointed at Ascalon. "Take that with you."

She picked up her sword and looked back at the dragon as Braeden spelled them back to Mirabilus.

The gypsy mage moved out of the shadows with a sigh to caress the beastie's ear. *"Yes, you were strong and brave. And, my sweet, you are well and truly loved. More than I ever could have hoped for you."*

She frowned and then slipped the chain holding the amethyst pendant from his ear. The mage studied the pendant before she looked around the ruined chamber. *"A love like that should never go unrewarded. You should never be without that love. You should never be alone."*

Using a broken piece of lumber, she cleared a circle around the unmoving beast then tossed the wood aside. After placing the pendant on the floor next to her beastie, she surveyed her handiwork and nodded in approval. *"And some morons need spells, blood, pain and death. The fool only needed to dance."*

She stepped inside the circle and began to do just that. Feet tapping, body swaying, she spun around and around dancing inside the circle's edge. Her swirling skirts brushing the dragon.

"Not a dragon born."

She clapped while spinning another round.

"Yet a dragon you shall be."

She turned, so her back faced the outer edge of the circle.

"Once this beast has taken form."

This time she danced so her back faced the dragon.

"It will answer only to thee."

She shrugged at her bad rhyme, but kept dancing, turning back and forth, facing the dragon then facing the outside of the circle.

"St. George will set you free."

Her magic spun, she continued to chant and dance faster and faster until her feet would carry her no more, then she fell laughing inside the empty circle.

The second her feet hit the floor of her bedroom, Caitlin headed to Sean's side. On the way she tossed Ascalon to her mother. "Tell Father we need to respell that."

Danielle reached out and took the baby. Heading for the bedroom door, she said, "Your mother and I will see to him for now."

Her mother followed, adding, "We'll manage just fine."

Caitlin sat on the edge of the bed and motioned to the door. "If there's nothing you can do, could the rest of you just go? I'll call you if I need you."

Cameron blustered something about being there for brothers, but Braeden pushed him through the open bedroom door and waved Aelthed to join them. "We'll be in the living room."

She nodded absently and leaned down to place her lips over Sean's. Uncertain whether sharing her life force would work or not, she exhaled a long breath.

After a couple tries, she sat up and felt his cheeks.

The coldness beneath her fingers drew a cry from her. "Sean, don't you dare die. Do you hear me?"

She leaned down again. Summoning all the energy she had, she exhaled again, her tears dropping onto his face.

When his lips remained icy and lifeless, she stopped. Stretching out next to him, she rested her head on his shoulder and wrapped an arm around him. "Sean, please, move. Say something. Stay. Don't leave us."

She didn't try to stop her tears; it wouldn't have done any good, anyway. They fell freely onto his shoulder, to seep beneath her cheek.

With a shuddering breath she closed her eyes, determined to commit every moment they'd had together to memory. Every argument, each kiss, every glare, each laugh—she wanted them all engraved in granite. Even though she knew that time would try its best to soften the memories, she didn't ever want to forget even one tiny detail.

A brisk wind blew through the sliding glass doors, sending a chill across her. Caitlin reached behind her to pull the edge of the quilt over them and froze.

Above the bed a smoky mist swirled.

She held her breath. It couldn't be. She'd watched him die.

From nowhere she heard a familiar voice chanting a familiar curse.

Not a dragon born, yet a dragon you shall be. Once this beast has taken form, it will answer only to thee. St. George will set you free.

The mist lowered. She moved aside to give it room. It flowed over and around Sean's body, enveloping him, pulsing with life, and then seeped into his body.

He jerked, his face contorted with pain. His arms flailed as if trying to fight off an invisible opponent.

Caitlin hesitated. Should she call for his brothers? Or was this normal when the beast and man became one?

As quickly as it had started, he calmed, easing back into a restful slumber.

She moved back to his side and placed her ear against his chest.

This time the tears that fell from her eyes were tears of happiness.

The beast crooned to her, erasing her fears, reassuring her that all was well.

Sean's arm came around her, holding her tightly against him in his sleep.

Chapter 19

Caitlin tossed the last of her clothes into the suitcase. She couldn't believe he was making her leave.

She glared at his back. He was standing in front of the sliding door in the bedroom, holding their son, not saying a word. Right now she was fairly certain he was using the baby as a shield against her outrage. He knew damn well that she wasn't going to start anything with little Sean right here in the room.

What was wrong with him? Less than twelve hours ago he had been at death's door. Today, with the rising of the sun, he acted as if nothing had happened.

Since the moment he'd woken up this morning he had treated her politely, like he would a guest at the Lair, or some stranger he'd met on the street.

Over breakfast, he'd informed her that the jet would be here to take her back to the States before noon.

She'd been speechless. He wasn't even going to give her a choice? Or a chance to change her mind?

Fine. She'd leave. But if he thought she was going to come running if he changed his mind later, he needed to think again. She was not a puppet to manipulate at whim.

Jerk.

A knock at the bedroom door tore her away from her fuming. "What?"

Danielle Drake entered. "I was wondering if I could have a little time with the baby before the plane arrives?"

Wonderful. He'd told the entire family she was leaving? Caitlin took a deep breath. Her anger wasn't at Danielle. She nodded. "Sure."

Once Danielle left the bedroom with little Sean, and Caitlin heard the outer door to the apartment close, she turned to stare at Sean.

He wouldn't even look at her.

She crossed the distance between them and tapped him on the shoulder. "You want to tell me what's going on?"

"I told you I wasn't going to stop you from leaving."

"You never mentioned throwing me out."

"I'm giving you what you want."

"Oh, really? You are, are you? Tossing me and my son out is what I want?"

"*Our* son."

"Fine." She corrected herself. "Our son. This is how you treat *our* son?"

"I'm not doing anything you didn't want."

"How do you know what I want? Are you suddenly all-knowing?"

"Have you changed your mind? Do you want something else first? The cabin wasn't enough, so you want another fuck before you go?"

A haze of pure red clouded her sight and mind. She raised her arm, palm open, and swung toward him.

Faster than she knew was possible, he spun around and backed her toward the bed. Before she could so much as gasp, they were naked on the bed, with him on top of her.

"Is this what you wanted? Do you need some energy to tide you over until you can find someone else to supply it?"

She didn't know what was wrong with him. But she did know something was. Not only wasn't this normal, it wasn't even rational.

She knew better than to physically fight him. There was no way she could win, and in his current state of mind she didn't know if he'd be able to stop himself from killing her.

So she wrapped her arms tightly around him and whispered, "Sean, where are you? What happened? Talk to me."

The rage in his eyes made his glare as hard and sharp as any cut gemstone. He hadn't heard her.

Caitlin closed her eyes and crooned to the beast inside. To her relief, the dragon listened and crooned back.

The man holding himself so tense atop her slowly relaxed. He buried his face against her shoulder. "Forgive me. I'm sorry."

"What happened? Where did you go?"

"A changeling isn't meant to separate from his beast. When I was by myself, I was filled with a rage I couldn't control. A cold fury that threatened to consume me."

She ran her fingers through his hair. "I noticed."

"I was trying so hard to get you out of here before it broke free."

Caitlin sighed. "And of course I just egged it on."

"I was acting like an ass. What else were you going to do?"

"Yeah, well, from now on, you don't ever—and I mean ever, ever, never—separate from your beast again."

"No fears there since I have no intention of doing that again."

"Good."

Sean rolled off her and spelled their clothes back on. "There's time for a walk before the jet arrives. We have a few things to discuss."

"Yes, we do."

He took her hand and led her out of the bedroom, down to the main floor and out of the castle. The entire Drake clan was gathered in front of the castle. But he didn't stop to chat, just nodded and kept walking to the beach.

Once there, he turned to her and took both of her hands in his. "You're pregnant."

Caitlin stared at him. "Beg pardon?"

"I said you're pregnant. With twins."

While that probably explained her emotional highs and lows these last few days, this wasn't exactly the way she wanted to discover the news. In fact, wasn't it usually the woman telling the man?

"And how long have you known this?"

"When we were at the cabin."

"Oh."

"So, are you going to marry me?"

She looked up at him. "No."

Before she could say anything else, like explaining why, he released her hands, turned away, shifted into a smoky dragon and took off.

Caitlin wanted to scream. If she did nothing else in

this lifetime, she was going to break him from this habit of running away.

She took three steps to chase after him and felt the wind rush through her skin. She frowned. Something was happening. Her body suddenly felt as light as air. She looked down at the beach, shocked to find it a good twenty feet below her.

She shifted her attention to her body, which was no longer there. No arms, no legs, no nothing.

Caitlin headed toward the water and glanced down at her reflection. If her eyes weren't playing tricks on her, she was the most gorgeous amethyst-hued smoky dragon alive.

She was lighter than a feather. Not just her body, but her heart. This was impossible, but it was fabulous. She was happy.

The cool breeze flowed through her; the colors of the earth and sea were more brilliant than she'd ever seen, brighter than she could ever have envisioned.

She flew over the castle, circled the people staring at her from the lawn.

Danielle Drake pointed to the left, shouting, "Go get him."

Caitlin wanted to laugh. Oh, she'd get him all right. If her mate thought for one minute he was going to escape his fate, he was sadly mistaken.

She veered to the left and instantly spotted him soaring over the ocean.

It took little effort to catch up with him, and she fell into line next to him.

He looked at her, surprise evident in the way he slowed down to study the form next to him.

Caitlin smiled to herself and then flew straight into him, her form and his blending into one.

"I'm not going to marry you because you haven't ever asked me to."

He welcomed her, filled her with warmth, cocooning her within the expanse of his misty wings. "And if I did?"

She snuggled into his warmth, breathing her life force into him and accepting the energy he returned. "If you did, you would never be able to get rid of me."

"Well, so tell me Caitlin St. George, milady Dragon Slayer, will you marry this beast who loves you dearly?"

She sighed at his words. "Yes, my love, I will marry you."

He took control of their flight, swirling, rising and dipping before he brought them both to a gentle landing on the beach.

Once they both returned to human form, he dropped down on one knee and took her hands between his. "I am honored. I swear to you that I will always love you, always care for you and keep you safe."

"Of course you will. You haven't broken a vow yet, why would you in the future?"

He kissed her hand. "I have to warn you of something, though."

"And what might that be?"

He rose to envelop her in an embrace and whispered against her ear, "Dragons mate for life."

Chapter 20

Mirabilus Island—Six months later

Caitlin lowered her oversize form down onto the lawn chair on the beach. She was fairly certain she'd be giving birth to hippos, not babies. Pulling a folding fan from the beach bag Sean had provided, she snapped it open and waved it in front of her face. Not that it helped; the summer heat was sweltering.

Alexia, sitting in the chair next to her, patted her hand. "It'll get better."

"Yeah, in three to four months?"

"That sounds about right."

Caitlin sighed. "So, is everything ready for the wedding?"

"Everything except for the bride."

Sean came up behind them. He handed Caitlin a glass of iced tea and massaged her shoulders. "What's Danielle's problem now?"

"Her veil was delivered this morning, and she doesn't like it."

Braeden dropped onto the sand at his wife's feet. "And she thinks Aelthed will care what veil she wears?"

"She just wants everything to be perfect." Caitlin tried to explain the woman's reasoning.

"Speaking of the happy couple." Braeden nodded toward the other end of the beach.

Aelthed and Danielle were walking hand in hand at the edge of the water.

Ariel snatched one of her children out of the water and joined them. "What do you think of Aelthed's new look?"

He'd shaved off his beard and cut his hair. The cleaner look made him appear younger than his nine hundred or so years. The blue jeans and sneakers helped with the overall look.

Caitlin mused out loud. "How long do you think he'll be here?"

Cameron shook water all over his wife, before sitting in the chair next to her. "Who knows? Does it matter?"

Sean answered, "Since none of us knows how long we'll live, I suppose not."

"Are your parents coming for the wedding?" Alexia asked.

"My mother says yes. My father just snarls."

Ariel laughed. "He's still not happy about that whole being married for an eternity concept the High Council imposed on him?"

"Considering he just bought my mother the house of her dreams and let her furnish it to her exacting tastes, he's obviously fine with it." Caitlin shook her head. "He just likes to kvetch, to hear himself talk."

"When are they bringing Sean back?" Braeden's tone

was a little on the sharp side. He still wasn't used to being related to the St. Georges and even though Caitlin had made her peace with both of her parents, he didn't trust them.

"They'll fly in tomorrow."

The babies decided to fight for space in her womb. Caitlin groaned and rubbed her hand over them.

Sean took the tea from her. "Come on, we're going in. You need to rest."

"That's all I do is rest."

"Now."

He helped her to her feet and looked at Braeden. "A little assist?"

In the next instant they were in their cool, air-conditioned bedroom. Sean pulled the curtains closed over the sliding doors to block out the sun.

He then helped her onto the bed and took her shoes off before stretching out next to her.

She had to admit, she was much more comfortable out of the heat, and the dragonettes seemed to like it better when she stretched out. Maybe it gave them more room.

Sean rolled onto his side and caressed the bulge that encased their babies. "Are you happy, Mrs. Drake?"

She placed her hand over his. "Very, Mr. Drake."

"Do you regret anything?"

No, she didn't. Not one single second of their time together. Not their first three days together, or coming to him for help when their son had been kidnapped, or their fights, or disagreements, or even their whirlwind justice of the peace wedding. "Yes."

His eyes widened. "What?"

"That we still haven't put any utilities in at the cabin."

"Woman, you'll drive me out of my mind." He

dropped a kiss on the tip of her nose. "But, darlin', I love you, anyway."

"That's good."

"Oh? And why is that?"

She reached up to cup his face and bring him down for a slow, leisurely kiss. Then she whispered against his lips, "Because, my love, dragons mate for life."

* * * * *

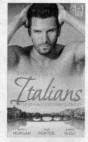

MILLS & BOON®

Want to get more from Mills & Boon?

Here's what's available to you if you join the exclusive **Mills & Boon eBook Club** today:

✦ *Convenience – choose your books each month*
✦ *Exclusive – receive your books a month before anywhere else*
✦ *Flexibility – change your subscription at any time*
✦ *Variety – gain access to eBook-only series*
✦ *Value – subscriptions from just £3.99 a month*

So visit **www.millsandboon.co.uk/esubs** today to be a part of this exclusive eBook Club!